SMOKELESS FIRE

a Fire Spirits novel

SAMANTHA YOUNG

FOR K MCJ AND ALL YOU DO. LOVE YOU LOTS.

PROLOGUE

The Stars Are Not Wanted but the Sky Will Submit

Her eyes attempted to overcome him. Everywhere he glanced those eyes of a thousand nights, eyes that had made love to every spectrum of color this realm and the others had to offer, were refracted on the cold glass and black marble of his home. He imagined those eyes had prevailed over many a worthy foe. Tonight he would pretend they had prevailed over him.

What happened after that was of no interest to him.
It would be of no interest to him unless He willed it so.

PART ONE

~1~

Ghost in the Soul

Ari's eyes followed the swipe of Mr. Dillon's eraser across the board, wiping out the poor chalk-figure hangman who had met his full and complete death - a head, torso, limbs and all - when the senior class had failed to figure out the blanks equated to *accumulated depreciation*. The last week of school. Business class.

Ari hid a yawn behind her hand and glanced worriedly out of the classroom window to the trees behind the parking lot. She wondered if he was out there already.

"God, I thought this class couldn't get any more boring," Nick Melua whispered across to her. Ari made a sympathetic noise and nodded in agreement. Waiting for graduation was a slow torture in hell. That the waiting room at present happened to be Mr. Dillon's Business Studies class only increased the banality.

Ari winced. She better get used to it. She would be heading off to major in Business at Penn after summer break. Pushing the future and the host of angry butterflies the thought of it created in her belly out of her mind, Ari concentrated on worrying about Charlie. Was he out behind the parking lot? *Again?*

"Miss Johnson?"

She groaned into her wrist and flicked her eyes up at the board. "W," she guessed without thinking and immediately felt the heat of the glares from her classmates.

"Nope." Mr. Dillon shook his head. "Nick?"

"E," he threw across the room belligerently and was rewarded with grateful smiles as the word became clearer.

"Entrepreneur!" Staci Pike shouted out with such enthusiasm you could be fooled into thinking she cared. Ari smirked over at her and rolled her eyes at Staci's sheepish shrug. Staci hated making anyone feel bad and the perspiration rolling down Mr. Dillon's face that told them he knew he was failing miserably at keeping them entertained, and was beginning to feel the pressure, was not something Staci could just sit back and watch.

Mr. Dillon smiled gratefully. "Correct. Do you want to come up, Staci, and choose a word?"

Ari grinned at her. *See, that's what happens when you're nice.*

Staci narrowed her eyes on her as she swept by her table. "Meanie," she murmured loud enough to make Ari snort.

Fifteen minutes later the class grew more fervent in their irritation as they struggled to figure out Staci's word. Finally Mr. Dillon sighed. "I'm afraid the hangman is definitely... dead. You'll have to tell us your word, Staci."

Her dark eyes were wide with disbelief. "You guys are terrible at this game."

"Aw come, Staci!" Nick beat his fist against the table, his voice climbing to a whine. "Just tell us."

"Fine," she huffed. "The word or words, rather, are 'Bill Gates.'"

Ari immediately began to laugh as the class exploded into an uproar.

"I still don't see what the big deal was." Staci shrugged as they headed towards their lockers.

"You were supposed to use a business *term*." Ari chuckled, plucking a spit ball out of Staci's hair and flicking it to the ground. She grimaced, wiping her hand against her t-shirt.

"Bill Gates is a businessman, helllllooo!"

"Hello to you too," a warm voice purred, an arm wrapping around Staci. She was pulled back into the solid embrace of her boyfriend A.J. Half Japanese (on her mom's side) Staci's slight frame was swallowed up in the stocky shadow of A.J.'s wrestler's body. Her almond-shaped eyes widened slightly before she relaxed into him, tilting her mouth up to his for a kiss.

Ari sighed and turned away from them, yanking her locker open with more force than she had intended.

"Is someone in a bad mood?" A.J. asked softly, grinning sheepishly at the glare Ari threw him over her shoulder.

Staci shook her head. "Nah, I think she's just bummed out after the longest class in the history of classes."

"What's there to be bummed about?" A new familiar voice entered the fray. Ari craned her neck around her locker to smile at her best friend. Rachel grinned up at her, her blonde hair swinging against her chin as she jerked her gaze back and forth between her friends with the excitement of a puppy. "We're officially free in a few days and... drum roll please." She gestured to A.J. who supplied the request with his imaginary drum sticks. "It's Ari's 18th birthday slash graduation party!"

As her friends began talking enthusiastically about their plans for the 18th birthday party her dad, Derek, was letting her throw in their house at the end of the week, Ari tried to smile with sufficient animation. It wasn't that she hated birthdays, or graduation even. It was more the promise of the future. A future she wasn't so sure about.

"Oh, guys, I have to bring the stethoscope Mom and Dad bought me to the party... it's awesome," Rachel chirped happily, her eyes glittering at the prospect of heading off to Dartmouth to do her pre-medical studies. After Dartmouth she was planning on applying to John Hopkins, and Ari had no doubt that whatever Rachel wanted, Rachel would eventually get.

"They bought you a stethoscope already?" A.J. snorted. "Dude, you're not even going to med school for another three years."

"Seven years of college. You are so insane." Staci shuddered. "I can't even imagine."

A.J. shrugged. "I don't know. Seven years making movies... sounds kind of fun."

Staci rolled her eyes at him but smiled indulgently. "Anything sounds like fun to you as long as it gets you off that farm."

Ari felt like sinking into the floor if only to disappear from this moment. Her friends were so clear about who they were and what they wanted... it terrified her. It made her feel like a freak. She glanced around at them as they started yammering on about college sweatshirts, roommates, the freshman ten, wondering what on earth happened to her that she didn't know what she wanted out of life like they did. Staci and A.J. were heading off to RISD together to study Film and Animation, something they had talked about doing nearly the whole three years they had been dating. Ari shut her locker, trying not to have a panic attack. Never before in her life had she suffered from anxiety but she'd had three attacks this last month. She closed her eyes, her back to her friends. When her dad suggested she studied Business at college Ari hadn't argued. What else was she going to do, right? Unlike her friends there wasn't anything she'd ever felt particularly brilliant at, or drawn to. How could they possibly understand that? She needed someone to understand.

She needed Charlie.

"Hey," Rachel said softly, her hand resting on her shoulder to tug her around gently. Her blue eyes were wide with concern. "You OK? You've been so quiet lately."

"I'm fine."

"Really?"

How could she not talk to Rachel about this? Rachel was her best friend. But then…Rachel hadn't always been her best friend.

Growing up Charlie had been Ari's closest friend. Her family really. He had been there when her dad forgot her ninth birthday, and the time she couldn't stop crying after the lie she told when she was ten years old caused her dad and his girlfriend to break up. There was also that time she'd gotten her first period and, even though she knew what it was, she had completely freaked out. She'd run off from school during lunch and Charlie had chased her into Vickers' Woods behind the interstate. When she'd bawled out what was happening, he had silently taken her hand and walked her all the way to his house and stammered through a blushing explanation to his mom. Mrs. Creagh had hugged her close and called the school and her dad to explain where she'd disappeared to and why. The phone call was followed by a trip to the pharmacy and a lot more hugging.

Anything good, bad, small or huge that had happened to her, Charlie was the one who had been there. And then something huge - too huge - happened to him and suddenly Charlie wasn't really *there* to be there.

"Are you worrying about Charlie again?" Rachel huffed.

Ari threw her a 'don't start' look.

"Let's go to lunch," A.J. interrupted, dodging any conversation to do with Charlie. He thought Charlie was a loser and hated that Ari 'wasted' so much time and anxiety over him.

Stemming a wave of anger at her friends and their attitude, Ari pulled away from them. "I'll catch up in a minute, save me a seat."

A frown appeared between Rachel's smooth brows. "You're not going over there?"

Clenching her jaw, Ari turned her back on them. "Just save me a seat," she called over her shoulder, dodging students in her path.

"You need to give her a break about him," she heard Staci say, but A.J.'s response was muffled as Ari moved further through the throng of teenagers.

Bursting out of the front entrance, Ari inhaled a lungful of warm summer air, shaking her hands out as if the gesture could shake out all her worries with it. Her eyes scanned the parking lot for Charlie but she couldn't see him, which meant he was out behind the lot in the trees where the teachers couldn't see. If he wasn't careful he was going to get kicked out. He'd already been held back a year. Not that he cared. A rush of angry wasps awoke in her stomach as they always did when she was about to face him. That hadn't been the case in the past. In the past, just the thought of him used to relax her. Pulling her shoulders back, Ari started off across the lot with a determined stride. She just had to know he was alright. They hadn't spoken in two weeks which was officially the longest they had gone without speaking.

As if coerced onto the scene by a sad Fate a little boy of nine or ten years old, with dark brown hair and eyes, shot towards her, puffing out of breath.

"Have you seen my sister?" he wheezed.

Concerned by his appearance at the high school during the day, Ari stopped, grabbing his arm before he could shoot off without an answer. "Who's your sister?"

"Gemma Hall."

Ari frowned. Gemma was a junior. "I'll-"

"Bobby!" They both spun around to see Gemma rushing down the school steps towards them. "Did you bring them?"

"Yeah, but you owe me, like, twenty bucks…"

Satisfied that there was nothing dramatic going down between the siblings, Ari left them to it, only glancing back once at the kid. He looked so much like Michael.

Michael Creagh. Charlie's kid brother. And the reason Charlie was so effed up. Two years ago, on Ari's 16th birthday, Charlie had taken his parent's SUV out to pick up his little brother from Little League. He was hurrying, trying to get Mike home so he could head over to Ari's to pick her up and take her out to celebrate. The cyclist came out of nowhere. Charlie had swerved onto oncoming traffic and the passenger side took the full impact of the collision. When Charlie had come to... Mike was already dead. Everything changed that day. The happy Creaghs stopped being parents to Charlie and Charlie stopped being…Charlie. He blamed himself for his brother's death and Ari wasn't so sure his parents didn't either.

Ari felt a rip of pain across her chest at the thought of how much agony her best friend was in. How did you live with that kind of guilt? Ari stopped hanging out at the Creagh's because Charlie didn't want her to. He told her his dad had started drinking and his mom had gotten her old job as manager at *FoodLand* back to keep them afloat financially and to avoid her husband and the son who hadn't died. Eventually, Charlie started hanging with a new crowd: slackers, potheads. He started skipping school, dropping grades. She'd even on occasion found him wasted in Vickers' Woods. She'd hoped he'd snap out of it eventually, that it was just his way of grieving. But it had been two years...

Before it happened... Ari had been psyching herself up to talk to him that night... the night of her 16th. After confiding in Rachel, her new Chem lab partner, she had been persuaded it was time. She had been moping after Charlie for three years. Ari didn't know when her feelings for him stopped being platonic. There wasn't a moment when everything shifted and suddenly she loved him. It was more that she turned thirteen and suddenly boys were cute and gave her butterflies. Charlie gave her butterflies. Not raging wasps like he did now. But tickling, exciting, beautiful creatures that fluttered their wings against her stomach, kicking her heart into a wild dance that matched their beat. She had been sixteen years old and in love.

And she still loved him.

Even though he wasn't Charlie anymore.

Ari's skin cooled as she stepped into the trees, winding her way over the worn path that took her into the clearing that was popular with stoners. Surely the faculty knew about this place but they were either too lazy to do something about it or just didn't care. Her eyes washed over the gathering, finding mostly sophomores and juniors. She only knew a few people by name and she nodded at them warily.

They were lounging around on the grass, leaning against one another and rocks, their pupils dilated, their features slack. Drifting through them, Ari headed towards a guy she recognized. He was tall, his long legs stretched out before him in dirty, ripped jeans, his *Smashing Pumpkins* t-shirt wrinkled and worn. His expression was blank as he gazed up at her, brushing his unkempt dark brown hair out of his deep brown eyes. He had a nice face, handsome in that boy next door kind of way. As she stopped before him, he tilted his head back and the corner of his mouth quirked up. A flash of emotion sparked in his eyes transforming him from cute guy next door to sexy and dangerous 'anything is possible with me' guy. Before her was a boy who could hurt her more than anybody else.

"Charlie." She nodded, trying to act casual, which was difficult considering the stares burning into her back.

"What's up?" he asked softly, reaching for the joint Mel Rickman handed him. Ari deliberately kept her gaze focused on Charlie. Mel was older than everyone else, in his early twenties, a complete waste of space. The guy gave her the creeps, and not because he was hanging out getting sophomores stoned, but because when he looked at her it was as if he were imagining her naked. The lascivious douche made her uneasy.

She glanced around to make sure no one was paying attention, suddenly feeling foolish standing there in her washed, un-ripped hipster jeans and plain t-shirt from *The Gap*. The grass tickled her feet in her flip flops and she looked down, her eyes wandering over to the steel toe cap boots Mel wore. She fingered the tennis bracelet on her wrist, trying not to flush. Most of the kids Charlie hung out with came from the east, the low income side of Sandford Ridge. It was a medium-sized town situated in the southeast of Butler County, not small enough for everyone to know everyone's business, but not big enough for people not to know if you lived on the east side or the west side. "I was wondering if you're still coming to my birthday party on Friday?"

Charlie gave her an inscrutable look, the silence between them stretching into irritating and unnecessary. Ari was *this* close to throwing the folder in her arms at him.

"I'll come to your party, babe." Mel winked at her. "Give me a private showing sometime and I might even buy you a present."

"Watch it." Charlie whipped his head around at him, his dark eyes glittering with fury. "Don't talk to her."

"Hey-"

"Just shut it." Charlie pinned him in place with a look of warning that would have made a smarter man pee in his pants. Ari shivered, unsettled by him even though he was only defending her. He glanced back up at her, the anger still etched in his features. "Of course I'll be there," he told her quietly. "I'll see you Friday."

Not wanting to leave him there, Ari jerked her head in the direction of the parking lot. "Do you want to come have lunch with me?"

He shook his head infinitesimally, his features losing expression again. "Go back to school, Ari, I'll see you later."

Feeling that familiar ache in her chest, Ari nodded and spun around, hurrying out of the clearing and the woods and wishing like hell her car wasn't in the garage and she could just head home.

She stopped on the hot asphalt, staring blankly at the Ohio plates of the Buick Lacrosse Rachel's parents had bought her as a graduation gift. *I can go home. I am going home.* Ari turned and began heading towards the gate. It was a half hour walk, it was nothing. She could do with the exercise.

"Ari!"

Closing her eyes in disbelief Ari huffed and slowly turned around to see Rachel running across the lot towards her. "Rache."

"Where are you going?"

"For a walk."

"Were you going home?"

"I thought about it."

Rachel shook her head, her eyes narrowing. "He's put you on a downer again, hasn't he?"

"It's not his fault."

"Stop making excuses for him, Ari. And you're not going home." She tugged on her arm, dragging her back towards the school.

"You're not the boss of me," Ari grunted, tripping on her flip flops.

"I am not letting Charlie ruin graduation for you. You think I don't know why you've been so sullen and quiet every time we mention college and graduation? It's Charlie! It's always Charlie. You're going to have to leave him to soak in his self-destructive soup and frankly I think it's a good thing. He is such a loser. You are so much better than that."

"Hey!" Ari yanked her arm away and shot her best friend a look so livid it was amazing waves of burning smoke didn't start weeping from Rachel's body. "You don't get to call him that. He's been through hell and I'm sorry if he doesn't fall into your perfect little bubble, but he's my friend, and I don't abandon my friends."

Holding her hands up in a surrender gesture Rachel nodded, her eyes wide. "You're right. I'm sorry. I shouldn't have called him that."

Ari shook her head, sighing heavily. "Whatever. Let's just get you back to the cafeteria before A.J. eats whatever you left on your tray."

Her eyes almost popped out of her head. "My Snickers!"

Ari gave a bark of annoyed laughter, watching Rachel lope up the stone stairs two at a time. Watching her friend, who knew herself inside out, Ari wished she was more like Rachel... or that she had more time at least, time to discover who she was supposed to be.

For once, Ari was glad to step into the airy house she called home, waving behind her to Rachel who was driving her back and forth to school while her car was in the garage getting fixed. She shut the door, dropping her bag and pulling off the light summer jacket she had needed when clouds had rolled in over the Ridge out of nowhere after lunch. She hung it up on the coat pegs, using the label to loop it securely to the peg. When it slid up and off, falling to the ground, Ari groaned and bent down to pick it up. She secured it again and headed off towards the kitchen only to hear the pinging of the metal buttons hitting the wooden floors. Exhaling heavily, she spun back on her heel and picked it back up, jamming the jacket down on the peg.

Her poltergeist was such a pain in the ass.

"I'm not in the mood, Ms. Maggie!" she called out, scanning the hall.

Two years ago, sometime after her 16th actually, a poltergeist took up residence in her house. When she tried to tell her dad about furniture being moved, an invisible person using her laptop, books taken down from the shelf and left around and open, he'd told her to stop being childish. For the last four or five years he'd been gone a lot, traveling the country and wining and dining doctors and hospital execs as a pharmaceutical sales rep. Her dad was good at his job and she never wanted for anything - except maybe for more time with him. Anyway, her theory about the poltergeist didn't really hit home until they got into an argument one day a year and a half ago. He'd raised his voice at her because she made the mistake of whining about him being gone so much and a book flew off one of the shelves and cracked him across the head. He hadn't imagined it and was now sufficiently freaked out by their house. Ari, on the other hand, had stopped whining at her dad in the hopes that that would make him want to be home more, and had gotten used to the company of the poltergeist. She was pretty sure the poltergeist was a woman because she seemed to take offence to sexist, anti-feminist jokes and had a considerate nature Ari had only encountered in girls. Sure she was mischievous, like with the whole jacket thing, but once Ari told her to stop doing something she would. Ari had named her Ms. Maggie after the dog her dad had bought when she was eight and then promptly gotten rid of when he realized how much work was involved for him.

Ari breathed a sigh of relief when the jacket stayed in place. "Thanks, Ms. Maggie. I appreciate it. It's been a rough day." She wandered out of the cold hallway into the even colder, empty kitchen. Their house seemed to lack the cozy warmth of her friends' houses. She didn't know if that was to do with the minimalist furniture or the lack of any *actual* family living in it. There could have been a family. But Ari had ruined that for her dad.

All of her life, Ari had lived with the knowledge that her mother, some mysterious woman named Sala, had broken her father's heart after a passionate and brief affair before returning nine months later with a baby she said was his. She'd left Ari with him and disappeared, never to be seen again. Her father had done the best he could, Ari knew that. And she knew that he loved her more than anything. He had tried. He'd read to her every night before bed, he'd taught her to swim, to play baseball, to throw a punch without breaking her thumb, but as she'd gotten older they had grown apart. Over the years there had only been a few girlfriends, for which Ari was grateful. Unlike other kids with no moms, Ari hadn't wanted one. To her, a mom was this creature who had stolen her daddy's heart and ripped it out, leaving them both in the cold, lost and alone. So when Derek had started getting serious with this one woman when Ari was ten, she'd started to panic. If her father married this woman, she'd be Ari's mom. What if she left too? She'd just break their hearts as well. And to be truthful, Ari didn't want to share her dad with anyone. The lie she'd told that broken up the relationship still ate at her conscience eight years later. In a moment of pure childish stupidity, with no real clue to the consequences of her actions, Ari had lied and told her dad that his girlfriend (Michelle) had slapped her when Ari had told her she didn't want to her to be her mom. Derek was furious. He believed his daughter over his four month old relationship and had swiftly ended things. There hadn't been anyone serious since. Ari blanched every time she thought about it. Her dad would so kill her if he knew the truth. Poor Michelle.

The upbeat melody of Sick Muse by *Metric* rang out from the pocket of Ari's jeans and she jumped, startled in the quiet of the house. Jerking her cell out, she smiled softly at the caller ID and pressed the answer call button. "Dad."

"Hey, sweetheart," his warm, deep voice reminded her of Christmas Day on the couch watching *Home Alone* and eating chocolates for breakfast. "How's things?"

"OK. Graduation in a couple of days," she reminded him.

"I know, sweetheart," he replied wearily. "I've asked Rachel's mom to take care of you and to take lots of pictures of you in your cap and gown. I'm so sorry I can't be there. You know I would if I could but I can't miss this meeting, it could be my biggest sale this year."

She nodded, feeling a little numb to the distance between them now. "I know. Don't worry about it, Dad. It's not a big deal."

"It is a big deal. That's why I want you to take the emergency credit card and buy whatever you need for your birthday party, OK?"

"Thanks, that's great."

"I've also got a fantastic birthday present for you. I'll be home in three weeks. I can't wait to see your face when you open it."

She smiled. Admittedly, her dad always bought her the most thoughtful presents. "I hope you didn't do anything extravagant."

Derek laughed. "It's your 18th, of course I did. I love you, kid."

"Love you too, Dad."

Their conversation was short and sweet, like always, and Ari spent the rest of the evening cooking pasta, watching cartoons, worrying about Charlie, and stalking his *Facebook* and *Twitter* accounts to see if there was any recent activity. There never was. She talked to Rache and Staci for a while on *Skype* and then slid back from her desk, falling, emotionally exhausted, onto her king-sized bed.

"Ms. Maggie... can you hit the lights?" Two seconds later the click of the switch echoed around the room and the bedroom was plunged into darkness. "Thanks, you're a doll."

Two minutes later a flash of light across her closed lids broke her fall into sleep and she groaned, prying her eyes open to see her laptop had been turned on, the glow of the screen flicking across her walls as it changed from a *Facebook* account to *Twitter*.

"Ms. Maggie," Ari groaned, flopping back against her pillows. "Can you Tweet in the morning. Please…"

The chair at her desk squeaked and the laptop went dark.

"Thank you," she breathed. "Today was already depressing enough without the reminder that my poltergeist has more followers on *Twitter* than I do."

~2~

A Fiery Lash for Her Crime

The black gates, with their swirling knots and lethal looking points sticking out of the top, swung open seconds after he spoke into the security box. Jai Bitar took a deep breath, pressing his foot to the gas and easing up the smooth driveway, watching the gates swing shut behind him. Already he wanted to be back in his condo in Hollywood. In fact he'd rather be anywhere than back home in the Palisades, called home to his family, to his father, to his boss. When his dad had a job for him he usually pulled him into their office Downtown. The fact that his father wanted to discuss this new job here... Jai sucked in a breath. Something big was going down. He parked the car at the bottom of the wide stone stairs that led up to his parents' massive home. It was a burnished clay color, more Spanish estate than the Moroccan architecture Jai favored, but his stepmother loved the design so who was he to argue.

Finally. Where have you been? I called you three hours ago.

Used to his father contacting him telepathically without so much as a warning, Jai didn't even flinch as he got out of the car. *I was in the middle of something. I got here as fast as I could.* Christ the old man couldn't even wait two minutes for him to climb those damn stairs to berate him for something.

Hmmph. I call you with an emergency you drop what you're doing and get your ass here. End of story. Why is the concept lost on you when your brothers have it down pat?

Jai glared up at the house, refusing to answer. His dad could talk to him when he got in the house. Correction. Rail at him unfairly. As usual. To stem off a tirade about how long it had taken him to climb the stairs, Jai envisioned the cold entrance hall of his parents' home with its high ceiling and black and white checkered flooring. There was an ugly ass abstract painting of his stepmother, Nicki, hanging on the main wall. As soon as he had it locked in mind, Jai relaxed, letting the flutter of wind brush against his skin. The blur of color and slightly dizzying sensation of using the *Peripatos* lasted merely a second and Jai found his eyes stuck on that ugly ass abstract.

"Where have you been?" a snide voice asked from over his shoulder.

Keeping his expression neutral, Jai turned to face his eldest half-brother David. His black eyes bore into Jai's with their usual disdain and for not the first time Jai noted they looked nothing alike. They could be strangers in appearance and manner for all anyone else knew. The Bitar's blood was very mixed. Two hundred years ago their Moroccan tribe took off for London to escape a blood feud with another Ginnaye tribe. From there they'd moved to the East Coast of America until migrating to the West. In that time they'd intermarried with other immigrant Ginnaye who had lived in Europe a lot longer than they had. Nicki was a European Ginnaye. Luca had met her on assignment in Ireland. Thus, the Bitar boys had a mixture of Irish and Moroccan heritage in their features. Jai was different. His features were harder, his skin olive-toned, his eyes green. He wondered often where his mother had hailed from to give him such unusual coloring.

Jai shrugged at his half-brother. "At my condo. Some of us live in our own apartments like big boys with big boy pants."

David narrowed his eyes. "Hilarious. But then I guess I'd need a sense of humor too if I were the only son Luca Bitar can't stand to have living with him."

They both knew the truth of that statement but Jai refused to give David the satisfaction of reacting. Instead he shrugged and strode towards him. "You still using the pool house to get laid behind Nicki and Luca's back? How is that working out for you, big bro? Bet the ladies are impressed by a thirty year old who lives in his parents' pool house."

"At least I get laid."

"As do I."

"Yeah but I use my natural charm. I don't have your mommy's evil succubus side to lure them in, asshole."

Despite the comment igniting Jai's blood with rage he was a master at deception. He threw David a lazy look as they entered his father's office. "I didn't inherit that part of her genetics, David. I get laid because fortunately you and I look nothing alike."

"Morning to you too," Luca Bitar's voice cut right through him.

Smoothing the triumphant smirk off his face, Jai stopped before his father's desk, his hands behind his back, his expression serious and ready. He and his father may not get along but Jai was one of his father's best guardians. Luca Bitar knew that. Even if he didn't want to admit it. "Good morning, sir." He nodded deferentially.

Luca nodded back stiffly, his eyes flicking to David. "Where's your mother?"

David slouched against his father's liquor cabinet, his arms crossed lazily over his chest as he eyed Jai with a twisted smile. "You know she likes to be a.w.o.l when the spawn is about."

Jai didn't even so much as twitch. In fact he enjoyed the way Luca's eyes narrowed on David in disappointment. It killed him that his eldest acted like a five year old when Jai, his offspring with one of the Jinn who had seduced him against his will, was the most professional and mature of his four sons. Not that he'd ever admit that out loud. Just as much as his stepmother, Nicki, liked to take Jai's unfortunate parentage out on him, so did Luca. Duty bound him to Jai, it made sure he raised his son with all the education and material comforts his other sons were given. But raising Jai with affection and love? No. That had been out of the question. It had made Jai the angriest son-of-a-bitch for the longest time. An anger he'd never shown, even when he'd been allowed to be beaten to a bloody pulp by his two elder half-brothers while the youngest watched, even under the disdain of their entire Ginnaye tribe who looked on him like some filthy half-breed. Rather than acting out he'd done the opposite just to piss everyone off. He'd worked and trained harder than all the rest, gaining the grudging respect from some of the elder Ginnaye, especially those from other tribes around the world. Now, at twenty three years old, he was one of the most respected Security Operatives at Bitar Security in LA. His father was the son of the last tribe leader out in California. For centuries their family had lived human lives, protecting Importants whenever they were contracted to do so. Back in the 40s, Jai's grandfather moved his tribe to California and set up Bitar Security at the height of Hollywood. As well as being guardians to Importants and Jinn who hired them, the Bitar Ginnaye were paid big bucks to protect starlets and rich folks. Still were. Jai's last job had been guarding a pop princess with a flagging career whose stalker had gotten out of control. Luca Bitar preferred to have jobs wrapped up quick, so he'd given Jai permission to go directly after the stalker. Using a little Jinn enchantment, Jai had ripped the darkness from the creepy little guy that compelled him to obsess over women to the point he believed they were objects for him to do with as he pleased. It left the guy almost slavering in a hospital somewhere but it was the best Jai could do without killing him. This way no one innocent got hurt.

Luca had been pleased with his son's work. Not that he had said so but Jai had known because his father hadn't criticized him in a week.

Until today.

"Fine." Luca ground his teeth, trying not to admonish David in front of Jai. Jai smirked inwardly, watching his father's internal fight. It wasn't that Luca didn't criticize his other sons. Jai had overheard him doing it plenty of times when he thought Jai was nowhere in sight. He thought showering his full-blooded Ginnaye sons with support and affection in front of him was another weapon of psychological torment. It had been at first. Until Jai realized Luca was the one tormented by the fact that Jai was more like him than any of his full-blooded sons. "You can leave."

"I want to see what he has to say about this? If he doesn't want it, I'll do it."

Luca flicked David an exasperated look. "You weren't requested. He was."

Jai frowned, his curiosity getting the better of him. "What's going on?"

"David, leave."

With a heavy sigh, David muttered 'yes, sir' before throwing Jai a look. *See you later, douchebag.*

Jai let his smirk glitter in his eyes where Luca couldn't see. *Go cry to your mommy, dick.*

Least I have a mom, dick. With that he slammed out of the office.

Jai slid his father a look. "So… what's so important you needed to talk to me here?"

Before his father could respond the air shimmered beside his desk and Jai held his breath, waiting to see who was arriving. The explosion of fire signaled their entrance, the flames shooting to the ground before disappearing. Jai blinked, bemused by the enormous amount of power that pulsed into the room from the Jinn before him. He was huge, at least six and a half feet, with long flame-red hair pulled back into a ponytail. He wore modern clothing and grinned congenially at Jai.

"So this is Jai Bitar." The Jinn strode towards him. He gave a little respectful bow to Jai which Jai returned out of good manners, still confused as to what the powerful Jinn's presence meant. Whoever he was he was someone important. Perhaps even royal. A minor prince perhaps?

"Jai," his father's voice curled around him coldly. "This is The Red King."

Not a lot of things could get a reaction out of him but that did. He quirked an eyebrow in surprise and The Red King laughed. An immortal? *The Red King*. One of the Seven Kings of Jinn was in his dad's office?

Why?

"You must be wondering why I have requested your services, Jai?" The Red King tilted his head, his light blue eyes washing over him, assessing him.

"I didn't know you had."

"Shame." He grinned, twisting around to look at Luca. "You haven't told him yet?"

"He just got here, Your Highness," Luca grumbled.

The Red King smiled knowingly as his eyes flickered between father and son. "Oh I see. Yeah. I see. Well, Jai," his huge hand came down on Jai's shoulder with a hearty clap, "it's well known that Jai Bitar of the Ginnaye has an unusual gift that gives him an edge in this whole guardian business. I need that edge."

At the mention of his 'gift' Jai squirmed a little. He had first realized his gift when he'd kissed their maid's twelve year old daughter when he was thirteen. It was something to do with hitting puberty or something but after he'd kissed her he'd found himself connected to her. He could feel exactly where she was when her emotions were heightened and then after a while he could just push his magic and tap into their connection to find her location. He couldn't read her mind or anything but he'd been pretty impressed by the 'gift' and had told his best, and only, friend Trey about it. Trey had thought it was too important to keep a secret and had told his father, Rik, who told Jai's father. They had an old Jinn woman in the Ginnaye with greater ability to 'see' things within people. She'd explained that the 'gift' of Jai's kiss was a trait that had somehow scrambled itself together out of his mother's succubus genes. It was like his guardian genes and succubus genes had gotten together and come up with something unique. They discovered over the years that Jai's kiss could be placed on a client to trace them. It had to be a real kiss and, like the succubus side, it only worked on those he could ever be sexually attracted to. Women. To discover if that was true or not, and not caring how humiliating it was for Jai (in fact, Jai was pretty sure his father saw it as another form of emotional torture), he'd demanded Jai kiss a boy when he was fifteen to see if it could work on potential male clients. At fifteen he was like any teenage guy. He *had* cared. It was mortifying. And getting another guy to kiss you... not such an easy feat. Trey had said he'd step up to the plate if he really needed to but Jai knew Trey's dad (a closet homophobe) would kill him. So Jai had refused, and not because he was terrified to kiss a dude, although it wouldn't have been the greatest thing to ever happen to a straight teen guy, but because he refused to be pushed into something just so his father could enjoy humiliating him. It was doubtful with his genes anyway that the trace would work on a guy. His father had come down on him hard for weeks after that.

For everyone else Luca Bitar was this strong, loyal Jinn who protected people. To his family he was the guy they could turn to for help. But when Jai's mother seduced him against his will, she'd stolen a piece of the love he had for Nicki and he'd blamed Jai for it for as long as Jai could remember.

Letting the memories fade into the background, Jai turned deferentially to The Red King. "How can I be of service?"

The Red King nodded, grinning widely. "I like you." He pointed a gun finger at him and Jai couldn't help but think this guy would do well in a Tarantino movie. "I do. I like you. That's good. OK, kid. Here's the deal. I have this extremely important *Important* I want you to watch over."

Well, if it was someone one of the Jinn Kings wanted protected they must be a huge deal. Jai felt his blood pump with excitement at the challenge. "I take it's a woman, if you want my particular gift?"

"You betcha. Now, she's real important to me, Jai. I need to know you got this."

Slipping into guardian mode, Jai stiffened with determination. "Of course, Your Highness."

"My son is the best, Your Highness," Luca assured him.

Keeping his face impassive, Jai nearly struggled to swallow a smile when The Red King laughed at Luca and then turned back to him with a twinkle in his eyes. "Bet that's the first time you ever heard that sentence uttered from his mouth - I mean when he was talking about you and not one of his pansy-assed full-bloods."

Rather than say anything disrespectful, Jai's eyes gave a non-committal reply. He kind of liked the King. He'd grown up on the stories of the Jinn Kings. He knew everything about them and Azazil and the so-called War of the Flames. Never in any of those stories had he imagined The Red King to be… funny.

"Well, you'll do." The Red King nodded again. "Look, this is an indefinitely long assignment and it's a 24/7 hour guard, so if you got any stuff you need to take care of in Hollywood, you got twelve hours to do it. I'll explain the whole… *situation*… when you meet me back here. I don't do Hollywood. I like the movies but the people…" he shuddered at the thought before abruptly exploding into bright, hot licks of fire.

When he was gone silence echoed around his father's office. Finally, Luca cleared his throat. "I don't have to tell you how important this assignment is. You're not the only reason The Red King came to us for this. When my great-grandfather was tribe leader one of his guardians killed one of the Jinn in an effort to protect an Important. He was taken to the Jinn Courts and would have been tried and killed if The Red King hadn't spoken up for him. The Red King is collecting on the debt we owe him. Don't mess it up."

Not even his father's disdain could ruin this moment for Jai. He'd just landed his biggest assignment ever. This would cement his position and power within the company. "No, sir." He nodded militantly and then visualized his apartment before using the *Peripatos*. He'd get his car later.

His condo was bright and airy and devoid of any clutter. There was little furniture and what was there was black and chrome and very masculine. Chicks hated it but Jai wasn't really a relationship type guy so it didn't matter. With nothing to wrap up before the assignment started, Jai flopped down onto his leather couch, staring out of the French doors to the view of LA sprawled out before him. The sun beat down strong in the morning light, causing eye-watering reflections to beam brightly off windows and buildings and cars. Jai sighed, throwing his head back. He could have waited in the Palisades until night fall but that would have meant having to be around his whole family.

No thanks.

He smiled slowly up at the ceiling as he thought of The Red King. *The Red King*. If this assignment went well all of the Ginnaye would have to treat him with respect. That would just kill Luca and his brothers. Sounded fantastic. Feeling the excitement build inside him, adrenaline already shooting through him with anticipation, Jai blew out a shaky breath and leaned forward to stare at the painting Trey had given him titled 'Palmyra'. The rich colors and exotic landscape soothed him. He wondered who the Important was he was guarding. It had to be someone really big. Someone with a massive destiny if The Red King was stepping in to see her protected. Jai felt a flutter of nervousness in his gut and grinned. He'd never been nervous about an assignment before.

This was so HUGE.

When his cell rang, Jai jerked in surprise, reaching deep into his jeans to yank it out. He laughed at the caller ID. News travelled fast.

"Hey, man."

"So," Trey's laughing voice echoed down the line, "The Red King, huh? Were you going to tell me or just take off to wherever he sends you without so much as a goodbye hug?"

Laughing, Jai relaxed into the couch. "Sorry, I just heard myself."

"So what's the assignment?"

"Don't know yet. Just know that it's a she and she's important."

"All Hail the Lord of the Obvious. Come one, dude, give me more than that."

Grinning he shook his head. "Trey, that's all I know. I swear."

"OK. I believe you. Well congrats, Jai. You deserve this. It'll show your old man what's what, huh?"

Lying, Jai replied, "Like I care."

Trey sighed. "Yeah. Yeah." No matter how much Jai denied it, Trey knew he was continually fighting for Luca's approval. It pissed his only friend off. They spoke for a little longer with Jai gazing up at the painting. Trey knew all about looking for a father's approval. He hid a lot of things about himself from Rik. He was a great Ginnaye, strong, powerful, and Luca Bitar counted him among his best, but Trey was also an artist behind his father's back. He painted under a pseudonym and did pretty well for himself. Not only that but... he was bisexual, something Rik would go ballistic over if he ever found out. The only person who knew any of it was Jai. Growing up, Trey had watched Jai get kicked to pieces, figuratively and literally, by his tribe. He'd stood up for him, befriended him, and taken crap from his dad for doing so. But they shared a bond and neither of them let anything come between it. Sometimes Jai wondered if he would ever have made it out sane growing up with the Bitars if he hadn't had Trey by his side.

When they hung up, Jai headed for the shower, his mind conjuring up all different kinds of scenarios for this job. It ranged from the disappointing to the fantastical. He was just about to kick back with a sci-fi novel (his weakness) when the doorbell to his condo rang. Frowning, he bookmarked *Treason* by Orson Scott Card and headed for the door, feeling for an energy on the other side.

It was Jinn.

When he yanked open the door, his mouth quirked up into a little cynical smirk.

Yasmin. She raised an eyebrow at him before throwing one last look over her shoulder to make sure no one was watching. She pushed past him into the apartment, breezing in with confidence. Jai shut the door and turned to watch her. Yasmin Lenz was the daughter of his father's best friend, Hugo Lenz. Luca and Hugo were pretty much the elders and leaders of their particular tribe here in California and Hugo was a nastier son-of-a-bitch than even Luca. Lenz despised what Jai was and never missed an opportunity to tell him or attempt to humiliate him in front of his peers.

His beautiful daughter Yasmin had been in the class below Jai and had been warned repeatedly to stay away from him. Hugo liked to play matchmaker with her and David, and Jai knew for a fact that David would say yes to dating her in a heartbeat. He'd been after Yasmin Lenz since he'd seen her thrashing their younger brother Stephen on their family's tennis court when Yasmin was sixteen. Pervy bastard. But Yasmin wasn't interested in that particular Bitar. In public Yasmin treated Jai like he didn't exist. Correction, in front of the tribe she was downright derogatory and hostile. Then something changed when she was eighteen. She started cornering him in private, giving him hot eyes and pretty much making herself available to him. Jai had walked away each time. He wanted nothing to do with someone who treated him like crap in public. Then a year ago, Jai had witnessed something that had shocked him to his core. He had been at Bitar Security offices in a meeting with his father and

David and second eldest Brother, Tarik. They'd been discussing a potential client and when Luca had asked for the files, David had realized he'd left them at the pool house. Like a dog, Jai had been sent to retrieve them using the *Peripatos*. He'd arrived outside the pool house and was just about to enter when he had heard *noises*. Bemused at the sounds of lovemaking, Jai had peered through the windows and nearly died of heart failure. Hugo Lenz had been with Nicki, his stepmother. It had shocked Jai because he'd thought Nicki was completely in love with Luca. He didn't think she'd fallen out of love. Stuff happened. People got weird. Had mid-life crises and such, but Jai knew if Luca ever found out he'd be devastated. Something inside him had felt broken up for his father, despite the way he treated him. He couldn't tell him. No one would believe him anyway. So instead he took his revenge out on Hugo.

Yasmin.

If Hugo ever found out his precious daughter had been banging the Bitar half-breed on and off for the last year he'd die of shame.

Jai kept his expression blank as Yasmin spun around, unbuttoning her blouse. She had the same look in her eye she always did. She thought *she* was using *Jai*. She thought somehow she had power here because he continued to be with her despite how she treated him in public. But *he* was using *her*.

He was using her to get back at them all.

It wasn't something he was proud of.

It was dishonorable and the one thing Jai had always counted on was his honor.

But then Yasmin wasn't a sweet innocent girl who needed to be protected. She was a manipulative, powerful female Ginnaye who believed he was worthless. Strike that. She thought he was hot so he had worth as a 'playmate'. But she'd rather die than let anyone else know that.

Jai sighed, reaching to grasp her hands and stop her from undressing. He'd been waiting for a moment to end it. Dumping her was part of the whole revenge thing but there had never been an opportune time. Heading off for his big assignment meant he'd be gone for gods knew how long. It was perfect timing.

He chuckled inwardly. He was going to enjoy this.

"Stop." He pulled back, watching her beautiful face darken. "It's not going to happen, sweetheart."

"What are you talking about?" she hissed angrily, frantically trying to re-button her blouse.

"I got a big assignment." He shrugged. "Don't know how long I'll be gone."

"So what has that got to do with anything?"

Jai narrowed his eyes on her and he watched the pulse jump in her throat. He couldn't help but enjoy the fact that he had such an effect on her. "What was it you called me at that meeting with Hugo and my father two weeks ago? A useless piece of dog crap with poison for blood?"

She shrugged, her dark eyes flashing. "It was a joke."

"Oh yeah, it felt like one."

"What's this about, Jai? You've never been pissed off before."

"I'm not pissed off. I don't do pissed off." He ran a hand down her neck, watching her shiver. "I don't care enough about you to do pissed off." Exhaling heavily, he stood back, placing a mocking regretful look on his face. "It's been nice, sweetheart, but I'm moving up and on. Time for you to hitch a ride back to your full-bloods."

It was hilarious, watching her jaw drop. Yasmin was not the kind of girl a guy broke up with. "Are you dumping me?"

"How can I dump someone I was never with?"

"You asshole!" she screeched, pushing him out of the way. "Wait until I-"

"Until you what, Yasmin?" he laughed now, eyeing her evilly. Yasmin was still that spoiled little girl who ran to her daddy when things didn't go her way. Hugo had threatened a number of boyfriends in the past. "Tell your daddy on me?" He shook his head, making a tutting noise. "You can't tell Hugo, sweetheart, cos' then he'd know just how naughty you've been this year."

Jai didn't think her face could grow any redder with rage. "I was right about you. You are nothing. You are worthless, Jai! No one wants you. Not for anything real."

He shrugged, not letting her see her words had affected him. "You really think I care?"

With a growl of rage, the air shimmered around her telling Jai she was about to use the *Peripatos*. Yasmin exploded into flames at the same time the vase on his phone table screamed, shattering into a million flying shards all directed at him. Jai cursed, wiping hand across the air in front of him. The shards sliced into his enchantment, turning into grains of sand before they could hit and cut him.

He grunted, leaning down to scoop at the sand on his carpet. The rug was one of the few splashes of color and comfort in his condo and was a genuine Moroccan Berber. Handmade. Expensive. Irreplaceable. It would take him forever to get the sand out without damaging the wool. "Should have dumped the crazy bitch weeks ago."

~3~

Push and Pull Too Much, My Heart Will Fall Right Out

The delicious, tingling impact of forceful sprays of hot water from her shower head woke Ari up in more ways than one. She frowned at herself, lathering coconut scented shampoo into her hair, her fingers digging into her scalp with frustration. She was not a negative, pessimistic person. She was… well… not exactly an optimist but she was not the depressed, 'bemoaning her fate' kind of girl she'd been projecting lately. No. She was a 'quit whining and do something about it' kind of girl. So OK, sure she didn't know if she had made the right choice about college, but since she hadn't a clue what she really wanted to do with her life, getting a degree seemed like the practical thing to do. So what if she wasn't looking forward to it? Ari was not going to lounge around all summer being pissy. No. She had a task to complete. Operation Save Charlie. A whole summer stretched ahead of them and Ari was dedicating this summer to pulling Charlie back from whatever hell he had dug himself into. He could be alright. Ari had to believe that someone as smart and kind and funny as Charlie still had a long, bright future ahead of him.

Determined to begin right away, Ari pulled her wet hair into a messy bun and threw on a light summer dress. Quickly checking her reflection before she left the bedroom, she noted the dark circles under her eyes and cursed. She took a couple of seconds to find some concealer and cover those bad boys up, her eyes washing over her reflection to make sure there was nothing horribly wrong. Usually she didn't much care but this morning she was hunting down Charlie and wanted to look at least OK. The fact was… it was kind of easy for Ari to look OK. Whoever her mom had been she had been pretty and Ari had inherited her exotic looks. Her long hair was thick and dark brown, although when the sunlight hit it, it had a reddish tint to it. Her smooth skin looked permanently tanned all year round and she had soft, pretty features, the most distinctive of which were eyes that seemed to shift colors in different light. No one was able to really pin point Ari's actual eye color, only that they were beautiful with thick, long lashes so dark Ari never wore mascara. She was pretty. It was a fact. But unlike other girls Ari didn't pander to the pretty. She wasn't vain, she wasn't egotistical;

she didn't assume things would go her way because of her face. But what she was according to Rachel was even worse. Indifferent. She didn't care. She knew she could throw on a pair of sweats and an old t-shirt and still pass for OK and according to Rachel that was an inverse vanity that bugged the hell out of her. Ari wasn't quite sure what that meant so she'd politely told her best friend to stick her inverse vanity up her ass.

Sure that she was presentable, Ari grabbed her school bag and hurried out of the house, foregoing breakfast, and texting Rachel to let her know she didn't need a ride to school that morning. Ari marched down the street, her long legs eating up the sidewalk, the lactic acid in her muscles burning as she forced them into sudden and intense exercise.

She made it to the Creagh's in record time *and* just in time to bump into Charlie as he slammed out of the front door. He stopped abruptly, pushing his messy hair out of his eyes, blinking at her owlishly. He took the steps two at a time and half-jogged over to her where she waited on the sidewalk. A waft of lemon danced up Ari's nose and she noted he was wearing a freshly-washed *South Park* t-shirt over a long-sleeved shirt. He'd done his laundry. Surely that was a good sign. Right?

"What are you doing here?" he grumbled, shouldering past her toward the direction of school.

Ari's heart was pounding as she took in his tired but un-dilated eyes. She brushed her hand across his arm to slow him down. "I thought we could walk to school together like old times."

Charlie frowned, throwing her a suspicious look out of the corner of his eye. "What's going on?"

Ari pretended to look affronted. "Does something need to be going on for me to want to hang out with you? We haven't hung out in forever."

"We don't exactly run with the same crowds these days, Johnson."

Here goes. Ari took a deep breath. "We could change that."

"What's that supposed to mean?"

The desire to start screaming and shouting at him that he was acting like a complete and utter douchebag bubbled under Ari's skin as it did sometimes when she forgot what he was going through, but she shook it off, pulling on every ounce of patience she had. "It means… you could stop hanging out with those bums and start getting your life back on track."

"I'm perfectly happy with my bums."

The distance Charlie put between them hurt, a painful hurt that was as fresh today as it was the first day he'd spoken to her in that infuriating monotone. "You used to be perfectly happy with me."

"Ari, don't."

"Don't tell me what to do," she muttered in irritation, frustrated that their meeting was already off to a dismal start.

Charlie grinned at her then, and her heart lit up at the sight of it. "Don't tell *me* what to do," he countered teasingly.

See, why can't he be that Charlie all the time? I love that Charlie. Giving him a soft smile, a smile meant to coax, Ari nudged him with her elbow. "How about we hang out this summer?"

"Yeah, sure."

Back to Mr. Monotone again. Great. "I thought maybe we could take a road trip or something."

"Yeah, whatever you want."

"Or we could do something you want to do."

He laughed bitterly, slamming his hands into his jean pockets and hunching over a little as they continued walking. "I wouldn't let you do what I want to do."

OK, maybe it was too early for patience. "What... get high? Get wasted. Sleep around with a bunch of STD-infected skanks."

"Ari," he moaned. "It's too early for this shit."

"Yeah well it's never too early to catch a disease," she snapped, attempting to conceal her jealousy and hurt that he slept with anything with breasts and yet treated her like an asexual house plant. "Have you even been to a clinic?"

"Two weeks ago." He tilted his chin arrogantly, narrowing his eyes to a smolder that should have annoyed her rather than cause the funny flutter in her lower abdomen. "Just because I'm eye-candy doesn't mean I'm stupid."

"Oh, ha-ha, funny."

"I'll have you know lots of girls find me attractive."

"Yeah and you don't turn down any of them do you."

"That sounds suspiciously like you're calling me a manwhore."

"I *am* calling you a manwhore."

"Ouch. I'm hurt."

"Yeah I can really see you're cut up about it."

Charlie grinned, his dark eyes glittering. "I miss you, Johnson."

Ari's heart stopped, a painful halt in beat that made her almost trip. She smiled sadly. "I miss you too."

He sighed, coming to a stop, eyeing her carefully. "A road trip huh?"

Her smile widened to a grin that made Charlie's eyes lighten even more. "Yup."

"OK, if it makes you smile like that I'm in. I haven't seen that smile in a long time."

Surprised, Ari attempted a casual shrug as she replied, "I wouldn't have thought you'd noticed."

"What? How sad you've been lately? I'm stoned, Ari, not blind."

"Didn't think there was any difference."

"Oh, ha-ha, funny," he threw her earlier words back at her. "So you going to tell me what's been bothering you or can I guess?"

A rush of overwhelming relief coursed over her at his question. This was Charlie. This was really, really Charlie. "Well I-"

"Hey, C-man, wait up!" a deep voice cut Ari short and they turned to see Mel Rickman trolling towards them in his beat up 1999 Subaru Impreza. He stopped beside them, leaning out of the driver's side window. "What's up?"

Charlie nodded tightly at him. "Not much."

Mel flicked a look at Ari, his eyes travelling up the length of her bare legs, resting on her breasts for a little too long, and then scanning her face with a twisted smile and burning eyes. "What's up, Princess?"

Charlie stepped in front of her, jerking his head towards the direction of school. "Ari, why don't you head in? We'll catch up at your party."

Furious at Mel for ruining their moment, for bringing reality crashing down on the remnants of what had once been a wonderful relationship, Ari clenched her jaw. "Why don't you come with me?"

His eyes narrowed. "Because I don't want to. I'll see you later."

"When?" she snapped, all pretense gone.

He sighed, rubbing a warm hand up and down her now chilly arm. "Your party. OK?"

Her eyes flicked to Mel, her anger over everything that had happened to Charlie in the last two years directed at him. He just kept smiling stupidly. She exhaled heavily and stepped back from Charlie's touch. "Whatever." She shook her head, her disappointment fighting her attempts to smooth things over between them and winning. Without looking back, Ari took off, her feet eating pavement in shovels.

"Ari!"

She stopped, her heart pulling at how sad he sounded. Smoothing her features to a placid expression, she spun around. Charlie's soulful eyes touched her even from so far away. He raised a hand in a forlorn wave and all of her angry resolve melted away. With a small, equally sad smile, Ari waved back and then turned, quickly marching towards the school, pretending her best friend wasn't just about to buy more pot.

Determined not to be a buzz kill again today, Ari tried to push Charlie out of her thoughts for once, making a mental list of everything she and Rache needed to get for the party on Friday. She was only at dip when a familiar voice brushed her ears, causing her to lose her train of thought. "Hey, Ari."

Yanked from her daze, Ari stopped in the middle of the school hallway and turned to find Nick Melua standing pretty close. She tried to take a step back without being too obvious. "Hey, Nick." She gave him a friendly smile, shuffling her books around in her arms in an attempt to not look uncomfortable.

"I'm really looking forward to your party on Friday." His blue eyes washed over her face with a familiar longing that made her want to stuff herself inside her locker and hide.

Nick was a friend of A.J.'s, they were both jocks, although Nick was on the basketball team not the wrestling team, both nice guys, kind of All-American types. After confiding to A.J. that he'd always had a thing for Ari, A.J. had begun a campaign to get the two of them together at the beginning of senior year. After weeks of pestering, and in attempt to get over Charlie, Ari had given in and gone on a couple of dates with Nick. Nick was good-looking, tall, tan, dark hair, blue eyes; he was smart, considerate, nice. But he didn't make her laugh and he could be kind of immature sometimes. She just… didn't feel that spark with him. According to A.J., Nick had been devastated when she'd ended their brief relationship (if you could even call it that). But he put on a good front, always friendly to her, and she was friendly back. But that little spark of longing hope in his eyes made her decidedly uncomfortable.

"I'm glad. It should be great fun."

He grinned again, shifting his feet, running a hand through his hair. He looked like a guy getting ready to ask a girl out.

Ari's heart plummeted into her stomach.

"Uh… I got to get to class," she mumbled and took off, leaving him in the exhaust fumes of her beat up social awkwardness.

They were doing jigsaw puzzles in Art History (all Art History related of course) and Ari was beginning to feel hot and claustrophobic as the classroom filled with the chatter of seniors and their talk of the future.

"I can't wait to get to Brown," Laurie Hollister chirped as Ari squinted at a puzzle piece she'd just inserted. It didn't look right. She took it out, hunting for another piece of crackled flesh. Their puzzle was the Mona Lisa. "Of course I'll need to get a new wardrobe and meet my new roommate but at least I know Staci and A.J. are on the same island as me. It's a small comfort right?"

Ari nodded mutely, her chest squeezing tight. God, were there no windows open in this place?

"I bet the babes are smokin' at USC," Jim Deebs said behind her to his puzzle partner. "I heard they wear bikini tops to class."

Ari couldn't even roll her eyes, she was too busy gulping in air.

"What about you, Ari?" Laurie asked. "Aren't you scared heading off to Philadelphia all by yourself? I know it's only a state away but the big city... kind of scary, no?"

Shut up, shut up, shut up, shut up...

"You'll probably meet some really nice guys there. Do you know what classes you're going to take yet? I'm still chewing over mine at the moment. Didn't your dad go to Penn? He must be so proud. Maybe he can help you pick out classes. Are you getting a single room or do you want a roommate too?" Unable to take it any longer Ari slid back from the desk with a loud scrape of her chair. Laurie looked up at her wide-eyed. "You OK?"

Trying to still the trembling in her hands, Ari nodded jerkily. "Just need the bathroom."

Grabbing the bathroom pass from the teacher, Ari ducked out into the school hallways, cold air from the a/c flooding her lungs and opening them up. She could actually feel the muscles unfurling with relief. Wanting some of the real stuff, Ari took off towards the front entrance, pushing the heavy door open with a muffled 'oomph' and coming to an abrupt halt at the sight that greeted her. Out in the parking lot, in the bright sun, Charlie stood with a sophomore, Vivien Meyer. He was smiling at her in a way that caused an aching wave of salt water to crash over Ari, nipping her eyes, disorientating her, knocking her off her feet. It was the kind of smile a guy gave a girl he wanted to kiss. Vivien raised a joint to her mouth in full view of the school. She inhaled, and before she could exhale, Charlie pressed his lips to hers, kissing her deep, his hand clasping the back of her head. He drew back and blew out the smoke, the two of them laughing.

It wasn't the first time she'd seen Charlie making out with someone else. And just like every other time she'd witnessed it, it hurt like a mother effing bitch.

The kiss settled in her stomach like a lump of solid stone, her day officially ruined. Ari trembled with fury, watching them head off across the lot towards the stoner's spot. If it was the last thing she did before she left Ohio, she would save that little tool from himself. Pissed off, she slammed back inside the school, marching towards her locker and ripping her bag out. She couldn't bear to listen to Laurie's college chatter and she couldn't bear to be even 100 yards from Charlie. Screw it. She was ditching.

As soon as Ari stepped outside the gates a feeling of relief flooded her. She glanced back at the school, bemused by the overwhelming sensation of disconnection. It seemed her mind had made the break from high school and was just waiting for the end of semester to catch up with her. Maybe she *was* terrified of the future… it didn't mean she was clinging to the school. It was one part of her past that truly was history.

The sun beat down on her back as she strolled homeward, the freedom of walking out of school brightening her day a little again as she deliberately avoided any thought of Charlie and the sophomore.

So busy trying to forget what she'd seen Ari stepped forward to cross the street without looking. Strong hands came down on her shoulders at the same time a horn blasted. Hauled back onto the sidewalk by the hands, Ari watched, heart pounding, as a truck blew passed her.

"Jesus Christ," she cursed at the near miss, inhaling her rescuer's delicious scent of sandalwood and dark spices. She turned to thank the hero, the words sticking in her throat at the sight of the empty sidewalk. There was no one there. The cologne she had smelled began to dissipate. Ari searched the space all around her. Nothing. She had not imagined those hands. If it weren't for those hands she'd be splattered across the front of a truck.

What the hell was going on?

Another poltergeist?

But she'd never felt Ms. Maggie. Ms. Maggie wasn't a solid shape. This thing had been a solid shape. Fear rose in the back of her throat.

"I'm going insane. I'm literally now going mental. I-"

"Ari, what are you doing?!"

Spinning around, Ari's eyes settled on Rachel, hanging out the driver's side window of her car. "Rache?" she frowned.

Rachel grinned at her. "I saw you ditching and decided it looked like fun and it's not like we can really get in trouble now, right? Come on, get in. I've already text Staci and A.J. to ditch and meet us at your house. I thought we'd go to the store, buy some snacks."

Hanging out with her friends sounded wonderful to Ari. So relaxing. So normal. So real. No kissing dopeheads or invisible hands. Perfect. She grinned shakily and skipped over to the passenger side door.

Ari struggled to open the jar of pickles. She slammed the edge of the top off her black granite kitchen counter, knowing her dad would have killed her for that if he had been there. She tried again. "Crap," she groaned, shaking out her reddening hand.

Rachel, who was leaning against the opposite counter munching on some *Pringles*, rolled her eyes. "Give it here."

"You're, like, half the size of me, if I can't get it, you can't."

Her friend quirked a blond eyebrow. "I'll have you know this tiny package is made of steel. Give it."

To her amazement the lid popped open in Rachel's hands. Ari eyed her suspiciously, taking a pickle out. "Have you been taking steroids?"

Again with the eye rolling. "Oh please, I leave the drug-taking to Charlie."

Ari glared at her.

Rachel laughed sheepishly. "Sorry, cheap shot."

"Mmmhmm."

"Really, I am sorry. How are you anyway? You seemed so down yesterday."

Not wanting to get into it with her, Ari shrugged. "I'm fine."

Her friend exhaled wearily. "I'm not stupid, Ari. I know when something is up with you."

God, how Ari wished she could talk to Rachel about college and how much she was freaking out, but Rachel, despite being her current best friend, was the last person Ari could discuss it with. Rachel had wanted to be a doctor since her cousin died of leukemia when they were eight. That kind of determination and single-minded focus was a huge part of her personality. Unfortunately she tended to think that people that lacked focus were flakes and unworthy of her time.

At her extended silence, Rachel grinned lasciviously. "I know what would help."

Ari grimaced. "What?"

"You need to trade in your v-card."

Nearly choking on her pickle, Ari watched as a rice packet flew out of one of the open cupboards and whacked Rachel across the head. She burst out laughing as her friend's eyes popped open in shock.

"What the hell was that?"

Ari chuckled. "That was Ms. Maggie defending my virtue, you tramp."

"Your frickin' poltergeist?!"

"Yup."

"I thought you were kidding about that!"

"No way!" A.J. suddenly loped into the kitchen grinning. "Ms. Maggie totally took me out last time I was here when I cracked a joke about women 'in the kitchen and in the bedroom'."

"Good." Staci strolled in at the back of him, Nick on her tail. Ari's spirits dipped a little at the sight of Nick and she hoped her expression hadn't said so when Staci explained, "Nick was in our class. We offered to rescue him."

"Of course." Ari forced a smile. "The more the merrier."

He smiled back. "Thanks. I thought I was going to die of boredom back there."

Ari nodded, trying her best to fake relaxation. "Can I get anyone a drink?"

"You got any beer?" A.J. asked, pulling the refrigerator open and taking out her dad's beers before she could respond.

They settled in her living room, eating and joking around as they took turns on the *PlayStation 3*. And by took turns Ari meant while the boys hogged the controllers. Hanging out with Nick was a little uncomfortable, but being with the group made it easier and soon he and A.J. were so engrossed in video games there was nothing to be uncomfortable about. Ari laughed as Staci made fun of the look of concentration on her boyfriend's face.

"Oh God," she mumbled to her girlfriends. "That's his sex face."

The three of them burst into loud laughter drawing the guys' attention.

"Uh, what's going on over there?" A.J. asked suddenly, looking worried.

"Nothing," Staci teased. She tried to sober at his suspicious expression and avoided his gaze by turning to Nick. "So, Nick, you excited about playing college basketball?"

Just like that the conversation switched to college talk and for Ari the temperature in the room abruptly dropped. A cold sweat erupted across her skin and she excused herself, hurrying into the kitchen, thrusting open the window above the sink and gulping in huge wafts of fresh air. She stood in perfect peace for a couple of minutes before she felt the heat of someone's gaze on her back. Craning her neck around, Ari's eyes caught on Nick's as he stood in the doorway.

"You OK?" he asked, his light blue eyes alight with concern.

She turned to face him as he walked further into the room. He lifted a hand, placing his empty beer bottle down on the counter. He had large hands. They reminded her of the invisible ones that had rescued her today from near death and another sheen of cold sweat broke out under her arms. "I'm fine," she responded softly, clearing her throat as the last syllable came out a cracked whisper.

He smiled shyly, this crazy cute smile that should have made her knees weak but didn't. "You know we're only going to be a state away when we go to college. Maybe I could visit you sometime."

Her heart fluttered in panic at the thought. "You'll be way too busy to come visit me."

Nick shook his head adamantly. "Not possible."

Oh crap.

"I-"

"You looked beautiful at Prom, by the way," he interrupted, grinning sweetly. "I never got a chance to say it to you that night."

Ari frowned. "Probably a good thing since you had a date, Nick."

"She was just a friend."

Oh this conversation was going downhill fast.

"Ari! We need more chips!" Rachel shouted from the living room.

I love you, Rache. She shrugged, grabbing them up off the counter. "Duty calls." She brushed past him, hurrying from the conversation as if the hounds of hell were nipping at her heels rather than a cute guy with a crush on her. What was wrong with her?!

For the rest of the day Ari never made the mistake of being in a room unattended again. Nick gave her a hug when he left and she couldn't stop herself from tensing in his arms. He noticed, shuffling back awkwardly from her and making her feel like the worst person alive. A.J. glared at her, the blow of that look softened by his girlfriend's sympathetic smile and Rachel's grimace that said 'when will that dude take the hint?!' She was never so thankful to be left alone in her empty home. Well... almost empty.

"Ms. Maggie," she called out, leaning against the front door. "You got a poltergeist friend who's corporeal but invisible?"

Knowing the poltergeist was unable to answer only added to her frustration because she could not get what happened on that street out of her mind.

"Knock the phone off the side table if you do have a poltergeist friend who can touch me."

Nothing.

"OK. Is there a poltergeist out there that can touch me who isn't a friend?"

The phone clattered to the ground with a sickening thump. Ari's stomach roiled, her heart racing hard and fast inside her chest. "Oh God," she whispered. "Way to scare the crap out of me."

The door reverberated against her back with three loud bangs and Ari yelped in horrified surprise.

"Ari!" Charlie's concerned voice shouted from outside.

"Holy macaroons!" She yelled, pulling the door open. "You scared the bejesus out of me!"

A frown wrinkled the skin between his brows and his eyes washed over her looking for injury. He shoved past her, glancing around the hallway. "You OK? What's going on?"

She slumped, suddenly feeling exhausted. It was too crazy to explain. He'd probably think she'd finally lost the plot. "I was just talking to Ms. Maggie. I wasn't expecting anyone at the door."

Charlie's shoulders seemed to drop, relaxing as he shut the door. "I thought you were being murdered or something."

"No. Ms. Maggie wouldn't let that happen."

"Yeah." He curled his lip teasingly. "Thank God for Ms. Maggie."

Now that her heart was returning to its normal rate, it suddenly occurred to her that Charlie was here. At her house. Of his own accord. "What are you doing here?"

He shrugged, heading towards the living room, eyeing the empty beer bottles and chip packets. "Thought maybe we could watch a movie." When he turned back around his dark eyes blazed, goading her to ask him why. There were two paths in front of her here. She could ask him and he'd start an argument and leave. Or she could just watch a damn movie with him. Easy answer.

"What do you want to watch?" she asked nonchalantly, heading over to her collection.

He seemed to let go a sigh of relief behind her, the couch groaning as he thumped himself down into it. "Action."

"*Universal Soldier?*"

"Sounds good."

Taking the classic Jean-Claude Van Damme movie her dad loved out of its case, Ari tried not to smile, the stone that had been in her stomach all day completely dissipating. Forcing herself to remain casual, she flopped down on the couch next to him and handed him the remote.

They watched the movie in perfect silence, the heat of Charlie next to her so unbelievably relaxing Ari had to fight not to curl into him and fall asleep.

At the end, as the credits rolled up, Charlie muted the television and stood up. He looked down at her, his dark eyes enigmatic and so deep Ari could feel herself falling into them as they locked onto her own. "Ari?"

"Yeah?" she whispered, not wanting him to leave.

"If you don't want to go to college, then don't go. It's a lot of money and you should know what you want to do with your life first. Talk to your dad, OK. Make him understand."

She nodded slowly, her heart hammering as she listened to his footsteps fade, the door opening and shutting behind him with a click that told her he'd put the lock on.

Before, when she'd thought Charlie wasn't Charlie anymore, the pain had been hard and deep.

Somehow, it was worse knowing Charlie was still in there behind this iron cast wall no one could get through. Today was just one of those lucky days when he slid back a little window to talk to her. But when her front door closed, she knew that window had closed with it.

~4~

Solace is Looking For You, Stop Hiding

*I*t was divine providence that's what it was, Ari thought, looking down at the cell in her hands. Charlie's cell. Clearly it had slipped from his pocket while he was watching the movie last night all so Ari would have an excuse to see him today. She clutched it tightly in her hand, tempted to scroll through the numbers and see how many girls his contact list had accumulated over the last two years. But that would be wrong. She shook her head. She wasn't that far gone yet. Smiling, Ari dropped the cell into her bag and set off outside, texting Rachel again to let her know she didn't need a ride to school.

Her stomach growled from lack of breakfast and Ari grimaced. The sacrifices she was making for love.

Feeling lighter than she had in some time (and all because she'd clocked more Charlie time this week than she'd had in the last two months), Ari turned up the volume on her iPhone, letting *Metric* sweep her through the suburban streets. Her neighborhood was quiet and neat. Very neat. The houses were pretty big but modest in appearance with lush lawns and white fences and lots of space between each one. The street curved around in a huge bend until it split off into two directions. To the left the town stretched out from the moderately well-off, to the rich, to the wealthy, to the even wealthier, and then to a couple of farms on the outskirts of town, like A.J.'s parents' grain farm. As for the center of Sandford Ridge it was literally that. The center. Stores, two 'malls', small businesses, a large car manufacturer factory… the usual. And best of all *The Smoothie Place* on Main Street, Ari's favorite place to chill out.

Ari took the right towards Charlie's house and the school. The Creaghs lived three blocks away in a noisier neighborhood that seemed much more real to Ari. She'd loved hanging out there. Unlike her street, where the only activity consisted of people jogging by quietly alone or with their dogs, Charlie's street was abuzz with the sounds of children's laughter and shouts as they played in one another's yards. Lawnmowers growled, dogs barked, music blared from car radios. It was like walking out of Stepford into Sandford. Charlie's neighborhood was still considered the west side, as was their high school, but only four blocks over from the high school was all the low income housing and two well-kept trailer parks. Overall Sandford Ridge wasn't a bad place to live. It just... wasn't *great* either.

Just as she was taking her first steps onto Charlie's street the smell of sandalwood and spices floated up her nose and Ari skidded to a halt, her heart suddenly thumping in her chest. Sniffing the air to catch the scent again her skin prickled as if someone were staring at her. Or standing right over her shoulder. Heart hammering now, Ari twisted her head around and stared. No one there. She sniffed again and couldn't find the scent. Thoroughly freaked out at the reminder of the invisible hands that had rescued her, Ari curled her arms around her waist, hunching over and picking up her feet.

Jittery, Ari felt her heart kick into super speed as she strode up onto Charlie's porch. She blew out nervous air between her lips, glanced once more to make sure there was no one behind her and rapped on the porch door. When there was no response she rapped again, only harder this time.

Mrs. Creagh appeared at the door, pulling it open and shoving the screen door open so hard it almost whacked Ari on the nose. Charlie's mom's expression cleared somewhat at the sight of her but Ari missed the huge smile she always used to bestow on her when she came around. "Ari. Haven't seen you in a while."

Ari shrugged apologetically. "Yeah, I know. Things have been... busy. I'm looking for Charlie, is he still home?"

Mrs. Creagh snorted and stepped back. "You'll be lucky. You can go on in and check his bedroom if you like. I'm late for work." She grabbed her handbag and keys and scooted past her, patting her shoulder almost affectionately before she left. Ari stared after her, watching her walk to her car with slouched shoulders and angry lines around her eyes. The bubbly, mothering woman who would have known whether or not her son was safe and home in his bedroom every night and every morning was gone. She'd died two years ago along with her youngest. Feeling anger at her loss and her subsequent treatment of the son she had left, Ari swallowed hard, trying to force the choking sensation in her throat away.

"Mrs. Creagh!" she called out before she could stop herself.

Charlie's mom nearly dropped her keys, her head jerking up in confusion. "Yeah?"

"He's not good," Ari told her, her voice cracking on the words. "Charlie." His mother gulped, her skin seeming to tighten even more across her cheeks, her lips trembling. Seeing the emotion Ari took a step towards her. "He still needs you, Mrs. Creagh. The way he's going… you'll be lucky to have any kids left."

Rearing back like Ari had slapped her, Mrs. Creagh's face darkened, her eyes narrowing. Ari waited for her to say anything, even if it was to tell her to mind her own business, but instead she jammed her keys in the car door before hauling ass into it as if she was running from a wall of flames. Feeling almost bad for what she'd said, Ari turned away and peered into the house. If Charlie was in, she hoped he hadn't overheard that.

Pushing her shoulders back, she walked slowly into the house, amazed by how familiar and yet unfamiliar it was. Mrs. Creagh had always been this TV mother, always baking so the house consistently smelled like mouthwatering heaven. She'd also hated clutter and there was never a speck of dust anywhere. Now the walls were faded, darkened by cigarette smoke; there were photographs of Mike everywhere, frames cluttering furniture and the walls. Ari stopped at the doorway to the living room and felt her chest twist in pain. Mr. Creagh, about thirty pounds heavier than the last time she'd seen him, was lying on his recliner in front of a flickering TV screen, his eyes closed, his mouth open in loud snores. A half-empty bottle of scotch and a glass tumbler lay knocked over on the floor beside him. Unable to keep looking at the unrecognizable man, Ari squeezed her eyes shut and headed up the stairs to Charlie's room. She'd read about situations like this, seen them on TV, thought they were so clichéd. But it wasn't cliché. It was real. And devastating.

It was unending mourning.

Ari stopped at Charlie's closed door, her hand grasping the cold metal door handle. She so hoped he was in there.

"Charlie?"

Silence.

"Charlie?"

Nothing. Taking a deep breath, she thrust the door open and strode inside, coming to an abrupt halt at what she found. The room was empty. Just... empty. All of the posters that Charlie had pasted to his wall of the bands and movies and books he loved had been ripped down, leaving cold, sterile steel blue walls. His furniture had been thrown out, his bed, his desk, his TV, his bookshelf. All that remained was a sleeping bag on the floor, his laptop, and a pile of books and CDs in the corner of the room. The bedroom smelled musty and there was just the sweet hint of marijuana in the air.

This wasn't grief, Ari shook her head, her jaw clenching with fury that his parents had let him strip his life to nothing. When someone dies, you mourn. After you mourn you grieve. And days, months, years later, something small can happen, like a familiar toy soldier suddenly appearing where it shouldn't, and you grieve all over again. But the mourning… the mourning should end. The Creaghs still mourned. Charlie still mourned.

Resisting the urge to throw a bucket of cold water over Mr. Creagh, Ari flew out of the house, trying to scramble through the people she knew Charlie regularly consorted with. There was only one house she could think of where there were no parents to worry that Charlie was there instead of at home.

Mel Rickman's.

She shuddered at the thought, but she was determined to haul Charlie's butt home. She pounded down the porch stairs and began marching towards Manchester Drive. Everyone knew where Rickman lived and, for such a stupid guy, not once had the police been able to prove he was the one dealing. Ari winced. She guessed that said more about the Sandford Ridge Sheriff Department than Rickman.

The porch screen had a huge tear in it, there was trash bags on the broken porch steps, the windows provided plenty of privacy with the sheer amount of filth accumulated on them and the mailbox was more of a stick stuck in the yard than a receptacle for mail. Ari felt sorry for the neighbors who must pass the house every day and wish they could just burn the eyesore to the ground. Feeling somewhat sick at having to be there, Ari had to take a minute. She was so going to kill Charlie for this.

No one answered when she knocked. Or rapped. Or called out. In the end, after Ari started banging the heck out of the front door, an unfamiliar guy with bloodshot eyes and a sickly pallor pulled it open. "Where's the fire?" he groaned.

"Is Charlie here?"

"Who?"

"Charlie?" Ari snapped.

The guy took a moment, his narrowed eyes searching the ground for clues. Finally he looked up and shrugged. "There's a C-Man."

Ugh, Ari sighed. C-Man. It made him sound like such an idiot. "His name is Charlie." She brushed past the smelly, unwashed miscreant, pushing him aside.

"Hey, watch it, girl."

She eyed the living room. There were five people passed out on the floors and furniture. Ari shivered as one of them came to, his bleary eyes all too familiar. Rickman. Desperate to get out of there before he became semi-functional, Ari turned back to unwashed guy. "Where is Charlie?"

He pointed down the hall. "Back bedroom, but I wouldn't go in there if I were you."

Not caring what he would or wouldn't do, Ari rushed down the hall to the door he'd pointed at, so determined to get out of Rickman's house she didn't think. She burst the door open and ignored the kick to her stomach at the sight of Charlie sprawled across the bed next to Vivien Meyer.

Well at least he's got his pants on, Ari thought, thanking God for small favors.

He jerked awake at the sound of her entrance. "W-what?"

Catching sight of his *South Park* t-shirt, Ari grabbed it up off the floor and threw it at him. "Get up. Now."

"Ari?" He mumbled, pulling the shirt off his face. His eyes widened and he sat up, swaying a little. He shot a look at Vivien next to him and then paled, glancing back up at Ari. "What are you doing here?"

She narrowed her eyes on his face and leaned closer. He reeked of tequila. "Are you wasted?!"

He winced, clutching his head. "Ari, keep it down, Christ."

"I'll keep it down if you get up and get dressed and leave here with me."

Charlie's expression changed instantly at her demand. He glared up at her. "What the hell are you doing here, anyway, Ari? You shouldn't be here. You're not my mom. I'm a big boy."

Fury shot through her. This wasn't the boy she loved. The boy who had wanted them to take a year out before college to travel the world together before he headed back to the States to study Architecture, hoping that whatever Ari decided to do she'd follow him. No… she didn't know who this person was. But she sure as hell knew she was never going to get him through his brother's death if she continued to let him wander down this path. "A big boy, huh? Well start acting like it, you drunken douche!" she huffed and dug into her bag, pulling out his cell phone and throwing it at him. It smacked against his chest and she enjoyed the look of surprise on his face. "You left your cell at my place. I thought I'd return it. And now I'm getting you out of Loserville. Come on," she snapped, kicking one of his sneakers towards him.

He kicked it back at her. "Ari, quit it. My head is pounding. Just go to school." He leaned back against his pillow, as if preparing to go back to sleep. Vivien hadn't even moved, clearly having passed out rather than fallen asleep. "I'll see you at your party tomorrow."

"What's all the noise?" Mel came up behind her and she sidestepped him, shivering at the feel of his breath on her neck. He reeked.

"Ari's just leaving," Charlie mumbled.

"I'm not leaving without you."

"Then I guess you're not leaving."

Mel chuckled. "Sounds good to me." He slid an arm around her waist, pulling her towards him. "We can have some fun, Princess."

"Get off!" Ari pushed at him, but he wouldn't let go.

Charlie was there in seconds, having moved pretty fast for someone who'd been complaining like a little bitch about his hangover. He shoved Mel up against the door frame, his face scrunched up with anger.

"Hey, man, relax," Mel laughed unsurely. "Me and your girl are just talking."

Repulsed at the thought of her and Rickman coupled together, even in just a sentence, Ari balked, "Ugh-"

"Shut up, Ari," Charlie growled, shoving Mel out of the door before turning to scramble for his things. He yanked on his shirt, stuffing his feet into his sneakers and reclaiming the cell she had thrown at him. Glad that something had convinced him into action at least, Ari ignored the biting pain of his fingers curled around her upper arm, dragging her out of the house.

She smiled as they stumbled down the porch steps and annoyance burned in his gaze when he caught her smug expression.

"Don't." He shook his head angrily, pale with the hangover. "You think you're so funny, don't you?"

"I think I got you out of there."

He laughed bitterly. "Yeah, well, now I have nowhere to go."

Ari sobered, thinking about the room back at the Creagh's. So cold. So empty. Such a stark reminder of everything Charlie's family had lost. Suddenly she understood why he truly thought that. Sighing sadly, Ari nudged him with her shoulder. "Come on. I know a place."

When she returned to her bedroom with a glass of water, a banana and some aspirin, Charlie was already out for the count. He lay sprawled across her comforter, his sneakers kicked off, his hands bunched up under her pillow, his pale face relaxed in sleep. Aching for him, Ari set the tray down on her bedside cabinet and scrawled out a note for him, telling him to take a shower when he woke up and to eat whatever he wanted.

She was late for school now, but it beat sitting around waiting for Charlie to wake up. She was afraid when she got home he wouldn't be there but on the other hand she didn't know what she'd say to him if he woke up to find her still there.

All day Ari half-listened to her friends as Rachel went over the final list of things still needed for the party and as Staci and A.J. had their usual 'cute' disagreements. Instead she pondered the fact that she had really messed this one up. For two years she'd had the opportunity to get Charlie the help he needed, to speak to an adult about what was really going on with him, to even talk to her dad. But she'd put it off and put it off, calling it a phase. And now Charlie was eighteen. He was on his own and Ari was just waiting for him to tell her that he had decided to drop out of school. She could feel it coming.

Ari had to let him know that she was there. Maybe she could convince him to talk to someone… like a therapist or something…

Maybe.

Although she doubt he'd go for it.

She had to make him talk.

She had to.

Somehow Ari had known that when she walked into her room she would find the bed remade, the dishes gone from the side of the bed, and no trace of Charlie in the house. He was like a ghost. She sighed, dropping her bag to the ground. Her blood twisted in her veins, hot with frustration. Her computer chair rolled out away from her desk towards her. She flopped into it.

"Thanks, Ms. Maggie."

Even her poltergeist was more real than Charlie.

~5~

Can You Party in the Past?

*R*achel's parents, Mr. and Mrs. Duff, were awesome. They hugged Ari close and congratulated her on graduating and told her how proud they were of her. They made sure she was in every photograph and when she had stood up on the stage to collect her diploma they had cheered just as loudly for her as they had for their own daughter. Graduation hadn't been so bad so far. Despite her own fears for the future, the atmosphere vibrated with so much excitement it was hard not to be positively affected by it.

Though Charlie should have been graduating with her.

She'd called him that morning but he hadn't picked up. Feeling lonelier than ever, Ari had wandered into her dad's room, picking up his favorite cologne and squirting a little into the air. As she'd glanced around his bedroom she'd realized how bare it was of anything familial. Derek's parents had died when he was eighteen, leaving him all alone in the world. Ari guessed that's why he didn't see anything so wrong about leaving her so much. He didn't mind the alone time, so he probably didn't realize how much *she* minded it. There weren't any photographs of her grandparents, nothing to give her any kind of connection to her lost family, and her dad never talked about them. He didn't talk about a lot of stuff. Her eyes had fallen to the one photograph in the room, sitting on his bedside table. It was a picture of the two of them, hugging outside Disneyworld the summer she turned ten. They'd gone with Michelle, who had taken the photograph of them.

It had suddenly struck Ari as she stood there in a conservative white dress her dad would have loved, her hair pulled back in a French plait, pearls he had bought for her sixteenth wrapped around neck, that she would be all alone at graduation. There would be no grandparents. No father.

No mother.

For the first time, a shocking breath of air escaped her at the thought. She'd never wanted a mother... but that morning, in that dress, getting ready to graduate, Ari had realized how wonderful it would have been to have her mother there. She saw how Rachel was with her mom. They were as close as two people could be. They told each other everything.

Shaken at the seemingly out-of-the-blue yearning that had taken hold of her, Ari had fled from the room, hurrying downstairs to wait on the Duffs.

"Let me take a picture of just Rachel and Ari," Mrs. Duff said. The grin she wore had planted itself there an hour ago and clearly refused to leave. Her good mood was infectious and Ari wrapped an arm around Rachel's waist, pulling the shorter girl close for a photograph that would forever capture that one moment of contentedness on this momentous day. "Beautiful." Mrs. Duff nodded, putting the camera down for the first time.

"My family's ready to leave," Staci said, sweeping over in her cap and gown, A.J. trailing at her back. She smiled sweetly at the Duffs. "Are you ready?"

The two families, plus Ari and A.J., were gathering together for a graduation lunch at *Nellie's* on Main Street, the best burger place in Sandford Ridge. Staci's mom had wanted to go somewhere a little more upmarket but the teens won the vote.

"Sure," Mrs. Duff began. "Let me-"

"*Everybody just wanna fall in love!*"

Ari winced as her loud ringtone interrupted Mrs. Duff. "Sorry." She shuffled around in the little purse she'd brought, pulling the cell out and cutting off *Metric* when she saw the caller ID. "Dad," she breathed happily into the phone, so glad he hadn't forgotten.

"Hey, sweetheart. Congratulations on graduating and happy birthday."

"Thanks, Dad. We're just heading off for lunch. Wish you were here."

"Me too, kid." He sighed heavily. "You got everything you need?"

The question sparked a riot of questions and longings. It was like graduation had flipped a switch inside her. Suddenly Ari felt a wicked slice of pain across her chest and she took a deep breath, wandering away from her friends as she replied, "I don't know."

Sensing her tone, her father's own grew clipped. "What's happened? What's the matter?"

"Nothing. I mean..." she glanced around, feeling lightheaded as she prepared to tell him. "I... just... I've been thinking about Mom today. Isn't that weird?"

Derek exhaled. "Ari, she's not your mom. She's your mother and she left you. She has no right to this day."

But you do! Where are you?!

"I know. I just... it would have been nice to have family here."

"Ari, are you trying to make me feel guilty? Because I already feel bad about missing your graduation."

"No." She trembled, trying to control the anger that was building up under her skin. She felt so off-balance. One minute she had been fine... the next... she was this. "I was asking about my mother, that's all, Dad. I just wanted to know what she was like."

"Why now? It doesn't make a difference, Ari. You're eighteen, you've gotten through life long enough without her and you've never wanted her before and you certainly don't need her now-"

"Dad-"

"I gotta go. Have a great birthday. I'll speak to you soon."

"Dad-"

The line went dead and Ari pulled the cell away from her ear, feeling stuck in slow motion. She was still staring at it when Staci appeared before her, her dark eyes warm with concern. "You OK?"

Ari nodded shakily, trying to force a smile.

"Oh, Ari…" Staci reached out a comforting hand. "Forget about your dad, OK. We're here. Today we're your family."

It had been two years since Ari last cried. The last time had been at Mike's funeral. Since then she'd sort of decided that tears were only for when something hurt so much it changed you deep inside. Today she wanted to cry. But she wouldn't. It had hurt… but she'd get through it.

Charlie had turned up twenty minutes ago, already drunk, eyes vacant as he nodded a hello at her and wandered off to find a beer and talk to Brady Richards who used to hang out with Charlie when he was going through his guitar phase when he was fifteen. She'd wanted to go to him, to ask him if he was OK, to be there for him as he grieved for his little brother on the second year anniversary of his death. But one minute he was there and the next he was gone. Now Ari couldn't see him anywhere in the crowds downstairs. The house was full to bursting with the senior class, more juniors than she remembered inviting, and even a couple of sophomores. Music blared loudly out of her dad's sound system in the living room, fighting with the TV and *PlayStation 3* to be heard as Nick and A.J. had turned it up to full blast. Ari was just waiting for one of her neighbors to cave and call the police. Having left Rachel in the kitchen with Staci as the two of them refilled the snacks that had disappeared in the first hour of the party, Ari decided to take the opportunity to do something that had been niggling at her all afternoon during lunch. She'd thought she'd have time after the celebratory dinner at *Nellie's* but she'd had to pick her car up from the garage and Rache and Staci had brought their outfits for the party with them and had insisted on going directly back to Ari's to get changed and set up for the party. They had done a good job, lots of food, drink, sparkly decorations everywhere. Rache had started piling up the birthday presents on the kitchen table and had taken over being hostess. Ari didn't care. Her mind was upstairs in her dad's room where maybe a hidden photograph or possession of her mother's perhaps could be found. Checking over her shoulder to make sure she had well and truly escaped Rache, Ari hurried into the hall, smiling at a junior she barely knew and skipping up the stairs. She passed a couple of people in the hall but everyone had been pretty good when Rache had announced the upstairs was off limits and anyone caught up there would be tried, judged and punished. There was no one there, and as she shot a quick glance into her room, she was glad to see it was empty. Desperate now to start her search, this inexplicable need that had come out of nowhere as far as she was concerned, Ari picked up the pace.

She strode into her dad's room with determination...

...only to stall at the threshold.

She backed out quickly before the couple realized they'd been caught. Her feet somehow carried her to her room, even though it was like wading through thick tar, and she collapsed on the edge of her bed, her heart racing as the image of what she'd seen kept rolling across her vision.

She'd caught Charlie making out with a girl plenty of times.

That was the first time she'd caught him having sex with another girl... let alone in her father's bed.

Ari wanted to throw up.

She made a harsh, choking noise.

The box of tissues on her bedside table slid towards her and Ari shook her head. "Thanks Ms. Maggie," she whispered. "But I'm not going to cry over him. I won't." Even though it felt as if someone had punched a hole in her chest, reached inside, and were now raking their fingernails along her insides in malicious torture.

"Please tell me you are not talking to that poltergeist again." Rachel grinned from her doorway.

"Her name's Ms. Maggie."

The smile dropped from Rachel's face as she stepped into the room glancing warily around. "OK, I thought you guys were really kidding. If you're serious that there's a poltergeist living here I may never be able to come over to your house again." She shuddered, jerking her head over her shoulder as if she had felt something behind her.

Ari would have laughed if she'd had it in her. "Ms. Maggie won't hurt you."

Rachel paled. "Seriously, Ari, it freaks me out. Stop?"

Taking pity on her friend, Ari nodded. "Sorry."

They were quiet a moment, each assessing the other. Finally Rachel shook her head. "I don't know what's happened between ten minutes ago and now but it can't be good."

"Charlie's screwing some girl in my dad's bed."

Rachel blanched. "You saw?"

"Oh yeah."

"I'm sorry."

Ari shrugged numbly.

Sighing, Rachel slumped down next to her. She nudged her with her elbow. "You know you're not in love with him, right?"

"What?" Ari snapped, shifting away from her.

"Oh come on, Ari. You're not in love with that guy!" she gestured towards the door. "You're in love with Charlie Creagh, sixteen year old cutie and all-around good guy. He's not there anymore. I'm sorry but he's gone. And you have too much going for you to pine over a ghost. So will you please, *please*, get over him?"

The words tumbling out of Rachel's mouth infuriated her for so many reasons but mostly because Ari *knew* she loved Charlie. It wouldn't hurt so much if she didn't love him. Right? She shook her head. "You're wrong."

Rachel's delicate jaw clenched but she was silent. After a few seconds she finally stood up, holding out her hand. "We'll agree to disagree. But for now... you're coming with me because your birthday surprise awaits you."

Ari found herself smiling despite it all. "What did you do?" she asked warily, taking her friend's hand.

Rachel grinned. "You'll see."

"**Uh…why is** there a half-naked hot guy in my living room?"

Sitting on top of a table that had been covered with a vibrant blue silk tablecloth with gold tassels on the end was some buff guy dressed as a… genie??

"Strike that. Why is there a genie in my living room?" Ari turned wide-eyed to Rachel who was grinning at their surprise guest; their surprise guest who at present was holding Staci's palm and murmuring something to her. Behind Staci was a line of girls. The guys were scattered around the room, looking a little doubtful and pissed that someone had turned the *PS3* off.

"He's here to grant us all a wish." Rachel clapped her hands together. "Isn't it cool? We thought we'd get, like, a psychic or something but instead we came across this guy. I tried to convince him that he was really a stripper trapped in genie's body but he wasn't having any of that so what's left of his clothes will unfortunately be staying on."

Thank God, Ari blushed at the mere thought of having this super tall, buff, exotic man with the bald head and gold hoop earrings, naked in her house. Her father would kill her. "Question," she murmured, her eyes washing over his bright red harem pants and

Arabic curly-toed slippers. "Since when does a genie do palm readings?"

Rachel shrugged. "Oh he's like a psychic too."

"I see."

"Birthday girl is here!" Rachel suddenly announced, grabbing her by the arm. "Make way, make way." She pulled her to a stop, shoving Staci none-too-gently out of the way. "Here," she said to the genie guy. "This is Ari. The birthday girl."

When Ari finally stopped glaring at Rachel for shoving Staci, she turned to look up at the guy perched crossed-legged on the table. His deep, dark eyes immediately sucked her in and Ari lost her breath at how intense his expression was. His beautiful features tightened and he reached out to her, taking her hand without permission.

"I am Rabir. What wish may I grant beautiful Ari on this special day?"

She heard giggling from beside her and all around but Ari didn't find it so funny with his abnormally hot hand clasped around hers. His energy seemed to flow into her, holding tight, begging her to make a wish as if it were somehow life or death to him that she did so.

"What do you wish for, Ari? Wish it inside, no words necessary, and I will make it a reality."

Her conscious told her it was a lot of crap but her heart... her heart held on to this gimmick genie/psychic guy and it wished for something she had never even known she wanted until today.

I wish I could see my mother.

As soon as she thought it the genie let go, a wicked smile stretching his lips. Ari stumbled back at his expression, a spark of fiery red glinting in his eyes. He looked... evil.

That's ridiculous. He's not evil. Right? She narrowed her eyes searching his expression for light. There *was* none.

She laughed nervously, shrugging it off, turning to Rachel as a means of escape.

"What did you wish?" Rachel grinned.

Ari took a few more steps back. "If I told you that it won't come true."

"Oh boo you." Her friend turned to the genie. "My turn!"

Feeling hot and thirsty, Ari snuck out of the room as the girls grew more animated about getting their wishes granted. She pulled the refrigerator door open and enjoyed the chill that wafted over her skin, trying to shake off the weird guy in her living room.

"Did you like your surprise?"

Having already been wondering if and when Nick was going to corner her, Ari wasn't surprised when she shut the door to see him leaning back against the kitchen counter. She shrugged. "Typical Rachel to pull something this weird on my birthday."

Nick chuckled. "The girls seem to like him."

"That's because Rabir is built like Jared Padalecki and is half-naked."

He laughed. "Yeah."

An awkward silence fell between them and Ari took a gulp of Diet Coke hoping when she drew breath he'd be gone. He wasn't.

Still unsettled, Ari pulled out a chair and flopped down into it. "You enjoying the party?"

"I was until Rachel shut off the *PlayStation*."

Ari snorted. "Yeah, sorry about that. When Rachel wants something done a certain way…"

"Yeah, I know, she was my lab partner this year."

That made her laugh. She could just imagine how much torture Nick had undergone. She smiled sympathetically and watched his eyes brighten.

"God, you are so special, you have no idea." Nick shook his head

Uh oh. Ari felt her stomach roil. She did not want to do this again. "Nick-"

"No, don't." He held up a hand to interrupt to her. "I know you just want to be friends, Ari. I do. And I know it's because of that knob Creagh. So OK. Let's be friends. Let's hang out this summer?"

Blushing, Ari looked at the floor, unable to meet his eyes as she replied, "You don't look at me like you want to be just friends, Nick."

"That's because I don't. I want more."

"Then we shouldn't hang out. I don't want you to get the wrong idea."

"I know where you stand. I do. I can be friends with you without making you uncomfortable. Just… give me a chance. Please?"

Feeling bad, Ari grimaced, finally drawing her eyes up to meet his. "Nick… I want to hang out with you this summer but I can't if you keep saying things like 'I want more'."

He laughed and stood up away from the counter. "OK. I won't. I swear."

"Do you know how many girls would kill for you to say that to them? You should be back in that living room, choosing one of *them*."

He shook his head. "I want someone special. I'll wait for her. And while I'm waiting I want to hang out with my friend Ari."

Flattered, despite it all, that he thought her so special, Ari stood up, pulling a fresh beer out of the refrigerator for him. "Come on," she said, clinking their bottles together. "Let's go get that *PS 3* turned back on."

Nick and A.J. kept her mind off Charlie for the rest of the night with their antics. She laughed a lot with them, letting her worries disappear, as she spent one last night with all the kids she'd hung out at high school with for the last few years. The genie mysteriously disappeared an hour after his arrival, an hour before his booked time. Rachel had been pissed because she'd paid to have him there for the two hours. Somehow, Staci talked her down. Personally Ari was glad he had left. The guy gave her the heebie jeebies and as for the thing she'd wished for... well... she didn't even want to think about that.

For a brief moment, when A.J. wasn't cracking a joke and she was left quietly sipping her drink, Charlie and the girl upstairs crossed her mind and the breath whooshed out of her body. She took a moment, not even pulling away when Nick wrapped an arm around her shoulder and hugged her close. The party played out around her in a blur of movement and color. Words were spoken, hands touched, lips kissed a cheek. But none of it meant anything to her. She let it happen, glad for the distance between her mind and it.

It was late when people started to leave. Rachel and Staci wanted to stay behind to clean up but Ari just wanted everyone out. Maybe she was more like her dad than she thought because all she wanted now was to be alone. She wanted silence. It took a lot of energy, and some pleading with her eyes at Nick, but between the two of them they managed to persuade Rache and Staci to leave. She hugged her friends as they stepped out into the cool night air, throwing themselves into the back seat of Staci's dad's car. God, she hoped they didn't throw up. She shut the door.

Alone. At last.

Ari turned the lock on the door and strolled slowly back to her living room. Paper cups, streamers, and wrapping paper littered every available space. Her gifts were scattered all over, some of them already broken. Drink spilled onto furniture, food was crunched into the floor. The thought of cleaning it up exhausted her.

"I'll do it in the morning," she mumbled, turning for the stairs.

The strange events of the day buzzed in the background of her mind and echoed in raw pain in her chest but exhaustion won out. Kicking off her shoes, Ari climbed into her huge bed with her jeans still on and collapsed back against her pillow, sinking into the cold mattress.

Her eyes were just closing when she heard the creak of her door. Her heart spluttered and she looked up, squinting in the dark. "Ms. Maggie?" she whispered, watching as the dark shape of a person appeared in the doorway. "Who's there?" She scrambled up into a sitting position, her heart pounding. An image of the creepy genie guy Rabir flashed across her eyes and she tried in her panic to remember where she'd put her baseball bat.

"Ari," a familiar deep voice croaked and her eyes widened as the shape formed in the dark, moving closer to her bed.

"Charlie?"

He gazed down at her, his hair all over the place, his clothes in desperate need of an iron. Ari felt the ache in her chest spread when she took in the haunted look in his eyes. They glimmered with unshed tears, blazing with the agony of his grief. Ari felt the choking sensation in her throat and tried to breathe through it. Somehow, everything that had happened up until that point disappeared and all Ari saw was the boy she loved... *needing* her. Silently she moved over to make room for him, watching quietly as he climbed onto the bed, stretching out beside her. Charlie's head rested against the pillow and he turned on his side to meet her eyes. A tear slid down his cheek. He made a rough choking sound and his body began to shudder with wracking sobs. Without making a sound, Ari slipped her hand across the comforter to grasp his. She felt his fingers curl around her hand, squeezing it tight. It was only when the sounds of his deep sobbing quieted and the echoes of them finally drew still, that Ari relaxed, watching as his chest stopped shuddering, easing in and out slowly as he slept. Assured his grief had been momentarily eased by slumber, Ari finally closed her own eyes, letting her conscious do the same for her, their warm hands anchoring one to the other.

~6~

Wishes are for Dreamers. I'm Not a Dreamer.

"Charlie, stop it," she mumbled, refusing to open her eyes. She was so tired. The tingling in her hand, the one that Charlie still clasped in his sleep, grew sharper until the uncomfortable numbness of it accelerated into acute pain. "Charlie." Ari tugged her hand from his, opening her eyes. Shifting her head on her pillow she was surprised to find her best friend still completely passed out, unconscious. Ari flexed her hand, willing the needle-like pain away, but instead it began to swim up her arm, nipping at muscle and agitating blood. She hissed, reaching out to clasp the arm with her other hand. A slight panic began to build as the pain escalated into her other arm.

"What the…" she trembled now, pushing herself up into a sitting position. "Charlie," she whispered, wanting to wake him up but reluctant to unearth him from his peaceful sleep when he so clearly needed it.

The tingling started in her feet now.

Her heart began banging in her chest.

Cold sweat broke out under her arms.

What the hell was going on with her? Was this some kind of food poisoning? That chicken at lunch *had* looked a little pink in a certain light.

As the pain grew steadily worse, Ari knew she needed to wake Charlie up. Something was seriously wrong with her. Holding in her panic, she reached over to shake him awake and bit back a scream.

Her hand.

Her hand was gone!

Ari watched in horror as the limb began to disappear, like some invisible mouse had come along and was *Photoshopping* her body out of the picture.

The organ in her chest slammed so hard and so fast Ari was sure it was going to explode. "Charlie," she squeaked as the fading began to accelerate around her body. "Char-"

Her body was no longer cushioned against the soft comforter and mattress on her bed. Cold seeped into her bones, blanketed by a hard surface that may as well have been a slab of Antarctic ice.

Had she fallen out of bed?

A sharp memory of her limbs disappearing before her very eyes sliced across her closed eyelids and Ari lifted an arm, patting her chest where her heart still raced.

It had been a dream.

Just a dream.

Thank the ever loving gods.

Groaning, Ari shifted her head and her neck complained with a crick, her hair sliding across a slippery surface.

What the…?

OK. I am definitely not in my bed.

Afraid to open her eyes, Ari took a minute, breathing slowly in and out, trying to calm her heartbeat, a heartbeat that was racing so hard she was close to throwing up. Another shock of icy chill slithered up and along her body from the floor. Ari's eyes popped open.

Her chest instantly tightened, feeling the familiar symptoms of an oncoming panic attack. Letting go of a shaky breath, Ari pushed herself up, glancing down at the cold mirrored floor beneath her. Her shadowy reflection, mottled by the artistic bubbling of the mirror, flickered back at her like a stranger waving a friendly hello. Patting herself down as she drew to her feet, ignoring the bout of dizziness determined to lay her flat out back on the floor, Ari realized she was still wearing the same clothes she had been wearing at the party. Raising her head, her eyes took in her alien surroundings and she shook it, trying to rationalize, trying to stay calm. She was dreaming. Clearly she was dreaming.

She pinched herself and winced in pain.

"Doesn't mean anything," she whispered, her eyes catching on the stone walls that glittered and sparkled in the romantic candlelight. She peered closer, realizing the twinkling flash of color here and there could be attributed to the small precious stones inset into the stone walls. They looked like emeralds. "I'm just dreaming." She nodded. "People have really vivid dreams like this. I've read about it. Maybe someone spiked my drink at the party and I'm on some kind of 'trip'." She exhaled heavily, glancing over the huge four poster bed with its billowing silk canopy made up of entirely fire colors. There was no comforter on the bed, which surprised her considering how cold the air in here was, but there was a decorative velvet blanket placed perfectly across the bottom of it, and millions of jewel-toned silk cushions scattered all over. The bed was the only splash of color in the entire place. The sparse furniture was as chilly as the atmosphere, cut and shaped from what looked like glass. "Must have been some drug," she murmured, confused by the lack of electricity in the room. There wasn't even a light switch.

So... what did one do on a drug trip? She glanced around. There was no one else here to entertain her. No TV, no laptop, no mus-

Oh.

A purple vase on the nightstand drew her attention. Heat seemed to radiate from it, making the vase appear as if it were pulsing with life. Intrigued, Ari moved tentatively towards it, her bare feet freezing on the mirrored floor. As she moved, the air cut around her and this musky, exotic scent tickled her olfactory senses, the floral headiness of it somehow familiar. It smelled like jasmine.

So she was dreaming in 3D IMAX with a scratch & sniff on the complimentary 3D glasses. Didn't mean anything. "This is just a dream," she whispered, reaching a hand out to the vase, sighing at the rush of heat that clambered happily up her arm when she placed her fingertips against the thick glass. Ari squinted. It really was unlike any vase she'd ever seen before. It was solid purple in color with a round fat bottom and a long thin flute of a neck. It reminded her of a genie's bottle.

Genie.

"No." Ari shook her head, stepping back. Creepy genie guy didn't do this. It was a dream. Just a dream. In fact she was probably dreaming about this crap *because* of creepy genie guy. Rachel was going to pay for that little surprise. A gimmick genie at an eighteenth birthday party... what had she been thinking? And not just any genie. Hot genie. With evil, soulless eyes. Rachel was such a pa-

What was that?

Ari pricked her ears, straining to hear it again.

There it is!

Heart pounding, she turned, almost slipping on the floor in her hurry to follow the sound of voices. Voices calling in the distance. Ari shot off across the room towards a door buried deep in the shadows. Wooden and medieval in appearance, Ari wondered what the hell she had been watching or reading in the last few days to make her dream this stuff up. Grasping the iron handle that looked more like a door knocker than a knob, Ari pulled the wooden door inwards and gasped at the blast of cold air that sliced across her skin.

Her chest tightened. "OK. That was pretty real for a dream."

Eyes watering from the sudden rush of oxygen, Ari blinked and tentatively stepped outside. Her feet were beginning to feel stiff and numb from the cold and the black flagstones beneath them weren't helping wake them up. As her eyes stopped tearing, they took in the long stretch of flagstones before her. She was on some kind of huge balcony. The roof arched above her in stunning architecture, swirls and patterns carved into the stone, almost Middle Eastern in appearance. The roof curved down to a halt on her right side, held up by carved columns interspersed evenly along a waist high wall. Ari's eyes drank in the colorful mosaic on the inside of the wall, mosaics depicting people and acts, almost like a story being told. It was like those ancient architectural reliefs her history teacher was always going on about. She followed the picture of a man on fire as his head reached the top of the wall and her eyes automatically looked out and over.

"Holy macaroons..." she gasped, stepping forward unconsciously. Beyond her perch in the balcony of this insanely amazing building, Ari took in the towering stone mountains that surrounded her, mountains that winked green under a winter sun. She squinted, trying to work out the flash and spark and realized the mountains were made out of the same stone and green gems as the walls of the room she'd been in. "Amazing." Built into the mountains were elaborate homes that reminded Ari of the pictures she'd seen of Morocco, architecture that favored curves and color and arabesques. The homes grew steadily more modest the further they were located down a spiral into a valley hidden by a sea of foggy clouds. Ari's eyes widened as she saw people in the distance, walking casually along rough-hewn paths teetering on the edges of the mountains. Just the thought of traversing those roads terrified the bejesus out of her. The voices she heard appeared to have been these colorful figures, who strolled back and forth, descending up and out of the fog in brightly colored, loose fitting robes and pants. *In this weather?* She shivered again, rubbing the goosebumps from her arms. These people were crazy.

They're not real, Ari. Figment meet Imagination.

"Right," she breathed. "*I'm* crazy."

Just a dream.

Ari's whole body froze; her muscles tensed, her shoulders hunched to her ears, her ears pricked up, her heartbeat did its best to drown out her hearing by rushing her blood around her body super-fast. It was the kind of reaction someone might have to the sound of a thief breaking into their house at night. *Ari* was reacting to the low, deadly growl that rumbled from somewhere over her shoulder. She gulped. *Just a dream, just a dream, just a dream.* Slowly, hands trembling, Ari turned, placing one foot carefully after the other. Her eyes widened as she turned full circle and faced...

"Holy mother of crap."

...the thing before her... *oh god, oh god, what is it, what is it?!*

The growling grew deeper and louder as she began backing away slowly towards the room she had just come out of and she felt the bile rise as the thing took an awkward unbalanced step towards her.

You are so seriously messed up if you can dream this kind of stuff up, Ari!

The monster – for that's what it was – snarled. As far as Ari could tell its mulch-shaped head was really only half of a face. It had one eye, dark and lidless with thick, pulsing red veins flowing out from under its mud-colored skin, skin that crinkled like paper when it moved. It had no nose cartilage, no bone structure, just a hole in the middle of its… face?... that grew bigger and then smaller as it breathed its fury at her presence. As for the thing's mouth…

"Just a dream, just a dream," Ari chanted, backing all the way into the room now, her knees dying to buckle in terror as it followed her predatorily, saliva dripping between its black gums and razor-sharp teeth. The ugly horror of the creature was only increased by its lack of a left arm and lack of a right leg. Its twisted malformed body slithered towards her, somehow balanced despite its deformities. Its long, blackened claws clacked and scraped harshly in a high whine against the mirrored floors as it continued to back her into a corner.

Feeling faint and nauseous Ari stopped, struggling to draw breath.

"It isn't real." She shook her head, trying to still her body. "It's OK." She exhaled, opening her eyes to stare the creature down. "Just let it happen. It'll attack and you'll wake up. That's what happens in dre-" She cut off into a silent scream as the monster launched into the air towards her, its mouth open wide. Ari threw her hands up to cover her face, closing her eyes tight and waiting for her subconscious to rip her out of the nightmare. Instead she felt the impact of it hit, her body slamming to the floor with a painful thud that knocked the breath right out of her, her head smacking against the mirrored floor in eye-watering pain. A sharp streak of light shot across her eyes and then she felt wet heat clampdown on her forearm.

Agony ricocheted through her whole system as the monster's teeth tore through her flesh. She screamed, her eyes rolling back in her head as a wave of nausea swept over her.

"Vadit. Heel," a deep, male voice commanded quietly and Ari felt the heat of the monster disappear. Air flowed across her wounds agitating the pain, and she felt the warm blood slip down her arm at too fast a current.

"It's not real," she whispered, tears leaking out from her closed eyes. *It's too real*, she shook, gulping back panic, her body starting to shudder with the shock. Her chest tightened as her heart raced too fast and she felt her brain grow fuzzy, like there was too much crammed inside it. *I'm going to die, I'm going to die.* She struggled to draw breath as the panic attack took control.

"Ari," a hard voice whispered in her ear and she felt the heat of someone bending over her. "Child, open your eyes."

Dad? The thought of the familiar, of having someone here on her side in a dream world she couldn't awaken from, eased the tightness in her chest and her heart began to slow. Despite her pain, the overwhelming belief that she was going to die dissipated and she pried her eyes open. "D-d-d-dad?" she stammered through the shock.

But it wasn't Derek who knelt beside her in dark trousers hand-sewn to his body, his muscled chest bare beneath his rich voluminous robes. The man was huge, perhaps in his mid-thirties, his dark face chiseled hard as if from stone. Ari's heart clenched at the sight of this mammoth man and not because he was a stranger but because of his bleak black eyes that blazed down on her without feeling.

They were empty.

"Yes," he whispered, stroking her hair back from her face, seeming oblivious to the fact that she was in agony and bleeding all over the place. "Child. It is your father."

Ari's heart stopped. "M-my w-w-w-what?"

Slowly her thoughts swam up out of the murky waters they'd been drowning in and Ari gulped, drinking in the air of consciousness. It took her a minute to remember the dream. The nightmare. The pain.

She groaned, feeling achy all over.

And then her body caught up with her mind.

The floor was still cold and hard beneath her body, except from her shoulders that seemed encased in inexplicable warmth. When she gasped at the feel of wet licks across her forearm, she gulped down the overwhelming scent of spices and jasmine.

Her eyes slammed open and met the belligerent one-eyed gaze of the monster who had attacked her and was now currently licking her arm. She jerked, choking down a scream.

"Stop," a soft, commanding voice whispered in her ear, stilling her movements. It was then she realized there were arms wrapped around her, that the heat behind her belonged to a person - to a 'he'.

"Vadit is a Nisnas. His saliva is the only cure to a wound made by him. I am his master but even I cannot control him if you incur his wrath while he saves what he would rather attack."

The wet slide of the Nisnas' (*what the effing eff was a Nisnas?!*) tongue across her flesh was nauseating to say the least. Ari's whole body was a live wire, vibrating under the creature's attempts to heal what he had ravaged. She watched in absolute silent terror and amazement as her flesh crawled towards itself, fusing the torn skin together under the swipes of the Nisnas' saliva. Finally it grunted and backed away on its sliding, malformed body.

"Vadit, leave us," the man at her back said quietly. He hadn't spoken above the low register and yet there was a chill, as icy as the room they lay in, in his voice, a treacherous black ice that you dared not ignore. The Nisnas did not. It left the room with screeching whines across the glass floor.

"What the hell is a Nisnas?" Ari asked hoarsely. It wasn't some weird, misshapen dog. It was too intelligent. There was a human intelligence in its eyes that scared the utter crap out of her.

Suddenly lifted to her feet by the stranger, Ari swayed back from him and tried to center herself, rubbing her wet but healed arm against her t-shirt. She was no longer in shock but her body still felt weak from the attack.

"A Nisnas is one of the Jinn," the man replied, coming around to face her.

Ari gulped, her neck arching back as she stared up at the weirdly-garbed guy who must have stood close to six and a half feet tall. "Jinn?"

He nodded, those emotionless eyes so deep and penetrating Ari found her own glued to them. "Like me. Like you. Like your mother."

All of a sudden the air felt thin and Ari pressed a hand to her chest, breathing deep. The pink skin of her healed arm caught her attention and she shook her head, disbelieving that this was actually real and happening. "This is a dream. I'm dreaming. I'm dreaming. I have to be dreaming because if I'm not dreaming you're telling me I was actually attacked by some monster and you're claiming that monster is Jinn and that you're Jinn and I'm Jinn and the mother that I don't know and how the hell do you know is Jinn and from everything I've read I can only assume by Jinn you mean frickin' mythological genies but the frickin' scary kind and I can-"

"Breathe," he interrupted, his features harsh and impatient as he placed one huge hand on her shoulder. "I do not deal well with hysterical women."

Ari blinked owlishly, her cheek blazing red at the insinuation she was some prissy idiot who couldn't handle a bad situation. This wasn't a bad situation. This was an EPIC situation. "I'm not your daughter," she responded softly. "I'm Ari Johnson. Derek Johnson's daughter. And this is a dream I would really like to wake up from now."

The man cocked his head, studying her, his jaw unclenching as his eyes washed over her. "You may ramble incoherently like a fool but the only tears you shed are ones of physical pain. Interesting."

Her patience snapped. She didn't care how huge or sociopathic this guy was. "Who. The. Hell. Are. You?"

He leveled her with that careful, expressionless gaze of his. "I am The White King."

"What?"

"The White King. You are in my home in Mount Qaf, the realm of the Jinn. And you, Ari Johnson of the mortal realm, *are* my daughter."

~7~

I Found Me in a Cold Promise

*H*er teeth chattered and she stepped back from the insane man before her, rubbing her arms briskly. "It's c-c-c-cold. Don't you think it's c-c-old?" She shook her head, refusing to believe anything he said, refusing to believe what she could see and touch and hear and smell. "This is too real for a dream," she whispered, shaking her head, feeling her chest tighten in panic. Did this mean she had become unhinged? Oh god. Oh god, she was crazy.

"It is winter on Mount Qaf but the Jinn do not feel the cold," the guy who called himself The White King explained, "You only feel it because you have never used the magic within you. Your body is waiting for your mind to catch up with the truth."

When Ari continued to look at him blankly, shivering, and hiccupping down little gasps of oxygen, he shook his head. There was no annoyance on his face but she got the feeling she was irritating him. "Rabir."

Before Ari could speak flames burst to life in the air in front of her, and as they swam towards the ground their flickering tails revealed a familiar face and torso, until all of Rabir stood before her, the last sparks of the flames hissing, extinguished.

Her eyes had widened at the sight of the flames, now they were as round as saucers, her heart pounding like crazy. "You?"

Rabir gave her a charming little bow and smiled. "Ms. Johnson." He held out a hand, a jacket with fur-lining dangling from his fingers.

In shock, Ari reached out unconsciously and took it, pulling the jacket on and shivering at the warmth of the silky soft fur against her chilled skin. The White King nodded at Rabir and the 'genie' went up in flames. She squeaked on a scream, the heat of the flames licking her face before disappearing completely. There was no evidence of him ever having been there, not even the scent of lingering smoke.

He had gone up in smokeless fire.

Ari gulped, shaking. "That was Rabir. The guy from my party."

"Rabir is a Shaitan. A servant Jinn. I sent him to the party to bring you here."

"I don't understand."

"There are rules. No being may be forced to the realm of Mount Qaf unless to be tried by the Jinn Courts. I feared coming to you would bring you to the attention of those I'd rather keep distant from you. So I had Rabir haunt your feelings with the thought of your mother."

That still made no sense. Ari snorted. Like any of this made sense. She was probably in a padded cell somewhere gazing blankly at a man in a white coat, saliva dripping down her chin. "Still… not getting it." She shrugged, burrowing deeper into the jacket, her eyes wandering over The White King's form. He was truly a magnificent creature, imposing and arrogant… and utterly terrifying. Those eyes of his. They were so black. So… *soulless.*

"I wanted you to wish to see your mother so that you would be brought here. Of your own free will."

"It's not exactly my free will if you manipulated me into missing my mom."

The White King smiled and Ari flinched back from it. It was the strangest smile she had ever seen. He stretched his lips into an approximation of a smile but it was more of a bearing of teeth. There were no lines to crinkle the corner of his eyes, no spark to make the black of his irises glitter. It was a dead smile. "You are clever. I am glad."

She shook her head. It was like he wasn't human. *Wait*, she reminded herself, *he said he isn't.* "I really want to wake up now."

"This is not a dream. Please stop trying to convince yourself otherwise."

The sheet beneath her was chilled from the winter air and lack of central heating, the mattress firm, contouring under her butt. The candlelight flickered when wind blew into the room from the door she'd left open, casting threatening shadows over the very real man in front of her. Jasmine still danced on the air and Ari doubted she would ever be able to smell the floral scent again without thinking about this alien room. Ari pressed a hand against the velvet blanket at the end of the bed, her hand smoothing over the plush fabric, its softness tickling her palm. Her arm didn't hurt but it still felt raw from the Nisnas' bite, the fur inside the jacket making the sensitive skin tingle. Oh God, she had been attacked. She really had been attacked! She glanced behind her to make sure the thing was definitely gone, fear prickling her spine and making her check once more before she turned back to The White King. She laughed a little hysterically inside. *The White King?!* It was like something out of Narnia. Inhaling deeply, Ari let the bitter air flood her lungs, opening up her panicking airwaves. Although her heart slammed in her chest and the blood rushed in her ears, she felt calmer knowing she wasn't crazy.

This was real.

She locked gazes with The White King and tried not to shudder. "You were right earlier. I'm not the kind of girl who cries very easily anymore. But I'm... scared. I thought maybe I was going crazy but... weird has already entered my life. I have a poltergeist, you know. And I'm pretty sure a poltergeist stalker. And at the party when Rabir took my hand I knew there was something off about him. Like really off. Like poltergeist living in my house off. This isn't a dream. And I'm not crazy. So what am I?"

He nodded at her and then turned, snapping his fingers over the air beside him. Out of an explosion of fire appeared a glass chair.

No wait. A throne.

He settled down into the high backed chair, arranging his colorful robes just so. "How would you like me to explain? From your beginning or from *the* beginning?"

"I think this is one of those occasions where the long version is preferable to the short version."

His opaque eyes remained trained on hers and he nodded again. "How much do you know of the Jinn?"

She shrugged, sucking in a shuddering breath, her stomach muscles clenching and choking the life out of the butterflies that had awakened in her belly. Her foot started to bounce on the floor and she had to press a trembling hand to her knee to stop it. "Not much. Just that Disney was waaay off the mark."

"You know nothing of your heritage?"

"Why don't we lead up to the part where you explain how it is my heritage?"

"Your tone is disrespectful. Do all children speak to their parents this way where you come from?" His voice had grown calmer. It had a rumbling, icicle-laden edge to it that stopped her from rebutting with a smartass comment. This wasn't a dream. If The White King over there wanted to take her out with a snap of his fire-breathing fingers there was no waking up from that.

At her continued silence he blinked those dead eyes and straightened up in the 'chair'. "Then we shall begin at the beginning." He curled his fingers elegantly in the air and little flames danced into the darkness, transforming into the outline of a man. "In your world, this, and the others, are Jinn. A diverse race of many colors spawned by Azazil." The figure pulsed more vividly in the air so Ari assumed it represented this Azazil person. "Azazil is the Sultan of all Jinn, created from Chaos; he is as powerful as time and a lover of destruction. Power like Azazil's causes fear, betrayal and death. Over the centuries the Sultan Azazil bore children - Seven Kings of Jinn, each a ruler of one day in the mortal realm. The Gilder King, ruler of Sunday. The Glass King, ruler of Monday. The Red King, ruler of Tuesday. The Gleaming King, ruler of Wednesday. Myself, The White King, ruler of Thursday. The Shadow King, ruler of Friday. And The Lucky King, ruler of Saturday."

Ari gaped at him, trying to process all the information. "OK, OK. Sultan guy is Azazil. And then there is you and your brothers, who are sons of Azazil. Have you got a notepad, because I already can't remember their names?"

The White King made a low humming noise from the back of her throat that creeped her out. "Try to keep up. I won't be repeating this. We live between realms, my brothers and I, interfering in the lives of Importants on the days we ruled-"

"Importants?" Ari interrupted, frowning.

"People with destinies that matter to humans. We helped shape those destinies, but only on the days we ruled over. However, my brothers began to betray one another. They began to interfere on days that were not their own."

"What do you mean?"

"I was told The Gilder King interfered with a very special Important on a Thursday when he should only have traversed into the Important's world on a Sunday."

"The Gilder King is the ruler of Sunday, right?"

"Exactly."

"OK, so you each started trespassing on one another's turf, is that what you're saying?"

"Exactly."

"So… what happened?" *And am I really sure I'm just not crazy?*

The White King turned his eyes to the dancing fire figures that had multiplied from one to eight. "Chaos. War. Distrust between the Seven Kings of Jinn. The order fell apart. We no longer control as many of the Jinn as we once did. And new half-breed races have sprung up in the human world, deliberately seeking to interfere with us." He sighed and wiped a hand over the fire figures, extinguishing them. "Only Azazil has the power to undo what has happened but my father enjoys chaos too much. So we exist without order, without structure, once great… now… empty of purpose. Life seems meaningless."

Ari's stomach roiled, her chest rising and falling in fast waves, feeling as if a million birds had been let loose inside it, as he gazed over her shoulder into a world she could not see. "You're not kidding, are you? This is real?"

He cocked his head. "What gave it away? The Nisnas attack or the Fire Spirits that keep appearing before you?"

"Fire Spirits?"

"Colloquial name for Jinn."

Her fingers bit into the velvet blanket beside her. "So... Jinn... there are different kinds? Ones like you and Rabir and ones like the Nisnas?"

He nodded. "There are many kinds. With many talents."

"Good or evil?"

If it was possible his dark eyes seemed to grow even blacker. "Why are humans so obsessed with that distinction?"

Ari snorted. "Because we like to know what we're dealing with."

"Good people have been known to do evil things, child."

She sucked in a deep breath, her nerves twanging as she found the courage to ask, "Are you a good person?"

The soft tap of his fingers against the glass arm of the throne made Ari jump and she watched his face twitch at her reaction. She cursed herself for revealing how much he unnerved her. "I am not a person. I am Jinn."

She shivered at his deflective response, somehow inherently knowing that this man - this Jinn - wasn't good. Wasn't... right. He couldn't be her father. There was no way. "Why am I here?"

"Because I willed it so."

"Can you maybe explain...?"

"My brothers and I are powerful. Powerful enough even to control whether or not we leave seed for a child to grow in the womb of a women."

OK, too much information.

"Nineteen years ago, I decided that I wanted a child. Perhaps a child would bring some connection to the world for me again. At the time I had gained the servitude of a very powerful Ifrit-"

"Ifrit?"

"A strong species of Jinn who have nearly all of our basic powers, including a gift specific to the individual. Sala's gift was the power of seduction."

At the name, Ari's heart seemed to unhitch itself from its rightful place and drop into her stomach, splashing up acidic bile that lodged at the back of her throat. "Sala?" She whispered, disbelieving.

The White King studied her reaction, seeming fascinated but unmoved by it. "Your mother. If I were to have a child I wished the child to be strong. Sala was the strongest and most desirable of my people at the time. She conceived you because I willed it."

Her face suddenly felt numb and she pressed the icy tips of her fingers to it, reassuring herself that she was still there, she was still her. But she wasn't. She wasn't Ari Johnson. She was...

... she wasn't even human.

"I feel sick," she mumbled, leaning into one of the bed posts.

"I have never understood the human reaction of uploading bodily waste at news you find discomfiting."

Suddenly not caring that he was scary Ari jerked her head up, her eyes flashing angrily. "Discomfiting news? You not only tell me I'm not... that my dad isn't my dad... but that I'm not even *human* and you think that that's discomfiting? How about mind-effing-altering!"

"I think you should calm yourself."

"I think you should go fu-"

He held up a hand cutting her off. "I think you should calm yourself before you insult me and do something you may regret."

She gaped and then laughed bitterly. "Are you threatening me? Your own daughter?"

"I am The White King."

That's his answer? I am the White King? This guy was like a frickin' robot! Ari shook. "You're not my father. You can't be."

"I am." He cocked his head to the other side now and Ari shivered in revulsion. She remembered watching this sci-fi movie with Charlie where these aliens began bodysnatching people. They looked like the humans they'd stolen the bodies from (obviously) but their features and eyes lacked total expression and when something managed to arouse their interest they'd cock their heads to the side, studying it as if it were some kind of lab rat. That's what this guy who claimed to be her father reminded her of. A sociopathic alien. "Sala and I argued during her pregnancy. To punish me she disappeared into the mortal realm and returned a month later. Alone. She told me she had hidden you from me to punish me. Ifrit's are powerful and Sala's powers of seduction are greater than any Jinn I have ever met but her use of enchantments are basic at best. The enchantment she used to keep you hidden with one of her mortal ex-lovers, Derek Johnson, began to wane after sixteen years. I could feel you but I couldn't find you. It took me two years."

Ari gripped the bed post tighter, trying to digest this news. This truth?

"If you were honest with yourself, child, you'd know that I speak the truth. From what I've seen you've been abandoned by the elders in your life. The people you care about have been abandoned by their elders. You feel disconnected to that world, Ari. You know you do. Your only connection is a troubled boy upon whom you cling to in desperation... like a life float." He sat forward, his robes whispering against the glass of the throne. "You have come home, child. You have come home and I will not abandon you."

She searched his face, his words piercing her with their knife-like perceptiveness. Perhaps what he said was true. She and Charlie were all alone. They did only have each other. But that wasn't the only reason she clung to him. And this Jinn? This king?

His was the coldest promise she'd ever heard.

He had a child to fulfill something within himself, not because he wanted to love the child. And her mother?? Her mother had told a lie to a man about her paternity, a good man whom Ari loved, and Sala had done this over some petty argument?!

Her parents were monsters.

Her father had gone to all this trouble to get her here for nothing. Making her wish for her mother, making her-

Making me wish for my mother.

Confusion rippled through her and Ari let go of the bed post, standing shakily to her feet. "If I wished for my mother, why didn't I appear before her?"

The White King shrugged and sat back. His eyes flickered to the nightstand and for once they expressed emotion: boredom. "You did."

The sick feeling intensified and she gaped at the purple bottle that had drawn her attention when she first arrived. "No." She shook her head. "That's crazy. That's like something out of *Arabian Nights*."

He blinked at her. "Where do you think the legends come from? Sala betrayed me; she incurred my wrath." He spoke of wrath but there was no fire in his voice. It remained quiet and chilling. "She is lucky I didn't strip her skin from her bones and hang her out for the Qaf vultures to feed upon."

Ari stumbled back in horror at his words. "Oh my God."

"You do not betray The White King and walk away unscathed. Sala was lashed for her crime and trapped within the bottle. She will remain there for however long I wish it. Perhaps another few centuries."

"You don't even care." Ari's mouth trembled, the fear crawling up her spine again. "You're a monster. You're not my father. I'm not related to you, you're a monster."

He stood up so swiftly Ari stumbled back against the bed. His tall figure towered over her, casting her in shadow and heat. "I am Jinn," he replied quietly. "You would not be horrified by my actions if you had been reared within our realm, among your kind, as you should have been. As is your right." He held out a cold hand for her. "Stay, Ari. You are a princess of the Jinn. I will not abandon you. Your father will not abandon you."

She bit her lip, terrified of the consequences of her response. But she wouldn't stay here. She had a home to return to and two people she loved. And she needed to get back there so she could have a suitable mental breakdown without this psychotic legend watching her. "No. You may be my father but you're not my dad. Send me home."

Gasping in surprise, Ari watched his black eyes light up like two flames. His body shimmered, shadows moving under his skin like black serpents fighting for freedom. "If you leave, child, you will regret it."

"You won't hurt me." She shook her head uncertainly.

That smile, that horrifying non-smile returned to his face. "You leave me… and I will find a way."

"You said you can't keep me here of my own free will. So send me back."

"You will regret it."

"Then let me regret it from the comfort of my home."

An explosion of noise bled her ears and Ari automatically threw her hands up to cover them, watching as the whole room went up in fire, including The White King. Flames danced around her, tasting her skin and yet leaving no burn. She heard the odd, disquieting sound of that strange humming noise he had made earlier, just before darkness descended across her eyes.

~8~

One of Many Bullets

Ari loved rollercoasters. She loved the feel of the wind rushing through her hair, slapping against her skin, making her eyes tear, making her feel more awake than anything had before. She loved the feeling of falling and rising and dipping and whirling through space, her stomach fluttering, her heart racing, her whole body free.

Rollercoasters were fun because at the back of your mind you know you're strapped into a tough metal car with very little chance of falling out of it.

This was just like that.

But without the car.

Wind rushed into her eyes, battering so hard against her body it knocked the breath out of her and nearly blinded her. All she could make out was a rush of colors blurring together before being spat out of the wind tunnel, or whatever it was, onto a hard floor. She groaned, lifting her head off the ground, her cheek tingling with pain after the harsh impact. Feeling bruised and sore and emotionally destroyed, Ari pushed herself back onto her knees and took in her surroundings.

She was back home. In her bedroom.

Relief rushed over her and she sighed, slumping on her butt, her back against the footboard of her bed. "You here, Ms. Maggie?"

Nothing happened. No light switch turned on, no computer chair moved. Ari bit her lip, shaking her head. Great. Just when she needed the poltergeist the most the damn spirit had taken off.

"Perfect." She coughed up some wind phlegm, feeling drained. Biting back burning tears, refusing to cry despite the life-changing insanity she was going through, Ari spoke out to the room as if Ms. Maggie was still there, "You would not believe where I've been."

The events of the past few hours flashed through her mind and Ari glanced down at her arm automatically as she remembered the creepy-ass Nisnas. Still wearing the jacket Rabir had given her Ari shuddered and began shrugging out of it. She threw it across the room, telling herself to remember to burn it later.

"I found out who my real parents are," she whispered sullenly. "You wouldn't believe it. Then again, you're a poltergeist so you might." She laughed, not seeming able to stop. "Oh," she tried to draw breath, her laughter slowly dying to choked tears. "I'd rather be crazy. I'd rather be crazy than this be real. My father sucks. Big time. And my mother... God... I wish you were here. In fact if I were wishing for things I would wish that Charlie was here but I-" Ari froze as she mentioned his name. Stumbling to her feet, she turned to stare at the empty bed. "Charlie?" Where *was* Charlie? He should be here. Oh crap, he must have woken up and seen her gone and-

Wait.

Ari strode over to the window, looking out over the day-lit sky. How could it be day when she had only been gone two hours tops? Heart pounding now, Ari spun around and dashed for her cell on her nightstand. It was dead.

Super crap.

Rummaging through her jewelry box, she pulled out the digital watch she hardly ever wore but was still set to the right date and time.

The numbers blinked up at her, taunting and teasing, so much so Ari could have sworn they were lying. The watch fell from her hands and she gasped for breath, shaking now from head to toe. It was too much. It was all too much. "I've been gone two days?! Two whole days." Ari's fake calm flew out of the window. If she hadn't been convinced that everything was real before, the two days lost on Mount Qaf certainly cemented the truth.

"Holy macaroons. I'm Jinn," she breathed, staring at her apparently magical hands.

A loud thud sounded from downstairs and Ari tensed, her fingers automatically curling into fists. She tried to slow her heart by reminding herself that it could be Charlie. When another thud sounded, however, she was also reminded by her father's threat that she would regret leaving him.

Not your father! She winced, mentally slapping herself. *The White King.*

Fed up of being scared out of her wits, Ari quietly delved through her closet until she found the baseball bat she kept there from her days in Little League with Charlie. Clutching it firmly between both hands, Ari stealthily made her way out into the hall, ignoring the pounding behind her ribcage and the rushing whoosh of blood waves in her ears. She strained to hear as she tip-toed downstairs. She couldn't call out for Charlie in case it wasn't Charlie so she knew she better keep her reflexes tight in case it *was* Charlie and she swung a bat at him. It took her less than five minutes to scope out the ground floor and Ari couldn't find anyone or anything that could have been the cause of the thud. Deciding it must have been Ms. Maggie, Ari dropped the bat on her living room couch and stood facing the window, trying to find calm in the neat, peaceful neighborhood that had no idea that Middle Eastern legends were true. That living next door to them was one of the Jinn. Jinn who was a child of a monster and a tramp. Was that what she was? Was that what she had been looking for all this time? She bit down on her lip so hard - trying to hold in the tears of despair - she drew blood.

"You know there was an Ifrit living in your house, right?"

Letting out a startled cry, Ari spun around to find two men standing in the doorway of her living room. No. Not men. Ari took in the one closest to her with abject dread. If it was possible he stood even taller than The White King, and there was a familiarity in the cut of his features that made her stomach flip. However, instead of bleak black eyes and a shiny bald head, this guy had bright blue eyes, brown skin tinged with a slight reddish hue, and long flame-red hair tied back in a ponytail at the back of his neck. The tip of the ponytail swung at his lower back as he took a step closer to her. Ari stumbled back, not fooled by the jeans and t-shirt he wore. He was Jinn.

She just wanted them to leave her the hell alone. Why couldn't they do that? What did they want from her? "What are you?" was all she managed.

He smiled at her, a genuine, beautiful smile that wiped any similarity to The White King from his face. "I'm your uncle," his deep voice boomed around the room. He didn't speak with that careful, old-fashioned correctness The White King had. He spoke like her. Like a modern American.

Ari shivered and glanced around for some kind of weapon since her baseball bat was too far away from her now. "I told The White King to leave me alone."

His eyes dimmed. "Oh I'm not here for your father. The opposite in fact. I'm The Red King. You may call me uncle if you wish."

She frowned as he slipped into a more formal speech. "I think not. What do you want?" She glanced warily over The Red King's shoulder at the guy standing in the doorway. Something about him made her pause. When his eyes glittered back at her from the shadows, Ari felt his gaze on her with a jolt, like sun peering through the crack in a curtain, waking one with burning eyes and a groan. It wasn't unpleasant but it was unexpected and intense. She eyed him back guardedly before shifting her gaze back to the enigmatic red-head before her. "I've had my fill of Jinn for the day. And not the good gin that my dad has locked in his liquor cabinet. The creepy Jinn that took a bite out of my arm and destroyed everything I've ever known."

"Yeah." The Red King heaved a sigh, sitting down on the couch. "Sounds like big bro."

Ari raised an eyebrow at how casual and relaxed he was. "What are you doing here?"

"The Sultan sent me."

Her eyes widened. "Azazil?"

The Red King scooted forward, his features suddenly taut with expectancy. "How much did bro tell you?"

"Bro?"

"The White King."

"Oh you mean the asshat who ripped me from my bed and coldly told me he was my real father and that I'm Jinn?"

"Asshat. I like that." He grinned and then promptly wiped the smile off his face when he noted she wasn't smiling with him. "Yeah, that guy."

Ari gulped. "Just *that*. That my mother hid me with my dad, with Derek, and that The White King couldn't find me because of some enchantment she put over me, hiding me from him. He said it wore off when I was sixteen."

She waited, somehow hoping that information would be enough to make him leave.

"It did." The Red King nodded eagerly. "Azazil had me searching to find you before The White King could get to you. Unfortunately my psychotic brother got to you just as we did. Well… I might have been able to stop him if *someone* had told me about Rabir a little sooner." He threw a dirty, pointed look over his shoulder at the guy in the doorway, and the said guy took a step forward into the light.

"Hey," the guy snapped. "If you had told me what the hell she really was," he jerked a hand in her direction, "I would have gone directly to you rather than to my father."

"Have you forgotten who you're speaking to, kid?" The Red King's voice purred threateningly, suddenly reminding her of The White King.

The guy, who Ari now noticed was younger than she'd first thought, stiffened. She noted, however, that he didn't look frightened by The Red King, merely annoyed, and that somehow reassured her. Instead he nodded tightly, the strong line of his jaw clenching. "Apologies, Your Highness."

He sounds way less than apologetic, Ari thought.

The Red King's eyes flashed and he turned back to her. "I like this kid." He jerked a thumb over his shoulder at the young guy. "He's got fire." He grinned and winked. "Get it?"

Ari almost rolled her eyes, amazed that this weird bizarr-o world was really her life now and that in just a few hours she'd reached a point she didn't even blink when someone introduced themselves as 'The Red King'. "He's Jinn too I take it?" She ran her eyes over the young guy who appeared to be in his early twenties. She noted his 'normal' height at a couple of inches above six feet. He was strong looking, however, broad-shouldered and fit. Like The Red King he wore black jeans and a plain white t-shirt, his olive skin formed over tightly roped muscle.

"He is," The Red King replied. "This is Jai. Jai is one of the races of Jinn who live as humans. He is also a highly trained member of the Ginnaye."

Jai nodded at her, all serious and growly, and she found she couldn't quite take her eyes from him. He smirked at her. "You need to watch where you're looking when you cross the street."

"Excuse me?"

"Corner of West and Frederick? The truck."

Holy macaroons! "You!" She cried, her eyes wide with disbelief. "You were the invisible hands that pulled me back?!"

"You're welcome."

"What?" she squeaked, anger bubbling in her blood dangerously. "I'm welcome? You made me think I was being stalked by some crazy poltergeist!"

"Just doing my job."

Ari looked to The Red King and she suddenly realized she was staring at him as if she were waiting for him to come to her defense. Irritated at herself now, she threw a disgusted gesture in Jai's direction. "What is he? Why has he been following me? Invisible stalking me, more like."

"As I said, Jai is one of the Ginnaye's youngest and most promising members."

She glared at Jai. "The who?"

"The Ginnaye," Jai answered in his rough voice. "Protectors. Guardians. We're high-paid security for Importants."

Eyes narrowed, Ari slowly sat down into the armchair that faced The Red King. "You hired someone to protect me because you consider me an Important?"

"I see my brother at least filled you in on Importants."

"I'm not an Important. I'm…" she gulped, hating to admit it. "Apparently, I'm Jinn."

"Well I just-." Jai's eyes glittered dangerously at The Red King as he held up a hand to silence the guardian.

Ari glanced warily between the two of them. "You just what?"

The two Jinn continued to stare at each other in strained silence until finally Jai lifted his head and pinned her to the wall with a strange and intense look that sent a shiver rippling down her spine. "I just found that out. I thought you were human."

"OK. Um…" she watched them both for a moment trying to work out her next move.

But she was just so tired.

Deciding she couldn't find anything remotely hostile or cruel about The Red King (upfront anyway), Ari leaned in towards him. "Just tell me why you're here? Please."

He sighed, clasping his large hands together in front of him. The White King had been so alien, so strange, apathetic and sinister in his emotionlessness. His brother was the opposite. If it weren't for his beautiful but strange skin and long flowing red hair, he'd almost pass for an ordinary guy. "Azazil has asked me to protect you. That's why I've hired Jai. Your father, Ari, may become persistent in his goal to retrieve you."

"But why?"

"My brother, did he tell you anything of the Seven Kings and Azazil?"

Ari pressed a hand to her temple to stem a gathering knot of tension. "He told me about your war. That you each trespassed upon one another's duty."

"Then he only told you part of the truth."

"What more is there? And what do I have to do with it?"

"My brother lives for power. Nothing else. He wishes to dethrone Azazil and he will do anything to attain that goal. He's divided my brothers in this war, destroyed the order he claims to want to uphold." He shook his head disgusted, seeming more Jinn now than he had five minutes ago. "He's gathering an army, Ari. And you... you're conception was merely to create another soldier for his cause."

It literally felt as if her stomach had dropped to the floor at her feet. She stared at the carpet numbly, noting her bare feet still looked red and cold from their time in Mount Qaf. Her toe nails sparkled with the blue glitter nail polish Rachel had forced on her at school last week when she was wearing flip flops. She smiled humorlessly thinking how funny it was that her feet seemed to sum up her life before and after she discovered the unbelievable truth. "Why? Why would he want me?"

"You were born. You are his. That is enough reason for him. My brother doesn't like losing what he considers his."

"Is that why he trapped Sala in a bottle?"

The Red King nodded. "Unfortunately Sala is one of many Jinn who walk the fine line between good and evil, only to discover when faced with true evil that they are not at all prepared to cross the line. She is being punished for her naivety."

Ari gulped, clenching her hand into a fist, wishing she didn't care if a mother who had abandoned her was being abused at the hands of the monster who called himself her father. "Will she ever be free?"

He sighed heavily, drawing her eyes up to his kind face. It was amazing that this man was related to The White King. In a weird way it made her feel better about being related to the psychopath. "Ari, you cannot worry for Sala. You have enough to worry about for yourself."

Her heart did this weird little jump in her chest, a jump that vibrated causing a wave of nausea to rise up and over her. She felt her skin prickle into a cold sweat and knew the color must have leached from her face. "Why?"

"For two reasons. One: my brother will not give up his attempts to lure you back to Mount Qaf to be with him. And two: your bloodline is significant. You may not have tapped into your magical abilities as Jinn but you emit an aura, an aura that only the very powerful emit. It comes from you being the daughter of a Jinn King and a powerful Ifrit. This aura attracts Jinn. It's already attracted Jinn."

Head whirling at this new information, Ari narrowed her eyes at his last comment. "What do you mean?"

He shook his head, seeming to marvel at the fact that she hadn't put two and two together. "The Ifrit living in your home for a start."

She frowned. "The Ifrit? There's no If-" she gasped, her eyes flying wide to the open hallway. "Ms. Maggie? My poltergeist?"

"Not a poltergeist," Jai replied from the doorway. "Ifrit. A solid, living being. She's just invisible. She's been using the *Cloak* to stay hidden."

Crushed, Ari tried to hide her upset. "I thought she was my friend. I mean she's been nice to me. She's been my friend."

Jai grunted. "Ifrits are rarely friendly."

Hugging her arms around her body, Ari tried to remind herself that she wasn't alone just because Ms. Maggie turned out to be Jinn. She had her dad. And Charlie. Charlie who was probably going crazy wondering where the hell she was. Oh God... Charlie. She needed Charlie. "I should call Charlie."

"About that..." The Red King had that sympathetic look on his face again and Ari felt her heart flip. "The brother. The kid that died... your Ifrit tells me that was a Labartu."

"You've spoken to Ms. Maggie? Wait... what... Mike? What's a Labartu?"

"Yes. I questioned the Ifrit for answers. I also sent her on from here while you were searching the house like a hellion with a baseball bat. I also cleaned up the mess from your party btw. You're welcome."

Ari blinked, looking around the living room, only now realizing in all the craziness that she hadn't noticed the house had been completely cleaned of any evidence of a party. She nodded wearily. "I appreciate it."

He shrugged. "It's cool. Anyway, according to the Ifrit, your friend Nick is possessed by a young Jinn attracted to you, and your friend Charlie... His little brother was killed by a Labartu; it's one of the Jinn that specifically gets off on the destruction of young children. The cyclist that apparently came out of nowhere wasn't human. It was a she. A Labartu. And she killed Mike."

Like someone had snapped their fingers everything that she'd been told, her father, her mother, her uncle... it all fell away. She stood up, her eyes wide. She had something she could fix. Something she could focus on. Something that she could make sense of. Something good out of all of this. She had to tell Charlie the truth. She had to tell him that he wasn't responsible for his brother's death. Of course there was the small matter of convincing him that she wasn't a complete head case. Ari glanced sharply at Jai. He might prove useful after all.

"And this guy." She nodded in his direction. "He's my bodyguard or something?"

Jai seemed to take offence at her tone but The Red King shushed any snarly retort by standing to his feet. "My brother wants to use you, make you learn your magic. Azazil would rather keep you hidden and protected."

There was something missing here. Why would some ancient, all powerful Sultan Jinn guy care about her? She shook her head. "Why does Azazil care what happens to me?"

Her uncle's eyes flashed and he cocked his head in a way that reminded Ari of The White King. She shivered and tried to cover her flinch, her reaction. The Red King wasn't looking at her as if she were a specimen to be examined. He actually looked impressed. He nodded at her after a moment, a small dry smile curving his lips. "He doesn't." He shrugged. "My father doesn't care about you. He cares that The White King cares. And Azazil will do anything to thwart my brother for his betrayal and attempt at usurpation."

Now *that* Ari could believe. "Fine." She nodded, the glint in her eye telling him she was grateful for his honesty. She crossed her arms over her chest and ran her eyes down Jai, wondering how the hell she was going to explain his presence to everyone. "So this guy is to protect me?"

"Yup. Jai will provide twenty four hour protection from Jinn that may become a nuisance and from any signs of my brother's threat. He will contact me if you are ever in need of my help."

Ari blinked. "Wait. A twenty four hour guard?" She shook her head. There was definitely no way she could explain his presence if he was hanging around *all* the time. Plus, she didn't want him hanging around all the time. She couldn't go from being a relatively solitary person to having some monosyllabic Jinn guy attached to her hip. "I don't think so."

"Yeah, uhh I do think so," The Red King argued back in a comically immature fashion that Ari would have laughed at under any other circumstance.

"No," Ari replied adamantly, and then smirked when something occurred to her. "It's not like the dude can keep a twenty four hour watch on me anyway. I have a car you know and I can leave his ass in the dust."

The Red King raised an eyebrow at her remark and sighed, turning to Jai. "That reminds me. Put the mark on her. That's why you were chosen."

Jai glowered before giving The Red King a hesitant but deferential nod. He then stood up from slouching against the door and strode towards her determinedly. Her eyes widened at his approach, only now fully measuring the broad width of his shoulders. He was bigger than she'd thought. Ari tried to back away from him. His hands shot out, taking hold of her upper arms with a firm grip.

"Hey!" she cried out, ignoring the heat of his body and the familiar delicious scent of his spicy cologne as she tried to pull away. His grip intensified until she was standing still. "Stop it!" she snapped. Up close his eyes were a vivid green. Not a blue-green or a hazel-green but green-green. They were darkly lashed and unbelievably hypnotic. She shivered under them, tugging away from him again. "What are you doing?"

"Jai has a rare gift courtesy of his mixed-blood. While his father is a high-ranking Ginnaye, his mother is a Lilif - succubus Jinn. The two objectives drew together when Jai was born and his kiss can be used to place a mark upon those he seeks to guard. It means he can track you down wherever you go."

Ari's eyes widened as she looked from The Red King to Jai. "No!" She tried to get loose. "You are not kissing me you big l-"

And quite abruptly her insult was swallowed in his kiss. His hot, deep kiss that shut down her brain and made her legs go like Jell-O. She felt a furious heat rush into her cheeks and swim downwards into the pit of her belly and she unconsciously gripped Jai's t-shirt, feeling his heart beat steadily beneath her palm. As if he were waiting for her to soften, Jai took advantage of her momentary daze to flick his tongue against her own, deepening the kiss. Shocked and excited at the same time, Ari had to find the strength to pull back from this stranger who had accosted her.

"Hey! Whoa, you are done!" she staggered back from him.

To her utter annoyance his expression remained the same. Arrogant and serious. He turned around to her uncle and nodded. "It's done."

"You mean you were telling the truth? You can like…sense me now wherever I go?!"

"Yes."

"Yes. Just yes. Just like that."

"Well." The Red King smiled. "I see you two will get along just fine. Remember, kid, call me if you need me." And in eruption of flames that was growing way too familiar to her, The Red King was gone.

Ari gaped, her mouth wide open at his abrupt departure. Slowly, in a daze, she turned to lock eyes with Jai, still feeling the sensation of his mouth on hers. He was staring back her calmly, his eyes blinking at the normal speed, his arms crossed over his chest as if he were waiting for her to make the next move. "He left."

Jai just looked at her blankly.

"Great. He left me here in the middle of a life crisis with Mute Boy. What the hell am I supposed to do with you? You can't be here 24/7."

Jai shrugged, not moving. "My job is to protect you."

She snorted. "So was kissing me protecting me?"

He sighed, letting his arms fall away so he could lean on the back of the couch. "Look, it was just part of the job, OK. Get over it."

"Get over it?" Ari raised an eyebrow. "It's just part of the job? Doesn't that make you some kind of whor-"

"Finish that sentence and I won't be responsible for my actions," he interrupted, his rough voice laden with ice.

Washing her eyes over his bristling physique Ari had no doubt he could follow through on the threat and she tried to ignore the blossom of goosebumps on her arms. She shook her head inwardly. She wasn't afraid of this guy. He was there to protect her. Buttons pushed, Ari cocked a hip, her hand planted firmly on it in a 'don't mess with me' stance. "That would go against the job description wouldn't it?"

Jai strode around the couch and Ari eyed his movement warily as he came to a stop in front of her. "Look. We're stuck together for who knows how long. So let's lay down some ground rules."

"Rules?"

"Rules. One: no calling each other names. It's petty and irritating and I don't have time for it."

"I feel like I'm in Kindergarten."

"That's because you're acting like you're in Kindergarten."

"Hey, I've had a really tough day. OK."

Jai exhaled heavily and gave her a brittle nod. "That's why I'm going to forgive the attitude."

Ari made a face. "What are you, like, forty?"

She had to ignore the strange little puff of warmth that flared up in her chest as he looked adorably embarrassed at her teasing. "No. I'm twenty three."

"You don't act like you're twenty three."

"That's because my job is a little more important than most twenty three year olds'."

Guessing that was true, Ari made a gesture to tell him to continue.

"Rule number two: no complaining about me being here. I'm here until my assignment is over so get used to it. And rule number three: no going anywhere without me. If I have to track you down using the mark I will be pissed off. I'll be even more pissed off if I track you down only to find you dead. *You* dead equals *me* dead. Got it?"

She studied his serious face for a moment, trying to figure out how she could possibly hide him from her dad and Charlie and everyone. Well... not Charlie. She actually needed him for the Charlie situation, and she had every intention of dealing with the Charlie situation in the next ten minutes. Jai's vivid (*and beautiful*, she admittedly grudgingly) eyes stared down at her without wavering, intense and grave, waiting for her agreement. When her eyes dipped to his mouth Ari flushed stupidly and she dropped her gaze to the ground. Her first kiss in months and it had been with Mr. No Personality.

It was a hot kiss.

"Was not," she muttered.

Jai frowned. "What?"

"Uh nothing. I mean... OK, I agree to the rules. But you have to do something for me."

Before he could ask what in that growly voice while he glowered, the phone rang, jolting Ari back into reality. They both stared at it and Ari felt her pulse leap. It was weird... the phone ringing. It was the first normal thing that had happened to her since last night. No. Correction. Two nights ago.

The answering machine clicked on and Ari's heart promptly stopped when her dad's voice echoed around the room. "Ari, where are you? Pick up if you're there, goddammit."

Hearing the fear and concern in his voice, Ari jumped over the coffee table, catching her foot on it and falling onto the couch. She reached for the phone, knocking over a lamp as she grabbed it. "Dad?" she asked, trying not to sound out of breath.

"Ari!" Derek cried, relief evident in that one word. "Oh Christ, where have you been?"

Oh crap. What was she supposed to say? She glanced back over at Jai who was staring at her unhelpfully. "I uh… didn't want to speak to anyone so I've just been holed up in the house."

"And you didn't think to check the answering machine?! I've left you a ton of messages. Charlie called me yesterday to tell me he couldn't find you, that you weren't in the house. I called the Sheriff's Department and they sent someone over. Why didn't you answer the door?"

Oh double crap. Ari gaped around, looking for inspiration for a lie. "Uh… I wasn't feeling well. I had my period." She winced, disbelieving that that was the best she could come up with under pressure. She slanted a gaze at Jai and blushed when she realized he was struggling not to laugh and losing. Scowling, Ari pressed the phone tighter to her ear. "Why did you call the Sheriff's Department?"

Her dad made a choking sound on the other end of the phone and Ari braced herself for an explosion. She had to hold the phone away from her ear as he started screaming at her that he had been worried sick, that he was at the CVG Airport and would be home in about an hour to kill her. She hadn't been able to get a word in and then he clicked his phone off. She didn't think she'd ever heard her dad so mad before.

"He's pissed." Jai relaxed casually into the armchair.

Ari rolled her eyes at the inconvenience of him being here. "Oh, you think."

"Sarcasm is such unattractive quality on anyone but me."

She scoffed, ignoring the somewhat sexy quirk to his upper lip. He had the kind of mouth movie stars would kill for, full pouty lower lip that made a girl want to nibble on it. Ari squirmed, thinking of Charlie and how worried he must be about her to have called her dad. "I doubt anything is attractive on you other than maybe silence."

He quirked an eyebrow. "I can see this is going to be a pleasurable assignment."

"Yup. Sarcasm definitely not attractive on you." Before he could reply, Ari stood up, hands trembling a little as she thought of facing her dad when he was in that mood. "Look, my dad is going to be here any second, so you have to... not *be* here."

Jai shrugged. "I'll just step into the *Cloak.*"

"The *Cloak?*"

"The enchantment we use to be invisible."

The thought of him in the living room listening to her argument with her dad and her knowing he was there but her dad not knowing was too creepy. "No way. I've already had one Jinn floating around my home invisible, I'm not having another one."

"Well, what do you suggest?"

"Uuhhhh... you leaving."

"Uuhhhh... not going to happen."

Exhausted and so not up to a fight, Ari threw up her hands. "Fine. You can stay. But you'll hide in my room."

~9~

I'm Right Here. Where Are You?

*J*ai grudgingly made his way upstairs to Ari's room and she watched from the bottom of the stairs, her heart thumping in her chest. Ari's whole body felt jittery and wired and it suddenly occurred to her that she must be running on pure adrenaline after everything that had happened, after all that had been revealed. Sure that Jai was safe upstairs, Ari made her way into the living room to wait for Derek. Her knee bounced up and down of its own accord and her teeth chattered together as she waited, her palms slick with cold sweat. Now that she had a moment alone all she could do was think about what had happened. Funny, it wasn't really the whole supernatural element to the truth that was getting her. Maybe it was her genetic makeup but she had always dealt with stuff like that with ease. She thought of how easily she had taken to Ms. Maggie, how it never freaked her out to believe there was a friendly poltergeist living with her even though it freaked everyone else out, including her dad. No, what she was struggling with was the whole parent thing. It was bad enough that Derek wasn't really her father but to know that her real father was such a... monster...

And now she had to face a good man who had been duped into thinking that he had a familial obligation to her. Ari loved her dad. But she was suddenly terrified that he would no longer love *her* if he knew the truth. It wasn't a stupid fear. He hadn't exactly been there for her these last few years. He'd let her make her own way through her teen years and where had it gotten her? She was going to a college she didn't want to go to. She had friends she couldn't really talk to. And she was in love with a boy who didn't want to be loved.

But I'm going to fix that, she thought. *That's the one thing I can fix.*

To Ari, then, it wasn't so irrational to believe that if Derek ever found out the truth he would walk away. Surely, all that had been keeping him from walking away entirely was his love for his 'daughter'. If Ari took that away from him, would there be anything left? Trying to hold down the anger she felt at that thought, Ari sucked in a deep breath at the sound of a car pulling into the driveway. She twisted around in her seat, waiting for the sound of the key turning in the lock. The scrape of metal against metal seemed overly loud and Ari flinched as the door gave away from the latch.

Derek Johnson stepped into his home, dropped his suitcase with a thud and slammed the door shut. Their eyes met across the room and Ari saw a war in her dad's gaze: relief fighting with fury and disappointment. When he marched into the room and grabbed her up into his arms Ari felt the burn of tears in the back of her throat. She gripped her dad tight, inhaling his musky cologne and the smell of detergent on the lapel of his suit jacket. His lips brushed her forehead, his large hands clasping her head between them as he pulled back to look at her. "I'm going to kill you," he whispered hoarsely.

She blinked, trying to remember the last time he had hugged her. "I'm sorry, Dad."

Derek shook his head, his eyes darkening as he stepped back, his features tightening. Ari's heart sank. She wasn't off the hook yet. "Sit." He jerked his head at the couch and Ari promptly dropped onto it. She watched anxiously as he shrugged out of his jacket and loosened the tie around his neck. Finally, he collapsed onto the armchair Jai had only minutes before vacated. And then it came. He fired questions at her, not waiting for her to answer, lamenting her poor judgment, vocalizing his disappointment, creating criminal scenarios as reasons for her stupidity, his voice rising and rising until he was shouting, his face mottled red with anger. He wasn't ready to hear her answers. Ari wasn't even sure he wanted answers, he just wanted her to know what an inconvenience the worry he had felt for her was. As she sat there, gripping her hands tightly together on her lap, aware of Jai upstairs listening to every word, Ari grew angry too. Her dad's worry wasn't supposed to be an inconvenience. It was supposed to be a natural element of fatherhood. And true, he might not be her real father, but *he* didn't know that.

Where had he been? Was he really surprised that something like this had happened? He had been leaving her alone for years. He was lucky something bad hadn't happened before now. He was lucky she could take care of herself.

As Derek ranted on and on about the humiliation of having to call the Sheriff's Department and tell them that she was fine, that she'd had a bad period and didn't want to answer the door or the phone, Ari's fears began to gnaw at her insides. Would he walk away from her if he knew the truth? Would the dad she loved, who had loved her when she was a kid… would he love her enough to still want her if he ever discovered the truth?

"I just can't believe that you would act so carelessly, so inconsiderately over… *nothing*. I didn't raise my daughter to act like that and she never has before. So tell me, Ari… what are you hiding from me?"

Gulping down the truth, Ari shook her head, the build-up of anger in her throat making it difficult to speak. "Nothing."

Derek's eyes narrowed, his lips pinched white. "No, I don't accept that. You never lie to me. Do not start now."

She scoffed, the noise escaping her before she could stop it. Her father's nostrils flared at the sound and she narrowed her own eyes on him, feeling dangerous. Feeling weightless and dangerous. "I never lie?" She shook her head, daring him to hate her. "Right."

"What's that supposed to mean?"

"It means… How would you know?" Her voice rose an octave on the last word as she jumped up from the couch. "You're never here. And when I complain you're never here you just call me a brat who doesn't know how lucky she is to have such nice things in her life because her dad works hard to give them to her. Lucky?" she whispered, eyes blazing, daring him to hate her and wanting him to love her all at the same time. "I'm all alone, Dad. I *have* no one, no one but Charlie and he doesn't want anyone to *have* him. So no... I'm not lucky, Dad. I'm eighteen and I'm alone because you're never here. You're never here and I made a mistake. I've made a few of those." She shook her head, watching the color leach from his cheeks and his eyes dim from anger to sadness. "You think I never lie? I lie, Dad. I lied about Penn. I don't want to go there. I don't want a business degree. And worse... I don't know what I want. I don't know who I am. And I lied about that. I lied because I want you to love me even though you're never here. And..." she sucked in a breath, that old lie still biting at her conscience. "I lied about your girlfriend Michelle."

Derek jerked back, the confusion on his face crumbling Ari's resolve a little. "Michelle?" he asked softly.

"Your girlfriend that I told you hit me."

His eyes lit up with recognition. "Michelle."

"You really liked her. I knew that even then. And you hadn't liked anyone so much before. I got scared. I didn't want a mom and I didn't want to share you. So I lied. She didn't slap me. She didn't slap me at all." She exhaled shakily. "I'm sorry. But I lied. I lied because I didn't want another mom abandoning us. I didn't want *you* abandoning *me*." She laughed humorlessly. "And that is just such a joke because... you abandoned me anyway."

The silence between them was so thick, so fragile. Ari waited, tense, her whole body – muscles, bones, nerves and blood - frozen as she waited for him to respond.

Finally, Derek lifted his head, his soft features hard, his skin stretched taut across his face. His dark blue eyes blazed at her as if he didn't recognize her. Without another word, he rose to his feet and walked past her. The front door slammed and Ari jumped at the noise, staring blindly down at the armchair he'd left empty.

Well, you wanted to push. You wanted to punish. Someone. Anyone.

Ignoring the ache in her chest, Ari turned slowly around only to come face to face with Jai as he entered the living room. His eyes glittered at her unfathomably but she noted a softening in his features that hadn't been there before. She dropped her gaze, not wanting his sympathy.

The shrill call of the phone broke the awkward moment and Ari reached over to answer it.

"Ari?" Charlie's warm voice asked in disbelief and relief.

"Yeah."

"Yeah? That's all you've got to say. Ari, I've been going out of my mind. What the hell happened the other night?"

She glanced out at the darkening day and sighed. "I'll tell you in a minute. You at home?"

"Yeah."

"I'll be there in ten."

This was not at all what Jai had imagined would be his assignment. One, the actual assignment - the girl - was a bigger situation than even he could have imagined. And two, she was different than he'd thought she'd be. Usually Importants were surrounded by people, had busy lives, were focused and driven. But then Ari wasn't exactly an Important. Not precisely. Jai watched her as she grabbed her keys, shoving her feet into white flats. She turned back to him, her long hair sliding like dark warm chocolate across her back.

"We're walking. I feel like walking."

Jai shrugged. Walking worked for him. It was just the destination that bothered him.

For over a week now he'd been following Ari, protecting her. He'd been surprised by how lonely she was, how abandoned she was by even the people who were supposed to love her. Her dad was an idiot, Jai thought so even more now after overhearing their argument. Her friends were typical teens too wrapped up in their own lives to see Ari was drowning, and her so-called best friend, Charlie, who she talked about all the time (even with that damn Ifrit who'd tried to bar him from the house) wasn't there for her. He seemed to come in and out of Ari's life, playing with her feelings, pulling her in, pushing her out. Jai felt like the punching the kid, but part of him also got where the guy was coming from. Anger, especially over something like losing your little brother, wasn't easily dealt with. Whereas some wanted an escape from it anyway they could, others, like Jai, channeled it into something productive. He guessed it all came down to how you were wired. Still, it bothered Jai, for some inexplicable reason, that the first person Ari wanted to run to after all that she'd been through was Charlie. Charlie who was too messed up to give her any kind of support.

He shot a look at her as she breezed down her sidewalk, her long legs working to get away from him. She better not be thinking about telling that kid any of this stuff. Jai sighed, rubbing the back of his neck. He shouldn't care what she did with her personal life, that wasn't part of this. But something about her had drawn him in since he'd been charged with following her. He understood what it was like to be all alone. And Ari was a nice girl. She was. Contrary to how she was reacting to him (but hey he was used to that), she was a nice girl.

With eyes a guy could drown in.

Jai frowned at that. Ari had Jinn eyes, clearly inherited from her mother. Those were powerful eyes, indistinct in color, but startling. She shot him a sideways glance, checking him out, and Jai hid a smile. She was only eighteen (and a virgin, according to her friend Rachel), she came from small town Ohio and she didn't really know herself. Jai sighed inwardly. She was an innocent. *In every way*, his thoughts suddenly depressed, darkened. It was unfair. The Red King should have armed her with the truth. Given her a chance to prepare. Jai glanced at her again. The Red King said he couldn't tell her… but that didn't mean he couldn't hint at it. Right?

~10~

Easing You Cuts Me

*J*ai hadn't said a word to her when she announced she was going over to Charlie's. He had followed her out of the door, past the now empty driveway (she'd put her own car in the garage before she'd been whipped into the genie realm), and down the sidewalk that would lead her out of her neighborhood and into Charlie's. An awkwardness still clung to them after what Jai had overheard between her and her dad and Ari kept shrugging as if that would somehow rid them of it. She glanced at him out of the corner of her eye, wondering how she could talk him into helping her.

When he sighed she realized he was going to break the uncomfortable silence first. "You know you can't tell Charlie anything right? Nothing about me, you, or any of the Jinn."

Her eyes widened and she drew to an abrupt halt, staring up into his dark, handsome face as if he'd gone mad. "Are you kidding me?"

Jai's jaw twitched and he leaned down so their faces were at eye level, his warmth breath whispering across her face. "No," he replied sternly before straightening back up. "I don't kid."

She grunted. "There's a surprise."

"So are we clear?" he ignored her jibe.

Ari reached out to pull him to a stop, feeling how hot his skin was under her hand. Fire Spirits seemed to run at a higher temperature than everyone else. She wondered if she'd also start radiating abnormal amounts of heat if she were to ever tap into her own Jinn abilities. It was ironic because she was much more of a rain and water person than a sun and fire person. The rain made her feel better, new, refreshed. She always imagined it gave her power somehow. "No, we're not clear," she argued. "I'm telling Charlie. I have to tell Charlie. He deserves to know that he isn't responsible for his brother's death."

"Look, that's very noble but the less people involved in that part of your life the better for everyone."

"You can't talk me out of this." Ari jutted her chin out defiantly and swooped past him, her long hair billowing at the back of her like a banner in the wind.

"Your uncle would be pissed."

"Don't call him that."

"The Red King then." It was now Jai's turn to reach out to her, his large hand clasping around her upper arm, the callouses on his palm rubbing against her skin and causing an involuntary shiver to wriggle down her spine. She stopped, jerking her arm from his. She met his stubborn look with one of her own. "Ari, the king might come across all cool and human and nice but he has his own agenda. And you do not want to cross The Red King. You don't want to cross any of the Seven Kings of Jinn."

She nodded. "I get you're doing your job. I get I can't get rid of you. But, other than making things right with my friends, I don't want anything to do with the Jinn world. I am going to pretend that none of it exists until I have no choice but to. I don't want that world, Jai. I want this one. I want my friends to be OK."

Disgruntled, Jai shook his head but didn't argue. He fell into step beside her and despite what she'd just said, she was kind of glad to have him there, now that she knew there were Jinn out and about trying to destroy the lives of the humans of Sandford Ridge. Nick was the next on the help list.

When they reached Charlie's street, Ari pulled Jai to a stop. "You need to hide for now."

He shook his head belligerently. "I'm not going anywhere."

"Question: what happens when I need to pee?"

Jai narrowed his eyes. "You're so juvenile, you know that."

She smiled sweetly. "Go away."

"No. I'll go into the *Cloak*." He tried to appease her.

Ari shook her head. "Nah, after Ms. Maggie it kind of freaks me out."

"Fine."

Before she could question that resigned sigh of his Jai surprised her by glancing surreptitiously around. He strode away from her, slipping in behind a large tree that hid him from the rest of the street. Ari frowned. "What-" She cut off at the hiss of flames, flickers of reds and oranges and yellows peeking out from behind the tree. Just like that it was gone and her eyes grew wide as a huge Great Dane padded out from where Jai had been standing. Ari gulped, remembering The Red King telling her that the Jinn could take the form of different animals. "Jai?"

He barked at her so she took that as a yes.

Eyeing him as he found step beside her, Ari had to curb the urge to pat his head. He was a white Dane with black spots all over him. His soulful black eyes still managed to contain a hint of disdain and Ari snorted. "Trust you to choose a Great Dane." Walking, Jai came up past her waist. She imagined when sitting his head would reach her shoulder. Ari had only known Jai a few hours but she already knew he exuded one word. Intimidation. She tutted. "How am I supposed to explain you to Charlie?"

He cocked his head up and Ari had to hide a smile at his comical expression. It pretty much said, 'Does it look like I give a shit?'

Not wanting to admit she was beginning to enjoy Jai's dry company, Ari picked up the pace and wasn't surprised to see Charlie waiting on the front porch for her. He moved towards her as if he were going to hug her and then seemed to think better of it. Her chest ached at the panic in his eyes and she hated herself for worrying him so much.

In a weird way, though, it was nice to know he still cared.

"Where the hell did you go?" he snapped and then his eyebrows drew together in puzzlement when his gaze dropped to the dog at her side. "What the hell is that?"

"That…" Ari shared a look with Jai. "That is… Hamlet."

"What?"

Ari shrugged, smiling stupidly. "Hamlet. He's a Great Dane. Get it?"

Charlie jumped down the porch steps, shoving his hands into his pockets as he glared at her. "Witty."

Trying to remind herself that he was just being a jerk because she'd worried him, Ari nodded her head in the direction of Vickers' Woods. "Can we go for a walk? Talk?"

He strode past her with a grunt.

Taking that as a yes, Ari smiled and followed him out of the drive. Feeling mischievous she turned back to Jai and patted her leg. "Come on, boy."

At Jai's little growl, Charlie threw the Great Dane a dirty look, gently moving Ari so the Dane walked beside him and not her. "That dog is freakin' me out."

Confused, thinking Jai was pretty cute as a Great Dane, Ari frowned. "Why?"

"It's so…" They both watched as Jai's eyes darted around the street, watching vigilantly for any signs of attack. Charlie made a face. "…human."

"Oh no," Ari replied dryly. "He's definitely not human."

Ari knew Charlie would bug her and bug her to tell him what the hell had happened to her that night of her party but she remained silent until they found one of the many rough paths that led into the woods. They passed the cherry trees someone had planted years ago without permission, the blossoms adding perfume to the dank smell of the dark soil. Settling on a large fallen trunk, Ari tried to relax, letting her mind and body calm, listening to the familiar sound of the interstate in the distance. Charlie stood before her, his legs wide, his arms crossed over his chest. She winced, noting that the dark circles under his eyes were even more prominent today. It looked like he hadn't slept a wink since she'd disappeared. Dried leaves and twigs cracked under Jai's paws as he padded over to her, sitting on his haunches, watching Charlie with a clear hint of disapproval in his eyes. Charlie saw it and eyed the dog with narrowed eyes.

"Where did you say you got the dog?"

Ari held up a hand. "I'm about to explain. It's just... really difficult to explain. You might think I'm crazy."

"I think your dog might be crazy," he mumbled, stepping back a little warily. "I get the feeling he doesn't like me so much."

"Charlie."

"What?" He finally dragged his eyes from Jai. "Sorry. You were saying?"

Ari suddenly realized something as she took in his overall appearance. His pupils weren't dilated and except for the dark circles under his eyes his skin had an almost normal color to it. "Are you sober?"

His brown eyes flashed at her. "Yeah, Ari. I'm sober. You disappeared out of your own bed two nights ago and I couldn't find you anywhere. I called your friends, I called your dad. No one knew what happened to you. Yes. I'm sober. I'm sober because I've been looking for you!"

She tilted her head, eyeing him sadly. "You should be sober because you're eighteen, Charlie."

He shook his head, his unkempt hair sliding into his eyes. "Look, I didn't come here for a lecture," he told her wearily. "I came here to find out what happened to you."

"What happened to me…"

Here goes…

"What happened to me… is… I met my real father."

For the first three quarters of the story Charlie watched her in taut silence, his eyes concerned and wary. She knew as she went on about being pulled into the realm of the Jinn, being attacked by a Nisnas, meeting her father, The White King, and discovering *she* was Jinn, that he thought she'd gone crazy or was maybe on some kind of drug. Then as she told him about coming home and finding her uncle, The Red King, in the house with a bodyguard named Jai, Ari noted his eyes grow anguished. Like he had lost her somehow.

The sadness turned to anger as she told him about Ms. Maggie being Jinn, about Nick being possessed by one of the Jinn and Mike… he grew so furious as she talked about Mike.

When she was done explaining about the Labartu who killed Mike, the silence between them pulsed with raw fury. She braced herself, determined to be brave.

"You think that's funny," Charlie hissed between clenched teeth. "You think that's fucking funny, Ari!"

Jai growled from beside her, standing up from his haunches to pad in front of her, guarding her. "Jai," she begged. "Show him. Please."

The Great Dane's head turned to her, his big eyes indignant.

"Please, Jai."

"You've gone nuts." Charlie stumbled back from her. "Only sane person in my life and she's gone nuts."

"No!" Ari jumped up, terrified she was losing control of the situation. "Charlie, I'm telling you the truth, you have to believe me. I know it sounds insane. I know. But it's the truth. You didn't kill Mike. One of the Jinn did. Because of me. And I'm so sorry," she choked. "I am so sorry. But I can prove it. The guardian I told you about. The Jinn. Jai. That's him." She pointed at the Great Dane.

Charlie's shoulders slumped, his face crumpling, his eyes glowing bright with unshed tears. "Ari... please."

"It's him!" she cried, turning on Jai. "Please. Help me."

The dog stared at her for a minute more and then the air around him shimmered. Ari released a breath of relief. Fire erupted in the air before them, crackling and spitting, the heat licking Ari's chilled skin. And then it was gone, leaving Jai standing in its place, his surroundings untouched by his magical flames.

He crossed his arms over his chest. "You owe me."

"Holy fu-" Charlie breathed, taking a few steps back, his eyes blinking wide.

"Charlie." Ari rushed at him, clasping his face in her hands. "Charlie." She shook him until his shocked gaze unglued itself from Jai and fell down on her face, so close to his. "Charlie, I told you I'm telling the truth."

"This is real?" he whispered, amazed, hurt, shocked, scared.

She nodded silently, stroking his cheek soothingly.

He jerked back from her and Ari felt the loss of him like a knife cut to the heart. "You're... Jinn? Jinn are real?"

"Apparently so." She locked her jaw, trying not to cry at the distance in his eyes.

That distance suddenly burned bright with wrath. "And... that's why Mike's dead? It was what... what did you call it?"

"A Labartu. They're like some kind of Jinn that targets kids. She was the cyclist that ran you off the road. It wasn't your fault, Charlie."

He gulped, trying to draw in air and Ari reached for him only to have him push her hand away. Heaving in rapid, jerky breaths, Charlie dropped his hands to his knees, tucking his head into his chest as he tried to collect himself.

"Charlie," she whispered desperately.

"Ari." She felt Jai's hand on her arm, attempting to pull her back.

Finally, Charlie straightened, his breathing still uneven, tears streaking his cheeks. When next he spoke, he didn't even look at her. "Was it yours?"

Ari shook her head in incomprehension. "What?"

"Was it your fault?" he bit out.

Feeling the rip in her chest lengthen and deepen, Ari's eyes blurred with tears. "I don't know."

Without another word, Charlie turned and strode out of the woods, leaving her there shivering in the aftermath of his silent blame.

She was surprised when Jai remained quiet for a whole five minutes, letting her gulp back the tears and gather herself. Her head felt too hot and her ears were buzzing with disbelief. She could barely breathe, her chest hurt so much from the fear that she'd lost Charlie.

Finally, though, Jai sighed at her back. "I know you're worried about him but we have bigger problems."

Ari shook her head, unable to look at him. "You don't understand."

"You think you're in love with him."

"There's no 'think' in that sentence."

When he didn't respond, Ari turned around and gazed up at him, trying not to let the defeat shine in her eyes for him to see. For everyone to see. "I guess you're right about the bigger problems though. So... how do we exorcise one of the Jinn?"

He shrugged. "You got Yellow Pages?"

"Seriously?"

Jai snorted. "Yes, Ari. There are Aissawa Exorcists in the Yellow Pages."

Huffing, Ari walked away from him. "You really need to work on intonation when you use sarcasm. That way people will know when you're being an asshole."

"And you need to work on your gullibility."

"Well, I was under the impression you have no sense of humor so forgive me for believing everything you say."

"Well that should be fun."

"See!" she threw over her shoulder. "No intonation. Jeez, Jai, drop the monotone."

Stepping into stride beside her, he sighed as if he were dealing with an infant. "You were less annoying when I was invisible."

"I think that says more about you than me." When she glanced up at him for a reaction Ari was surprised to see something spark in his eyes – like he was enjoying himself with her. The ache in her chest refused to ease but for a moment, as they shared a long look, she had to work hard not to give him a sad smile.

Abruptly, Jai cleared his throat, shifting his gaze directly in front of him. "I take it you want an Aissawa Exorcist for your friend Nick?"

"I would say yes if I knew what an Aissawa Exorcist was."

"The Aissawa Brotherhood are experts in exorcising homes, buildings, material goods and people that have been possessed by the Jinn. I'll make a call."

After muttering a thank you Ari let silence fall between them, suddenly realizing that after years of being alone for much of the time, she was never going to have a moment's peace from this guy for the indefinite future. Sure, Jai could turn into the Great Dane again so her dad was only questioning her about a mutt rather than a hot, older guy in jeans that did wonderful things to his ass, but where was he going to sleep? Did he intend to sleep in her room? With her?

The heat of someone watching her brought Ari blinking out of her thoughts and she glanced up to see Jai looking at her out of the corner of his eye. "What?" she asked warily.

He shook his head in disbelief. "Hamlet?

PART TWO

~11~

Let Me in to Your World, I Don't Belong in Mine

"*M*aybe you should stop calling him," Jai offered without looking up from his copy of *Earthborn* by Orson Scott Card. He was lying on the floor in her bedroom, propped up against the wall, sitting on top of the sleeping bag he'd conjured since he refused to leave her side for more than five seconds. It had been a few days now and if Ari never had to see another copy of a Scott Card novel it wouldn't be a bad thing.

Ari threw her cell on her bed and glared at the Jinn who had taken up permanent residence in her life. True to The Red King's word Jai lived like a human for the most part. He ate all her food and used up the hot water in her shower. Yes, he could magically conjure clean clothes but other than that he was like any houseguest. Well… you know when he wasn't padding around on four legs as a Great Dane when Derek was about. As for her dad he still wasn't speaking to Ari. Adamantly not speaking to her. So much so he'd looked at Jai in Great Dane form and not even said a word. He hadn't even asked why there wasn't any dog food, or bowl, or bed. He was that pissed off.

He wasn't the only one.

Ever since Charlie had walked away from her in the woods she'd been calling and leaving him messages but he still hadn't responded. She tried to fight her growing fear by irritating the life out of Jai but despite first impressions he wasn't easily irritated. He didn't answer any personal questions and every time she asked him when the Aissawa Brotherhood would arrive he would just say 'soon' and return to reading. As far as stalkers went, Ari guessed he wasn't so bad, although the less he told her, the more curious she grew about him. Attempting to work out the mystery that was Jai was easier than attempting to work out all the relationships she'd messed up over the last few days. Not only was she in the bad books with her dad and Charlie but also with Rachel and Staci. They were furious at her for not providing a suitable reason for disappearing on them for two days. Rachel had yelled at her for fifteen minutes on the phone before hanging up. Thinking she might try to mend fences by contacting Staci she wasn't surprised when her ten calls were ignored. Rachel had gotten to Staci before she could.

Great.

So now she was going stir crazy in a room with Jai, who only offered up an opinion on subject matters she had no wish to discuss with him. "Did I ask for your input?" she snapped.

He sighed, casually turning the page of his book. "Nope. But as a guy I can tell you the whole desperate thing would just be pushing me further away."

Insulted, Ari threw a cushion at him only to watch it dissolve into ash before it even hit him. That was the second cushion he'd destroyed. Never mind it was her own fault for forgetting he was one of the damn Jinn. "I am not desperate," she huffed.

"Stop calling him then. Be patient. You're either going to lose him or not."

"No." She jumped off the bed, her heart crying out in outrage at the thought. "I have already lost my dad, and my humanity, and my friends... I am *not* losing Charlie too."

Jai sighed again. "What is it about this kid?"

Disgusted by his seeming callousness, Ari shot him a dirty look. "Don't you have any friends, Jai?"

She was surprised when he actually glanced up to meet her eyes. "One."

She stopped, frozen. "Yeah?" She smiled tentatively, amazed he had actually offered up something personal. "What's he or she like?"

Jai rolled his eyes. "He's... a friend."

"Wow, you're descriptive skills are outstanding... it must be all that reading you do." When he ignored her teasing Ari blew out an impatient breath. "Oh come on you tool, I'm bored. Tell me something. Tell me about your friend."

"We grew up together. He's a friend. End of."

"You're killing me."

"Yeah, well, you're not exactly a day at the beach."

Deciding to ignore that, Ari flopped down at her computer desk and logged into her *Twitter* account. She scrolled through her friend's tweets, her eyes narrowing at a certain comment.

Sometimes friendships are a one-way system. Sad but true. A hard lesson I learned this week.

"Bitch," Ari hissed, clicking the unfollow button on Rachel's profile. One guess as to who the little anal, straight-A, genie-hiring suckass was talking about.

"Was that directed at me? Because if so it was completely uncalled for," Jai muttered, pressing the corner on the page he was reading down before he shut the book. He looked up at her. "You're bored."

"And pissed off."

He nodded. "Me too."

She relaxed back on the chair, swiveling away from the laptop. "Yeah? What would you usually be doing now?" Ari knew it was a personal question but she was hoping he had reached the same level of boredom she had and would say or do anything to dispel it. Besides, there really was no arguing with it anymore. She was curious to know more about the hot guy who was sleeping on the floor at the end of her bed every night, making falling asleep incredibly difficult. He made her aware of everything. What she wore to her bed. If she snored… Oh god, she hoped she didn't snore.

Jai sat up, drawing his knees up to his chest. "Training. Working. The Ginnaye are disguised as major personal security companies around the world. My father is the head of an LA company."

"So you get paid to protect people?"

He nodded, his expression careful, not giving anything away. "When the Jinn hire us we put them first, but we make our living by not only training humans to be security officers but sometimes also doing human security jobs ourselves. It's quite lucrative."

"Must be pretty cool working with your dad." Ari smiled wistfully, wishing her dad would start talking to her. What kind of dad didn't question a random Great Dane in his house?!

Instead of answering, Jai sat forward. "You know I could teach you things about the Jinn. That would pass time."

The smile slid off Ari's face and she looked away from him. "I don't want to learn anything about them."

"Ari, it's my job to protect you. If I can teach you about different kinds of Jinn it could act as an early warning system if you ever encountered one."

"No."

"This is your heritage, Ari. Don't you want to learn about your heritage?"

"No!" she snapped, jolting out of the chair, sending it careening across the floor. "I don't know who or what I am, OK. Before this I didn't know and I still don't know. But the one thing I did know was that I was Charlie's friend. That's the only thing I have. So, I don't want to talk about the Jinn. I don't. I'm just going to sit here and wait for my friend to remember that that's all I have and call me."

Silence fell between them and Ari was certain Jai wasn't going to comment.

She was wrong.

When he cleared his throat, she turned back to look at him expectantly. She was surprised to see he was angry. He shook his head at her. "You're smarter than that. Don't make out that who you are is dependent upon who you are to someone else. Being Charlie's friend isn't who you are. It's a part of what makes you tick. But it's not who you are. And sitting back on your ass while life happens to you... is that really who you are, Ari?" He tutted and grabbed his book up again, opening it to the placeholder. "I guess I was wrong about you."

"He's right, you know," a new voice entered the fray and Ari's head shot up in surprise to see Charlie standing in her doorway. He looked worn out and unsure. He jerked a thumb over his shoulder. "Your dad let me in. I take it he doesn't know about..." his eyes fell to Jai on the floor, Jai who kept reading his book as if nothing was going on, as if he hadn't hurt her with his painful perception of her.

Ignoring him, Ari turned to Charlie, letting her heart thump at the sight of him standing there. Of his own accord. Relief blossomed across her chest. "He does the Great Dane thing when dad's around." She smiled crookedly. "You're here?"

Eyes wide, Charlie nodded and stepped into the room, shutting the door carefully behind him. He heaved a sigh and turned around, leaning back against it. She saw a world of hurt in his eyes: trauma, shock, disbelief, relief, fury. Charlie had always felt so much and now she could see he was battling to control how overwhelming it all was. "I don't blame you," he whispered, those dark eyes searching her face for reassurance. "I'm sorry I made you think I blamed you I just... God... it was a lot, Ari."

Afraid to scare him off or do anything to make him change his mind, Ari took a tentative step towards him. "I know. I know. Believe me I know." She stopped at the pile of ash made from the cushion Jai had burned and tipped her toe into the pile nervously, moving it around. "So... you took some time to think about everything... How do you feel? I mean... how are you?"

Charlie shook his head. "Forget about me for a second. How are you?"

Ari smiled tremulously. "Coping."

"I can't believe all this is true. I mean I can because I saw it with my own two eyes but still... Jinn. Jinn are real. How freaking weird is that?"

She laughed at such a natural response and nodded, grateful when he returned her smile with one of his own lopsided ones. "It *is* weird."

"So what are you going to do about it?" he asked, pushing up away from the door. Charlie glanced down at Jai who was still reading his book like they weren't having this momentous conversation in front of him. "Are you going to learn, you know, to be Jinn?"

Scowling at the thought Ari shook her head violently. "Hell no. No. No way, I want nothing to do with any of it. Once I have a couple things sorted out I am going to continue my very human life like none of this ever happened."

Charlie looked doubtful. "It's not that easy, Ari."

"Yes it is. I mean I can't right away but I will. The Red King refuses to drop the protection so I'm stuck with Jai until I can figure out how to get rid of him."

"Thanks," Jai replied dryly without looking up from the book.

Charlie frowned down at him, clearly mystified by him. "So... that's it? No Jinn stuff... nothing?"

His look of disappointment baffled Ari. She wanted to question him about his reaction but she was afraid of what'd he say, afraid it would spoil the tenuous thread they'd sewn in their torn friendship in the last few minutes. "No. Well... yeah. You remember I told you about Nick? How he's possessed by one of the Jinn?"

"Jesus." Charlie's eyes widened. "After everything... I guess that part I kind of forgot."

"Understandable under the circumstances. Jai and I are waiting for these Brotherhood guys-"

"Aissawa," Jai interjected before yawning.

"Aissawa Brotherhood guys who specialize in exorcism."

Charlie's eyes lit up, such animation on his face so old and forgotten Ari gaped at him stupidly for a moment. "You're doing an exorcism?"

"Yeah." She nodded, so happy to see him *awake*. "Yeah we are. Once we figure out how to get Nick in a quiet, secluded place where we can, you know, depossess him."

Jai snorted. "*Exorcise* him."

"Whatever." Ari rolled her eyes at him.

"I want in," Charlie said, glancing up and down between the two of them.

"What do you mean you want in?" Jai lowered the book now, his rough voice all serious and antagonistic. Ari wanted to punch him.

"Just that. I want to help."

"No wa-"

"Of course you can," Ari cut off Jai's obnoxious shut down. Charlie was actually offering to do something that didn't involve sex, drinking or drugs. There was no way she was leaving him out of this. "I'll call you when it's time."

He smiled at her. "Great. Look I have to go because Mom and I are you know... well... we're actually talking so I said I'd be home for dinner..."

Warmth spread through her and Ari grinned happily at the news. "Charlie, that's great news, that's-"

"Yeah, yeah." He stopped her, leaning down to press a kiss to her forehead. "We'll talk soon, OK. Lots to discuss." He winked at her and then turned, casting another puzzled and wary look at Jai before disappearing out of the door.

When Ari finally stopped mooning at the doorway, she looked down at Jai only to find him glaring at her. "What?"

"You invited Rehab to help with the exorcism?"

"Don't call him that."

"He's not coming."

"This is my exorcism. I say who goes."

"You're such a child," he huffed.

Ari guffawed. "Excuse me? I am not the one that just nicknamed someone suffering from substance abuse Rehab."

"Oh so you admit he has a problem."

"*Had*," she argued. "*Had* being the operative word. I haven't seen Charlie that sober or that animated about anything in two years. If coming along to a freaky Jinn exorcism keeps him that way then fine by me."

"Just be careful with him, OK. You don't know what his agenda is."

"You know, Jai, some people don't have agendas. Some people are just... friends."

"God, Ari," he groaned.

Surprised by the entreaty in her guardian's voice, Ari spun about to look down at him, blinking in confusion at the begrudging smile he wore on his lips. She snorted. "What?"

"You." He thumped his head back against the wall wearily. "Your loyalty is exhausting."

Ari flushed at the backhanded compliment, ignoring the flutter of butterfly wings in her stomach. At the feel of them, she suddenly grew irritated and confused. She shook her head at Jai in disbelief. "I am going to the bathroom and you better not follow me."

"Child," he muttered as she blew past him.

Ari was surprised but pleased when Charlie called that night to talk. They hadn't talked on the phone for a long time. He asked her to tell him more about her visit with The White King and as she recounted the terrifying tale, she really wished Jai would disappear so she could have some privacy. After a while the conversation puttered out a little and she realized it was going to take more than the revelation that 'genies' lived among them to repair the damage to their relationship. But the call had been a start, and when Ari hung up, she felt eager and hopeful.

As she lay in bed in the dark, listening to Jai's soft breathing as he slept, she wondered what his story was in all of this. She knew her own. She knew Charlie's. She even knew Azazil's and The White and Red King's. She knew her dad's. But what about Jai, who liked science fiction and one word sentences and black coffee? Who was this guy who was sharing her life? What life had he left behind? Surprised that he was beginning to take up so much of her thoughts, Ari rolled onto her side to look out the window. It was only natural. It was only natural to wonder about the guardian assigned to her.

It was only natural, she promised herself and let the sound of Jai's breathing slowly lull her to sleep.

With his Jinn eyes Jai could make out every detail of Ari's room as if the lights were still on. He waited, watching her, relaxing when she finally closed her eyes and drifted off to sleep. Waving his hand over the floor, he drew on his magic to conjure and began thinking about everything he thought was useful for Ari to know about the Jinn, about her heritage, about the truth, without overwhelming her or going directly against The Red King's orders. He'd tried now for a number of days to get her interested in the Jinn but she was in denial. She thought if she buried her head in the sand about it, it would all go away.

But Jai didn't want her to get hurt.

Of course, he never wanted a client to get hurt. It was his job to make sure they didn't. But... a 24/7 gig with this girl should be killing him. He should be going out of his mind with boredom.

He wasn't.

He liked being around her.

Not good.

So instead of thinking about how unprofessional that was, he was going to do something to protect his client. From them all. From The Red King. The White King. From himself. Even from that little dick Charlie who looked oh so disappointed when Ari said she wasn't going to be looking into the Jinn. He was suspicious about this guy. And not because Ari couldn't see past her memories of a childhood sweetheart to the exceptionally messed up teen who walked in his shoes, but because if Jai had found out someone was responsible for murdering his kid brother he wouldn't be accepting that so easily. So Jai's question was... what did Charlie really want with Ari? And was it going to get her hurt?

Jai felt his muscles tense at the thought and his blood grew even hotter. Glancing up at her again sleeping in the dark, he felt an ache in his chest, a feeling he'd never felt before. Angry at himself now, he concentrated back on the job at hand, pouring his magic into his creation for Ari.

He was going to force Ari to discover her heritage. He was going to force her to be prepared so that when the time came she'd actually be able to handle herself.

The next morning she was literally shaken awake. "What?" she groaned, prying her eyes open only to look up into the blurry face of Jai. "What is it?"

"Wake up. The men from the Aissawa Brotherhood have arrived."

Jolting up at the news, Ari brushed back her tangled hair and gaped up at him. "Here? Now? What about my dad?"

"Your dad left for the office early this morning. He never saw them."

"Well these Brotherhood guys can't stay here."

Jai smirked. "That's why you need to get up so we can get on with the exorcism."

"Right, right. I still have slumber brain. Give me a minute."

"Slumber brain," he snorted, shaking his head at her.

Too tired to be teased, Ari pushed him aside and stumbled out of bed. "I take it taking a shower would be out of the question?"

"Not if you hurry."

"Great."

"Not a morning person huh?"

Ari rolled her eyes. "Do you have to ask that every morning when you already know the answer?"

"Yes. It's fun."

She made a rude gesture at him as she pulled some clothes out of her wardrobe and he snorted in response. She was discovering it was really hard to offend him.

"Oh, here." Jai suddenly reached out, stopping her before she went into the bathroom. Ari shivered under the heat of his touch and jerked away. His face darkened and he grabbed one of her hands, flattening the palm out before slapping a worn leather-bound book into it.

Making a face, Ari gripped the book with no title, tilting it at him. "What's this?"

When he crossed his arms over his chest and straightened up to his full height, Ari felt a tingle of warning. Uh oh. Whatever it was he meant business. "That… is a copy of a compilation of facts about the Jinn. Different races, different behaviors, different cultures, as well as some of our very important history, including stuff about the Seven Kings of Jinn and Azazil."

She thrust the book at him angrily. "I don't want it."

Narrowing his eyes on her, Jai shoved the book back at her, lowering his voice to a growl. "Read it, Ari. Read it… or I will spend the next few weeks reading it out loud to you for every minute of every day."

"Why?"

He frowned. "Why what?"

"Why do you care if I know this stuff?"

"Because…" he shook his head, as if searching for the right words. "It's… it's not easy not knowing who you are or where you belong. In the end you have to accept whatever you find out about yourself and make a place for you to belong to. But you can't discover *who* you are, Ari Johnson, if you don't accept *what* you are." He tapped the top of the book. "This is a good place to start." He threw her a cocky smile, rare and as deliciously warm as the sun after a day spent too long in the shade. "Knowledge is power."

Feeling things Ari couldn't even name, things that made her breathless and trapped in this air bubble with Jai, Ari couldn't help but gaze back up at him a little dumbly. When he eventually took a step back, Ari flushed, feeling foolish for staring at him too long. "Thanks." She managed, holding the book close to her chest. "You're right. I'll read it."

"Good." He nodded stiffly, back in his no nonsense guardian mode. "I'll go keep the brothers company." He stopped at the doorway and turned back with a little frown. "Do you have any pineapple juice?"

"Pineapple juice?"

He shrugged. "They want pineapple juice."

Ari snorted at the weird request. "No. I have OJ."

Jai shook his head. "Nah. I'll just conjure some."

Marveling over how weird her life was now, Ari sighed. "You do that."

~12~

Rip Me Out and Maybe I'll Be Different

*T*he Brotherhood was strange to say the least. They stood clustered together, ten Moroccan men from the city of Méknes, dusty and rumpled in their plain shirts and slacks. Somehow Ari had been expecting hooded robes and sinister moustaches. The Brothers regarded Jai with a mixture of awe and fear, and whatever 'aura' they got off Ari they refused to even look at her. Even when she was the one detailing the plan. The plan that sooo could not go wrong. After everyone agreed to the plan (well, the Brothers agreed once *Jai* reiterated it), including Charlie, Ari left the Brotherhood downstairs and went up to her bedroom to make the call. She was sure she would have to leave some long-winded, pleading voicemail that would beat the hell out of her pride, but to exorcise Nick she was up for it. It had occurred to her in all of this that poor Nick probably didn't have a crush on her at all. The infatuation belonged to the creepy-ass Jinn that had taken over him.

A whole year and a half of Nick's life was gone and he wasn't getting it back.

She bit her lip praying Staci would pick up. Ari had to make this right. It was her fault. She had to make it right.

"Hello?" Staci's soft voice asked tentatively.

"Staci," Ari breathed in relief. "Wow, it's so good to hear your voice." She was surprised by how true that was.

"I'm sorry, Ari. I shouldn't have ignored you like that. I was just... overwhelmed by Rachel. She's pretty mad at you. You know she hooked up with that teaching assistant she's been drooling over for the last few months. She was mad about other stuff I guess but also because you weren't there to talk to about the TA."

Ari felt a twinge of guilt and tried to shake it off. "That's great for her. But she won't take my calls so..." there was an awkward silence and Ari cursed inwardly. This wasn't going to plan. "Um... you know that's not why I called. I just wanted to say sorry, once again. And... also to ask you for a favor."

"A favor?"

"Well... after everything that happened with Charlie at the party I decided that Rache is right and I need to move on. I had a good time with Nick that night but I'm still a little... a little nervous, I guess. So I was thinking maybe you, me, A.J. and Nick could go on a double date later this afternoon. Go to the movies. It'll be fun."

"Really?"

Ari's heart leapt triumphantly at the excitement in Staci's voice. "Yeah. I mean if it's not too late notice."

"No, no. Me and A.J. were going to hang out anyway. Look I'll call him and get him to call Nick and then I'll call you right back!"

She smiled. "Sounds perfect."

"Oh, Ari, I'm so happy you're doing this. It's going to be sooo much fun. I'll call right back."

The line went dead and Ari drew her shoulders up.

This was going to be anything but fun.

A.J. and Nick rode up front, arguing over which radio station to tune into and cracking stupid jokes. Every now and then Nick would look in the rear mirror and smile at her and Ari would have to force a warm smile back while in her head she was thinking 'creepy jerk Jinn stealing my friend's body, I'm going to rip you out of there, you toad!'.

"I hope you don't mind but I told Rache we were doing this," Staci said quietly from beside her, drawing Ari's attention away from her possessed friend. She tried to concentrate on what Staci was saying but she was distracted. Had there had been any notable differences in Nick's behavior over the last eighteen months? It was hard to tell for her because they'd only really gotten to know one another in that time. Crap.

Wait. What is Staci saying?

"Rachel?" Ari frowned.

"Yeah." Staci smiled pleadingly. "I think if you call her again she'll be more amenable to a discussion. She sounded kind of excited that you were going out with us today."

Ari grunted. "She wrote on *Twitter* that I treat our friendship like a one-way street."

"Oh." Staci batted the words away with her hand. "She was just upset. She didn't mean it."

Guessing now was not the greatest time to alienate her friends, Ari nodded. "You're right. I'll call her, smooth things over."

"Good. It's silly to fight over something so silly."

Grinning, Ari shook her head at her friend. Staci was the kind of old-fashioned sweet that made you smile no matter what mood you were in.

They pulled into the parking lot at the cinema and Nick got out real quick so he could open Ari's door. The smile she gave him was almost feral and he frowned a little, seeming puzzled.

Do better, Ari. Do better.

It was hard though, especially when he put his hand on her lower back to guide her across the lot. She just couldn't get it out of her head that there was a *being* inside Nick, controlling him, using him... and all to get into her pants! Trying not to shudder and give herself away, Ari relaxed into his touch and gave him a soft smile. His eyes glowed happily back at her and she had to look quickly away before she punched him in the face.

"So, what are we watching?" Nick asked as they strolled inside, their eyes automatically reading the schedule.

"I vote *Vampires of Doom 4*," A.J. growled mockingly, bearing his teeth.

Staci snorted. "And this from the film student. I vote *The Apple*. It's supposed to be beautifully shot - it's mostly hand-held, oblique angles, blue filter, with some great location shots. It was filmed in Budapest."

Nick looked at Ari questioningly. She didn't particularly care because she wasn't going to be watching the movie, but if she *were* going to be watching the movie a cheesy vampire horror film and a pretentious love story were not her thing. Her eyes flicked down the schedule and then lit up. "Ooh they're reshowing *Harry Potter and the Sorcerer's Stone*."

A.J. scowled. "A kid's movie?"

"No. *Harry Potter*."

"Yeah, a kid's movie."

Ari made a face at him. "It's a wonderful fantasy adventure for children and grown-ups alike."

"It's got my vote." Nick shrugged.

Staci nodded, smiling sweetly up at A.J., her eyes glittering mischievously. "Mine too."

So it was with much grumbling from A.J. they bought tickets for the movie, some popcorn and drinks and wandered casually into the screening. Ari's heart immediately began to race a little harder as she talked the guys into taking seats near the aisle so she wouldn't have to shimmy by people when the time came for her to leave.

Which should be pretty soon.

Sure enough, just as they were settling in and Nick's arm was casually sliding along the back of her seat, Ari's cell beeped and she opened it to see the text she had been waiting on.

I'm outside. Bring Emily Rose.
Charlie

Here goes.

Pulling on her best acting chops, Ari muttered a curse and turned to Nick with big wide soulful eyes. "It's Charlie."

"Charlie?" Staci squeaked, leaning over Nick. "What's wrong?"

"He's outside. I told him I was coming here with Nick. He's upset. He wants to talk."

"Oh God, no, Ari." Staci shook her head. "I mean you know I like Charlie, but…" she glanced at Nick meaningfully. "Not now."

"I have to." Ari grabbed her bag and then looked back at a scowling Nick. "Will you come with me? I just… I don't want to leave him out there but I don't want to go alone."

Nick's expression cleared and he smoothed a hand down her back comfortingly. "Of course. Let's go."

As they walked across the cinema foyer the sickly scent of popcorn made Ari's already nervous stomach turn. She couldn't believe they were doing this. They were actually doing this.

"So what do you think he wants?" Nick asked, trying to appear casual, but she could see he was struggling *not* to ready himself for a fight.

Ari shrugged. "I don't know. He just said he wanted to talk, but last time we spoke we had a huge fight. I just don't want to deal with him alone."

"You're not alone." He gripped her hand tight in his and she had to force herself to not tug it back out of his hold.

Charlie was waiting way across the thankfully empty lot by Nick's SUV. She noted his eyes flicker down at her hand clasped in Nick's and she scowled back at the dark look he gave her.

"What do you want, Creagh?" Nick dropped her hand, striding towards him aggressively.

Great, he's being a chump.

Charlie nodded at her over Nick's shoulders and she shoved a hand into her bag, pulling the pouch that Jai had given her out. While Nick squared up to Charlie, Ari opened the pouch and scrunched it down on her palm, revealing the glittering black dust inside. "Nick, don't," she said, tugging on his shoulder.

"Ari-" He turned and as soon as he faced her Ari blew onto the pouch, the black dust coating Nick's face. He flinched and then stiffened, his eyes rolling back in his head before his legs gave way. Jai hadn't explained exactly what the dust in the pouch was, only that it would incapacitate someone without leaving any physical trace of injury. The incapacitating also only lasted on a possessed human for five, ten minutes tops. They had to move fast.

Charlie gripped Nick's collapsing body into his strong hands and together they shoved him into the back of the SUV. He dug in Nick's jeans, pulling out the keys, his eyes darting around the lot to make sure no one had witnessed the attack. As they jumped into the front of the car, he turned his dark eyes on her, noting her trembling hands. "You OK?"

She nodded, clenching her teeth together to stop them chattering. Her heart was racing out of all control.

Charlie decimated the speed limit and they pulled off at a quiet spot in Vickers' Woods where Jai was waiting at the edge of the trees for them. Together, he and Charlie dragged Nick's lagging body into the woods to the clearing the Aissawa Brothers had taken up residence. Ari watched from the sideline as Jai gestured for Charlie to get back. He stepped beside her and she tried to capture his attention but his eyes were glued to Jai, Nick and the Brothers. He seemed mesmerized by what was going on. Feeling a tingling of unease at his expression, Ari turned back to the group, watching as Jai tied Nick's hands and feet and left him to lie on the dirty ground. He then stepped out of the circle the Brothers made around Nick's body and took up his place on her other side.

"What happens now?" she asked him, watching curiously as one of the Brothers produced a small drum and began beating on it. She winced, hoping it wouldn't attract any attention.

"Don't worry," Jai murmured in her ear and she couldn't help but shiver at the feel of him so close, his dark, exotic scent tickling her every sense. "I've put up an enchantment to muffle the sound of what we're doing. The Brothers will do their thing and probably make Nick drink an herb called Indian Costus. It repels Jinn from the possessed."

Ari frowned. "Couldn't you have told me that? I could have just slipped the stuff into his Coke at the cinema or something."

Jai shook his head. "Doesn't work like that. There's a whole ritual. You'll see."

And she did.

The Brothers began to chant ominously in a language Ari couldn't understand. The sound of it, however, made her shiver and shake, like she was coming down with the flu. When she threw a quick glance up at Jai she noticed he looked similarly affected, his skin pale, a bead of sweat forming on his forehead. She touched her own clammy forehead with a trembling palm and fought to keep upright. She wasn't given much time to ponder the ill feeling that came over her so suddenly because at that moment the Brothers each produced a knife from their boots and drew the sharp blades over their wrists.

Ari gasped at the horrifying action and looked up at Charlie to see what he was making of all this creepiness. She was terrified that what happened here would reflect badly on her and he would never want to speak to her again. But instead he watched in utter fascination, his eyes rapt on the scene, chewing on his lip, something he did when he was busy concentrating. Shaken, Ari looked back over at the Brothers only to feel her stomach turn as they drank from their own bloody wrists and began chanting again, thick blood slipping down their chins as they did. Nick's body began to shudder on the ground, his eyes rolling back in his head.

"No," he croaked. "No, stop it. You can't…"

One of the Brothers stepped forward, a cup clasped in his hand. Carefully he tipped a vial of the herb Jai had spoken of into the cup and bent down next to Nick. He whispered something in that strange language that made Ari sweat cold sweats and then he pinched Nick's nose closed, tilted his head back, and forced him to swallow the drink. When he was sure Nick had, he returned to the circle and the Brothers chanting grew louder. Nick's body began shuddering harder until he was thrashing on the ground, groaning and choking on screams. Ari tensed, disturbed by the sight, and was glad for the warm hand Jai placed on her shoulder when she visibly flinched as some weird black stuff oozed out of Nick's eyes and mouth and ears. "Oh God," she breathed and Jai squeezed her shoulder harder.

Finally, to Ari's everlasting relief, Nick cried out one last time before flames burst from his body. One of the Brothers dropped to his knees, a bottle, like the one Sala was trapped in, clasped in his hands as he muttered frantically. The flames gave off a high-pitched hiss, almost like they were screaming, and then they spiraled tighter until they were sucked down into the bottle. The Brother promptly stoppered it and gasped out one last chant.

The woods were deathly silent.

The Brother with the bottle stood up and turned to Jai. "It is done." He bowed formally at him and he and the Brothers began making their way past the three of them like they hadn't just cut open their own wrists and exorcised an evil spirit from a teenage boy's body. One of the Brothers stopped before Jai, who handed him over a wad of cash. Ari frowned. She hadn't known this was going to cost Jai money. Great. Now she was even more in his debt. Literally and figuratively.

"Thanks," Jai said gruffly. "Appreciate it."

The Brother merely nodded and followed the others out of the woods.

Ari gaped. "Where are they going?"

"To call a cab back to the airport."

"But what about..." she trailed off, tentatively taking a step towards Nick who lay unconscious on the ground. She gulped down guilt. "Will he be OK?"

"He'll be fine," Jai said and then seemed to think better of it. "He won't remember a thing of the last eighteen months so... actually he won't be fine. But he'll be physically fine." He pulled out a cloth and handed it to Ari. "Clean the gunk off him and then you and Charlie load him back into the SUV."

Nick lay in the back of the SUV, unconscious but black goo-free. Ari gripped the dashboard as they pulled back into the cinema lot.

Charlie sighed, cutting the engine. He turned to her, his dark eyes concerned. "This isn't your fault. You didn't get him possessed OK. It happened."

Ari laughed humorlessly. "He's going to wake up any minute now and he's not going to remember anything about the last eighteen months. How will he get over that?"

Her oldest friend reached across the seats and took her hand. "He'll get through it. Just like you're getting through all of this. Did I tell you how proud I am of you?"

She smiled sadly. "Me? What about you? I want to throw up all the time but you - you're handling all of this amazingly well."

He shrugged. "It fascinates me. Plus… I feel different."

Glad that Charlie was no longer carrying around the weight of his brother's death, she squeezed his hand. "Freer?"

Just like that the temperature in the car dropped and the momentary happiness she had been feeling fled as Charlie's eyes darkened and he withdrew his hand. He didn't say a word in response and Ari felt her skin prickle uneasily.

"Ari!"

She turned at the sound of Staci yelling. She and A.J. were running across the lot towards the SUV. Ari and Charlie jumped out and walked around Nick's car to meet them. A.J. looked ready to launch himself at Charlie so Ari dived between them.

Staci's pretty face was pinched with concern. "You were taking so long we decided to come out and check everything was OK. Where's Nick?"

Reciting the story they'd come up with, Ari put on an innocent and, not entirely untrue, frightened expression. "He passed out. We were just talking and he collapsed so we were taking him to the hospital."

"Passed out my ass!" A.J. yelled, moving towards Charlie. "What did you do?!"

"A.J., A.J." Ari grabbed his arm, pulling him towards the back of the SUV and away from Charlie, who looked far too willing to engage in a fist fight. She wrenched open the back door and pointed in at Nick. "See, not a mark on him. We have to get him to the hospital."

Nick chose that exact moment to groan and A.J. practically shoved Ari out of the way to lean in and slap his face gently. "Dude, dude, you OK?" he asked frantically, making Ari feel terrible for their deception.

"What happened?" Nick mumbled, smacking his mouth open and shut. "My mouth. Oh God, my head." A.J. put an arm around his shoulders, helping him sit up and Nick opened his eyes wide, taking the four of them in, staring at him. "What happened? Where am I?"

"Ari said you passed out," A.J. explained.

Nick frowned. "Ari?" He looked over A.J.'s shoulder and his eyebrows drew together in confusion. "Ari? Why, where am I?"

"Dude, at the movies. The four of us came here together."

"We did?" He glanced around, shaking his head. "I don't remember."

Staci tutted. "A.J. we have to take him to hospital if he can't remember even getting here."

Charlie sighed and pushed forward. "What's the last thing you remember?"

Jesus Christ, Charlie! Ari pinched him for asking such an asinine question and he winced, batting her hand away.

Nick looked near tears now and she watched A.J. grow pale with concern. "I don't know. I was in my bed. I just got home from my date with Louise."

"Louise?" Staci frowned.

Nick nodded, glancing warily at Ari. "Louise. *Louise.* Louise Buckman."

"Your ex-girlfriend?" Staci looked up at A.J. in horror. "Were they dating again?" she whispered.

He shook his head. "No. Definitely not. He can't stand her." He gulped and turned back to Nick. "Nick, what year is it?"

"W-why?" Nick asked frantically now, his eyes growing larger and brighter with unshed, confused tears. "Why? You're scaring me, man."

"You're scaring me. What year is it?"

"2009. December 2009."

As a collective they gasped, even though Ari and Charlie knew it had been coming.

A.J cursed and patted his friend's shoulder. "We're going to take care of you, man." He turned now to Charlie, glaring at him. "Give me the keys, I'll take him."

Charlie handed them over somberly. "You need help?"

"Not from you."

Nick and Staci drove off with Nick towards Ridge Heart hospital, towards the disquieting revelation they'd discover pretty soon. Shivering, Ari wrapped her arms around herself, hating her father and her mother for doing this to the people she cared about. They might not have done this with their own two hands, but indirectly they had caused this. Their actions had put a dangerous being like Ari in amongst good, ordinary folks and she'd drawn evil towards them.

A strong arm came around her shoulders and Ari was folded against Charlie's warm chest. She breathed him in, clutching a hand to his *Nine Inch Nails* t-shirt. He smelled like lemons and damp soil and fresh musky sweat. She wanted to curl up inside him and never let go.

"You didn't do this," he murmured against her forehead, pressing a soft kiss to her skin. "Don't do this to yourself."

"I'm trying," she whispered.

He rubbed her arm comfortingly. "Try harder. Nobody beats up on my friend Ari. Including my friend Ari."

She smiled weakly, glad that at least one good thing had come of all this. Every second she was growing closer to getting her old Charlie back.

~13~

Years of Stars I've Yet to Know

*W*hen Ari and Jai finally returned home that night there was a message from Staci on her answer machine explaining that Nick had lost his memories from the last eighteen months and the doctors couldn't figure out why. There didn't seem to be any physical injury and there was no head trauma so they'd decided to keep him in overnight. She said she'd keep Ari updated and then quietly added that A.J. was wondering if they had told them everything that had happened in the parking lot.

"I'm really sorry, Ari," Staci whispered, as if she didn't want to be overheard. "But if my dufus boyfriend has his way he'll get the Sheriff involved. Nothing happened... right?"

Swallowing down the guilt Ari had deleted the message and listened to the one Rachel had left explaining how she had heard what had happened with Nick and was wondering if Ari was alright. Not one to hold a grudge against Rachel for her sporadic brattiness, Ari called her back and they arranged for Rachel to come over to the house in the morning to catch up. All the while, Jai sat on the floor reading *Enchantment* by Orson Scott Card. The only time he shifted was when they heard Derek coming upstairs. Jai changed into the Great Dane in a burst of fire and flame and they waited with bated breath to see if Derek would knock on her door.

He didn't.

His footsteps echoed on down the hallway to his bedroom and the door closed quietly. When Jai changed back she could feel his eyes on her questioningly, but she didn't want him to see her hurt or disappointment in Derek so she grabbed up the leather-bound book he had given her, too wired to go directly to bed. Her breathing eased when she heard him rustling back down onto the sleeping bag to read. Suddenly realizing how selfish she'd been acting with Jai (he had to move when she moved, eat when she ate, sleep when she slept) Ari lowered the tome in her hands and let her gaze fall on Jai's dark head. His hair was cut pretty close, almost military. He suited the severity of the cut but she thought perhaps he'd look younger, softer, with longer hair. Feeling her eyes on him, Jai lifted his eyes up from his book without moving his head.

His mouth quirked up under her unflinching stare. "Something wrong?"

Ari sighed. "I haven't been the best hostess, have I?"

His eyes glittered under the lamp on her computer desk and the quirk turned into a half-smile that transformed his hard face. She ignored the tiny flutter in her chest somewhere near her heart. "You're not supposed to be a hostess here. I'm not a guest. I'm a guardian."

"But if you're tired and want to sleep I'll turn off the lights."

"I'm fine, Ari. Read the book."

"If you're sure?"

He shook his head, lowering his gaze again. "Ari, guys aren't like girls. When we say we're fine *we* actually mean it."

Snorting at that, Ari picked the book back up. Opening the pages, she felt a shiver cascade down her spine, the crinkling of the paper seeming obnoxiously loud in the quiet of her bedroom. She stared down at the first page, her stomach churning. She was afraid of a book. Afraid of discovering more about her-

Say it, Ari.

-kind.

She wasn't human.

Without meaning to her eyes drifted over to Jai again. He wasn't human either. But he seemed human. He seemed... like one of the good guys. Of course, she couldn't know that for sure, but she felt it somehow.

Her fingers trembled as she traced the bold black script on the page in her lap.

JINN: A HISTORY
BYANONYMOUS

Ari wondered who Anonymous was and why he/she felt the need to be anonymous. That seemed a little *ominous* to her. Maybe people weren't supposed to write down stuff about the Jinn. Maybe the book was taboo. Shrugging off her unease, Ari turned the pages and began to read. The first few chapters were about the different kinds of Jinn, the most powerful ones, the more common ones. Her eyes trailed over one of the lists and she wondered if she'd ever be able to remember this stuff.

Jinn: This term is a collective one, used to describe individual Jinn and tribes of Fire Spirits. Jinn in their varied forms, like man, carry good souls within them or evil souls.

Hierarchy of the Jinn:

Azazil (also known as Iblis) : Sultan of the Jinn, Azazil is the first and most powerful of his children. He was born out of Chaos but legend tells us he has also fought on the side of good. As such, Azazil's mercurial nature lends itself to good and evil.

The Seven Kings of Jinn: Azazil's seven sons. Each king reigns supreme over one day in the mortal week. They have jurisdiction over their allocated day and can interfere in the lives of Importants (see page 112 paragraph 2). In descending order:

The Gilder King – Ruler of Sunday (neutral in the War of the Flames [see page 245])

The Glass King – Ruler of Monday (subject to Azazil in the War of the Flames [as above])

The Red King – Ruler of Tuesday (subject to Azazil in the War of the Flames)

The Gleaming King – Ruler of Wednesday (subject to The White King in the War of the Flames)

The White King – Ruler of Thursday (inciter of the War of the Flames [see page 243-245 onwards])

The Shadow King – Ruler of Friday (subject to The White King in the War of the Flames)

The Lucky King – Ruler of Saturday (neutral in the War of the Flames)

Intrigued by the so-called 'War of the Flames' Ari wanted to skip through all the other stuff to page 243 to learn what it was and why The White King – *her father* – had incited it. But if there was one thing Ari knew when studying for her SATs it was to never skip the boring parts because that's usually what came up in the exam. She drew her knees up to her chest, the book balancing on them, and she narrowed her eyes over the top of it to study Jai.

He wasn't going to quiz her on this was he?

"Keep reading," he murmured turning his page.

Her mouth fell open in amazement. How did he do that? Flushing at having been caught staring, Ari sunk deeper into her pillows to hide behind her knees and bury her head in the book.

It is argued whether the next in the order of hierarchy should come before the Seven Kings of Jinn for none truly understand the extent of his power...

Asmodeus: Often referred to as Prince Asmodeus, he is Azazil's 1ˢᵗ Lieutenant and the very first of the race of Marids (see page 87 para 4). Terrifyingly powerful and born of the evil Jinn, Asmodeus is loyal to Azazil – it is unknown why he is loyal to the Sultan, but his loyalty is absolute.

The lesser royal Jinn that followed weren't nearly so interesting as this Prince Asmodeus guy but Ari read on, her eyes glazing over every now and then until she snapped herself to attention at a list of the most common Jinn.

Marid: Always evil, the Marid have extraordinary power and are known to live as long as 2500 years, although Asmodeus is far older (his true age remains unknown, although some postulate he is almost as old as Azazil).

Ifrit: Like all Jinn, the Ifrit are telepathic and can converse with other Jinn this way. Like most Jinn the Ifrit can shapeshift, possess, shield themselves with invisibility by stepping into the Cloak, conjure with magic and enchantments, and place curses upon lesser beings - although their magic is not as powerful as the Marid's. However, each individual Ifrit has one gift specific to them that can even overshadow the power of the Marid. The soul of the Ifrit is more ambiguous than the Marid. Although some are evil, some have been known to be good.

Shaitan: Children and servants of the Sultan, the Shaitan have never been known to be anything but evil and are loyal only to those strong enough to call themselves their Master.

Ari read on, discovering the names of some pretty disgusting creatures, along with the Nisnas she had encountered and the Labartu that had killed Charlie's little brother. The majority of the information concentrated on the bad Jinn and Ari was left with a sick feeling in her stomach as the information planted itself firmly in her brain. It was weird. She had never wanted to know about her heritage but as she read on it became impossible to put the book down. Now that she knew what was out there, she had to know what else was out there. She had to arm herself in some way against the force of the Jinn. She was fascinated to learn that there existed half-breed Jinn – half-human, half-Jinn – that the Jinn called Hybrids. There were two kinds: Sorcerers and The Guild. According to Ari's findings, Sorcerers were rare because most Hybrids had no idea about the Jinn and therefore didn't connect with their magical abilities. The rare few who did were usually unable to handle the strength of the power without it turning their minds. They utilized talismans, seals and inscriptions to channel their magic. Theirs was considered 'illicit' magic for they often used it for their own means and to enslave Jinn. On the other end of the spectrum was The Guild, tribes of Hybrids who grew up learning 'licit' magic to hunt down Sorcerers and prevent any harm to humans from them or evil Jinn. They technically got away with killing Sorcerers because they were half-human but if a member of The Guild killed Jinn, rather than merely disarming them, they were called to Mount Qaf to face trial in the Jinn Courts. Wincing at how unfair that was, Ari moved on, surprised to discover that The Guild was created centuries ago by The Gilder King. Apparently he was known among the Jinn as the most benevolent of his brothers. It made Ari feel easier about The Red King; maybe he wasn't so bad after all too? Maybe, she really could trust him? She felt like she could trust Jai anyway.

Skimming through, Ari finally stumbled upon the history pages. What was written was only what 'Anonymous' considered the most important of Jinn history. She read about stuff The White King had already told her: that for centuries he and his brothers meddled in the lives of Importants, shaping destinies, building empires, destroying cities. Soaking it up, Ari turned the page to a new chapter and felt her heart pick up for no good reason at all.

Chapter Four: The Seal of Solomon

Religious scripts called him a Prophet, the son of David, but here he is known simply as King Solomon, enslaver of Jinn and master of the Seal of Solomon. Stories differ as to who bestowed the Seal of Solomon upon this Important but what is known is that it was a god. Placing into Solomon's hand a ring of brass and iron, this god offered the mortal king the greatest of power. With the brass part Solomon could stamp his written commands to the good Jinn and with the iron part, he stamped his commands to the evil Jinn. With this unlimited power, King Solomon enslaved many Jinn, using them to build his great temples and provide him with whatever he wished. Over the years, out of pride and greed, he began to abuse his power, and Azazil the Great Sultan grew uneasy for the first time. Enlisting Asmodeus to determine the true power of the Seal, Asmodeus was astonished to discover that with the Seal upon his finger, Solomon could feel his presence spying upon him even when hidden within the Cloak. Demanding he reveal himself, Asmodeus was bound before King Solomon and trapped within a bottle as punishment for his attempted treachery. Unknown to any of us, the being who had bestowed the ring upon Solomon grew furious with his subject for treating the Jinn so carelessly. He stripped Solomon of his crown and the Seal and sent him out into the desert to die. To prevent unrest among the people He freed Asmodeus from the bottle and in exchange for the Seal of Solomon, Asmodeus shifted to appear as the mortal king and reign in his stead until his death. When his time as Solomon was over it is said Asmodeus returned to the Jinn Realm of Mount Qaf where he offered his master the Seal. Azazil attempted to destroy the ring but discovered it was indestructible. Confident in his own mastery over his people – for Azazil needed no ring to be obeyed – he offered the ring to Asmodeus, commanding he protect it with his life and never use it against the Jinn. Asmodeus is said to be evil but he is also honorable to his word. For centuries he has guarded the ring, wearing it in confidence on a strip of leather tied around his neck, daring lesser Jinn to steal it from him.

None have.

But as the tension grows between the Seven Kings of Jinn and their father, the Seal has taken its place as the most important weapon in the War of the Flames.

Chapter Five: The War of the Flames

It is said that the Seven Kings suspect their father of causing the chaos between them, and for upsetting the balance of order in their world. None can prove it. But what is universally acknowledged is the Sultan Azazil's reluctance to restore order. He has the power to do so. But he does not. One son, one king, has grown intractable in his need to punish his father for what he considers negligence to their people. The White King. It is known throughout the many realms that The White King wishes to take his father's place as Sultan of the Jinn. It is known also that he plans to use the Seal of Solomon to do so. He has attempted many times to steal the ring from Asmodeus, each attempt ending in the bloody and violent death of the servant sent in The White King's stead to do so. Until his victory or failure to steal the Seal, the War of the Flames rages on, the Seven Kings of Jinn and their loyalties split into three factions: Azazil's, The White King's, and a place of neutrality where The Gilder King and The Lucky King refuse to be embroiled in the war. It is a sly war - for the most part it is not a physical war and will never be until the Seal passes into The White King's hands. For now... the War of the Flames remains an 'understanding', and a *promise of usurpation should the time ever present itself to Azazil's treacherous son of Thursday.*

Ari slammed the book shut, the crack of pages slamming together echoing around the room. Her heart was racing hard in her chest and she had no idea why. The words kept running through her mind over and over. *Azazil. The War of the Flames. The Seal of Solomon. The White King. Asmodeus. The War of the Flames. The Seal of Solomon. The White King. Azazil...*

"Ari, you OK?"

She jerked her head up, her eyes refocusing on Jai who was leaning forward on the sleeping bag, his eyebrows drawn together in concern.

Somehow, Ari began to breathe properly again and she nodded. He frowned in consternation and sat back. "You sure?"

Feeling better Ari reached over and placed the book on the nightstand, and when she glanced back at Jai she raised a questioning eyebrow. "So... you're a telepath, huh. What's that about?"

~14~

There Are Some Things Even a Dog Shouldn't Know

*J*ai was frustratingly closed-mouthed about the whole being telepathic thing. His literal reply had been, "Jinn can talk to each other with their minds."

That was it.

Frustrated, Ari wanted more but he was annoyingly vague about the whole thing and would only answer one of her questions - could Jinn read minds? Her heart had spluttered in mortification at the thought of Jai being able to read her thoughts. Thankfully, he promised her the Jinn could not mind read and then promptly lay down on his sleeping bag, turning the lights off with his Jinn voodoo.

The next morning Ari tried not to think about the book and all she'd discovered. Derek was in his office, still slinking around the house without talking to her, and Rachel was on her way over to 'make up'. When the doorbell rang, Ari was jerked out of her daze - she'd been staring stupidly at the book on her nightstand, the haunting pages of it rolling around in her mind like spooky little ghosts. Jai came out of the bathroom with questioning eyes. She nodded to let him know that Rachel was at the door and the air around him shimmered before he exploded into a fire that quickly burnt out, leaving behind Hamlet the Great Dane.

The knock on her bedroom door told Ari her dad had let Rachel in. Bracing herself for the multitude of moods Rachel could have picked from to face her after their 'fight', Ari sat down on her bed. "Come in," she called and smirked with amusement as Jai jumped onto her bed beside her, curling up lazily on the comforter before staring determinedly at the door. Rachel came in tentatively, an apologetic smile on her face as she closed the bedroom door behind her.

"I come in peace," she said softly.

It was weird. Rachel was this completely anal, bossy, know-it-all, bratty, self-important type-A pain in the ass a lot of the time. But as Ari smiled back at her, warmth gathered in her chest and the tension in her shoulders unknotted, and all she could see was the sweet, concerned, funny Rachel that had made Ari want to be her friend in the first place. "Come in, sit down." She shimmied over, nudging Jai to make room for her.

Rachel's eyes widened as she approached, her face lighting up. "Oh my God, who is this enormous bundle of gorgeousness?"

Ari smiled, swearing she could hear Jai make a snorting sound from the back of his throat. "This is Hamlet. He's replaced Ms. Maggie."

Rachel's shoulders hunched as she glanced around the room. "Is the poltergeist gone?"

"Yup. All gone."

"For good?"

"Looks like. So I got Hamlet here to keep me company."

Rachel giggled and sat down next to him, running her hands over his head and back. "Oh I sooo prefer Hamlet. And how cute is that name btw?" She grinned up at her. "Very witty."

Ari laughed. "At least one person thinks so."

"Oh sooo cuuute," Rachel squeed, pressing soft kisses to his head. Jai didn't growl or snarl or anything, but he was trying desperately to get away from her mouth. When Ari laughed at his predicament he shot her a dirty doggy look in protest. Finally taking pity on him, she reached out and touched Rachel's arm. "So... we OK?" she asked, drawing some of her attention away from Jai.

Rachel looked up, still patting his head. Ari could see the confusion in her eyes but she nodded. "Yeah. I don't know what happened to you but... the reason I got so mad was because I knew it was a Charlie thing. I thought you were freaking out about him. You were so out of it at your own party, and I just felt frustrated, you know. I was so worried about you. I'm sorry for not handling it the right way, Ari. I really am." She patted her hand, smiling apologetically. "But since then, Staci said you're taking my advice and moving on from him, so whatever those two missing days were they were at least a very good thing." She grinned now, reaching out to pull Ari into a hug. "I'm proud of you."

For thinking I abandoned a friend?

When Rachel pulled back Ari had smoothed the scowl from her face and put a fake smile on in its place. "So have you heard any more news from Stace about Nick?"

"Oh, he's going to be OK. The doctors can't work it out. There's no physical sign of injury, external or internal. It's just this weird phenomenon. Sooo weird. I feel bad for him, but you know he's alive, he's young and fit and he can get through this. We'll all be there to help him. Although, not yet." She frowned. "His parents are being wicked weird about visitors right now."

"Is A.J. still mad at Charlie?"

"I don't think so. I mean he'll never like the guy but Staci convinced him that Charlie was just there at the wrong time, wrong place. Although I hear he was going to take Nick to the ER so that's like a point in his favor right?"

"Right."

"So anyway!" Rachel suddenly cried, her mouth stretched in a cat's-got-the-cream grin. "You have to hear about my time with Paul Schwartz."

"Uhh." Ari looked down at Jai who was watching everything they did and listening to everything they said. She really didn't want Rachel discussing her love life with the T.A. in front of him. "You hooked up, that's great. Any plans to see him again?"

She nodded, her eyes glittering. "I'm going to have such a ball with him this summer before I head off to Dartmouth. So... OK... I invited him to your party; you were kind of out of it that night so you didn't see him flirting with me all night long. Nothing happened but he texted me the next day to go to the movies. Well... we got to the parking lot of the movies." Rachel wiggled her eyebrows suggestively. "And that's as far as we got. Next thing I know my shirt is off, my hand is down his pants-"

"Uh Rachel!" Ari stopped her, glaring at Jai for not leaving the room like a gentleman. "Are you sure you want to discuss this in front of the dog?"

Rachel burst out laughing, her eyes washing over Ari's flushed face. "Jeez, Ari, come on. You know you wouldn't get all embarrassed about sex if you just traded in your v-card already. I know, I know, you were waiting on Charlie to give up the old virginity but you are *too* pretty to be missing out on this stuff. Seriously at one point I thought my-"

"My dad's home." Ari bolted up off the bed, totally mortified that Jai now knew she was a virgin.

Rachel's eyebrows drew together in a glower. "So?"

"He might hear you."

"Ari, what is your damage?"

"You know... you're right." She blushed even harder. Rachel must think she was a total schizo. "Let's go get a soda and some chips or something. I'll put together a snack while you give me all the gory details."

"Oh sure."

Jai stood up to jump off the bed as the two of them made their way to the door. Ari turned back on him. "Stay," she snapped.

"Oh, Ari, he can come, he's sooo cute."

"No, he can stay." Ari glowered at him, his doggy eyes burning through her with indignation. "He chewed on my diary this morning. Chewed on stuff even a dog shouldn't know." She narrowed her eyes on him pointedly.

"I didn't know you kept a diary," Rachel mused, as Ari ushered her out the room and slammed the door on Jai.

Ten minutes later, as they sat in the kitchen - Rachel having already regaled Ari with her tale of sex with a TA in the back parking lot of the movies - a familiar click of nails on tile brought her head up and she watched as Jai wandered in with a lazy doggy smirk on his face.

"Wow," Rachel breathed. "How did he get out?"

"He got out because he's too damn nosy for his own good."

"You're pretty harsh on your dog, Ari." Rachel held out a cheese puff. "Here, boy."

Jai took it, crunching on it comically, his tongue licking the cheese powder from Rachel's hands as she giggled. Ari wanted to kill him. Wasn't it possible for her to have at least an hour in a room without him listening in on every little thing? Thankfully the conversation steered back to Rachel's excitement about attending Dartmouth. Not quite able to find the courage to discuss the whole probably not going to Penn thing with her just yet (she hadn't even talked to her dad about it because he wasn't speaking to her), Ari threw all of her excitement about college at Rachel for Rachel. And she *was* excited for her friend. This was everything Rachel had been dreaming about since she was a little kid.

A few hours later, assured that she and Rache were back on track (for now), Ari walked her to the door, surprised to hear Derek call out to them.

"Nice to see you, Rachel." He nodded from the armchair in the living room. He had his briefcase out, lots of work papers scattered over the coffee table.

"Oh you too, Mr. Johnson." Rachel smiled back and then hugged Ari goodbye. She bent down to place another slobbery kiss on Jai's forehead before she left. When the door clicked closed behind her Ari snorted, watching Jai lift a paw to try and swipe the saliva from the top of his head.

"Ari."

Taken aback, Ari jerked her head up sharply. Derek was speaking to her?

"Dad?"

He stood up, exhaling heavily, his features drawn and tired. He began gathering up his papers, slotting them into his briefcase. Finally, just when she was about to snap with impatience, he strode over to her, his familiar scent making her wish she could fall against his chest for a hug like she used to do when she was little.

I'm lonely.

"Ari, I'm..." he shook his head. "I haven't been acting very adult lately and for that I'm sorry. But... I am just so... so disappointed in you, kid."

Biting back the rush of anger his words incited, Ari nodded tightly, unable to respond.

"The things you told me. Said." He heaved another sigh. "I just…"

Despite her anger, Ari was terrified her dad was never going to forgive her. She *needed* him to forgive her. "I am so sorry," she choked out. "I am so sorry. I don't know what else…"

Seeing her fumble, Derek reached out and squeezed her shoulder and she leaned into his touch. "I know. I know, kid. I said I was disappointed. I didn't say I didn't still love you. Of course I still love you."

The tightness in her throat eased. "I love you too."

"But." He grew all stern again. "I think we really need to discuss Penn. I still think it's your best option at this point." Before she could feel any more deflated he went on, "Now I'm leaving tonight, I've got a plane to Boston to catch. I've got a big meeting with a few of the partners of a medical center out there, so we can't talk now. I'm going out to the office to get a few things and I'll be driving directly to the airport and I won't be back for a few days… but when I get back you and I are having a discussion. Including about him." He pointed at Jai. "Damn, that is a big dog, Ari."

"He was a birthday gift. From Charlie."

"Yeah, well… I'm not crazy about the idea but if it has to be a dog at least he looks like a real dog and not one of those yappy things girls put in their purses these days."

Ari grunted.

"And I like the name." His smile warmed her right through and she found herself tugging on his arm like she did when she was little.

"Do you really need to go, Dad?"

"Don't start, Ari." He shook his head impatiently. "On that note, when I get back we're also going to talk about some of the things you said."

Nodding numbly now she couldn't even muster a smile when he kissed her on the cheek. She watched, an ache in her chest, as he grabbed the small suitcase she hadn't seen placed by the door and shrugged on his coat.

"See you in a few days."

"Bye, Dad," she whispered.

The door had slammed shut behind him five minutes ago and Ari was still staring at it in a pained daze. Finally she heard the hiss of flames beside her, the heat licking her skin and bringing her back around. She turned to stare up at Jai, his beautiful eyes capturing hers. The green of them was broken up by bright gold striations that made them glitter in the light. She had always considered her eyes to be her best feature - they were pretty unique. But Jai's... Jai's eyes made you want to dive deep into them.

He crossed his arms over his chest, a deep frown gathered between his eyebrows. "You OK?"

Ari gave a little humorless laugh, moving into the living room where she collapsed on the armchair that was still warm from her dad's body. Jai followed her, his gaze never leaving her, and she realized how comforted she was by his presence. She flushed, looking down so he couldn't catch the thought in her eyes. He sat down on the couch across from her, and after a few minutes of him waiting patiently Ari finally looked back over at him. "Do you get along with your dad, Jai?"

Not really expecting an answer since so far Jai didn't do the whole personal question thing, Ari was surprised to hear him snort. It was a bitter sound. "My dad's name is Luca Bitar. In the world of Jinn and the world of Security he's known as a top gun. He's the head of Bitar Security in Los Angeles. He's successful, respected. He's married to Nicki Byrne Bitar, a born and bred female member of the Irish Ginnaye. They met when they were really young when my dad was on assignment in Ireland, they fell madly in love. They have three sons together. Two older than me, one younger. Some would say they had it all... but..."

Ari was leaning forward now, eager to learn all she could about him. This was the most he'd ever said in one sitting. "But?" she prompted quietly.

His eyes found hers again and he offered a bitter smile that made him look harder, older. "My mother came along. I never met her but I've heard all about the damage she did. I've... been reminded of it every day of my life. The Red King told you she was a succubus Jinn – called a Lilif - which is true. She was one of the bad ones, Ari. When she seduces a human she takes a huge part of their life force from them. It's what she feeds on. But when she seduces Jinn it's a little different. She made Luca think he loved her and she seduced him against his will. In doing so she placed on him, for lack of a better word, an imprint. He knew afterwards he didn't love her but it was as if she had taken a part of him anyway. He couldn't love Nicki the same way he had before. And they both knew it. Nicki tries not to blame Luca. When my mom turned up pregnant with me and left me on their doorstep, she just blamed me instead. So did Luca. And my half-brothers. The worst is Luca though. He pretty much hates my guts." He laughed, an unhappy sound that ripped at Ari. She wanted to reach for him. Take his hand. Do something to comfort this man who had come so suddenly into her life, pretending to be some untouchable, uncaring being when there was clearly so much more to him than that. And that he was sharing stuff so personal with her made her feel... privileged. "So... I guess the answer is no. I don't get along with my dad." He leaned forward now too, their gazes fused. His drifted for a moment over her face and, Ari didn't know if it was wishful thinking or not, but she could have sworn his eyes softened a little. "I know what it's like to be disappointed in the man who is supposed to be your father. Supposed to take care of you and support you. I know what it's like to watch him turn his back on you too many times to count and leave you standing in the dust."

"How does that make you *feel?*" she whispered, her eyes straying to the window to look out on the empty driveway.

Jai made a huffing noise that drew her attention. He was sitting back again, his cynical little smirk firmly back in place. "How does it make *you* feel?"

A sensation, a warm *tension*, a bubble of understanding, drew around them, closing them in together, their breaths seeming to match one for the other. She didn't answer. Because she didn't need to. Somehow, in all of this, Jai Bitar of the Ginnaye, one of the Jinn whom she wished to be nothing like, *got* her. She smiled shyly, dropping her gaze, trying not to think about the hot kiss he'd placed on her to trace her movements. Jai *got* her. And just then... just then she didn't feel so lonely anymore.

~15~

How Can I Lean on You When You're Lying Down?

*T*he dramatic (and somewhat cheesy) opening credit music of *CSI* enveloped the living room and Ari snuck another peek at Jai. He was slouched on one of the armchairs, his book under a lamp. He'd read all of his Orson Scott Card novels and had been looking for another sci-fi to conjure. Ari had given him *Oryx & Crake* by Margaret Atwood from her bookshelf instead. He'd been a little skeptical and a little sexist because it was sci-fi written by a woman (oh the horror!) but since his head hadn't lifted from the pages since he'd started reading it after dinner, Ari could only assume he was enjoying it. She drew her legs up onto the couch, curling them under her and attempting to concentrate on the television, but it was difficult with Jai sitting there... looking like that. Ari held in a huff of annoyance, wishing they could go back a few days. Yeah sure she'd thought he was attractive (she had eyes after all) but until today he'd just been this slightly annoying, hot, older guy she enjoyed trading insults with. OK, a slightly annoying older guy she enjoyed trading insults with and who also happened to intrigue her. A little. Now, not only was he hot, but he had shared himself with her. He had a story. A story she wanted to know more of. Needed to know more of. Crap.

In an attempt to shrug off whatever it was Jai made her feel, Ari had called Charlie, but his cell went straight to voicemail. She wondered if he and his mom were spending some more quality time together. God she hoped so. Still, it would have been nice to talk to him, tell him about her dad. About 'the big talk' Derek had planned, the one in which she was pretty sure he was going to bully her into going to Penn. She knew she should stand her ground but... it would be easier to let her dad have his own way. She didn't want to disappoint him. Again.

Without meaning to Ari's eyes drifted over to Jai. She was surprised he had told her that stuff about his family. He'd let down his guard and let her in so she wouldn't feel so alone in this thing with her dad. It was incredibly sweet of him. Settling her chin on her hand her eyes followed the way the light cast over his face. When Jai was talking to someone his whole face was tight, his jaw flexed a lot, and his eyes glinted like sharp cuts of emerald. But when he was reading he was more relaxed, his eyelashes long, casting shadows on the crest of his cheeks. He turned a page and Ari followed the lines of his large strong hands. They were nice hands, masculine and rough, but somehow graceful. The tendons on his muscled forearm twitched as he moved and Ari felt something in her lower belly tug, her heart picking up speed as her eyes feasted on him. Flushing at her wayward thoughts, reprimanding herself for being disloyal to Charlie (and yeah she was aware they weren't actually a couple), Ari wanted to tear herself away. But she couldn't. Jai had crawled in somehow and now she wanted to know more.

"So what The Red King said? You live a completely human life?"

Jai jerked his head up at her soft question, his brows furrowed together as he processed it. He cricked his neck, looking over at her. "What?"

"What he said... you live a completely human life?"

Frowning he pulled himself up into a sitting position so he could look at her without craning his neck. "Uh... yeah. The Ginnaye are among the Jinn who live a mortal lifespan... although... well..." he rubbed the back of his neck, seeming uncomfortable. "...with my mother's blood I don't know what that means for my lifespan."

"Your mother is immortal?" Ari's eyes widened.

Jai made a face and put the book down on the coffee table. "Ari, didn't you read the book I gave you?"

"Yeah. It was surprisingly interesting. Despite the revulsion I felt reading about my so-called father, I'm glad I read it. You were right. I needed to know this stuff. I especially found the whole Seal of Solomon thing fascinating."

His gaze sharpened on her. "Really? Why?"

She shrugged. "I don't know I just did."

"Interesting."

"Why-"

Jai cut her off before she could question that little murmured adjective, "The only immortal Jinn are Azazil and his sons. And Asmodeus for some reason that we can't fathom."

"Yeah, but there are Jinn who live a long time?"

"Yes."

"How old was your mom?"

Jai's eyes narrowed, his features tightening, and Ari immediately regretted the question. "I don't know. But her kind have been known to live for hundreds of years."

"OK. So beside the possible extended lifetime, you live a normal human life? You what... you have an apartment in LA? A life? A car? A girlfriend?" she threw in.

"Yes. Yes. Yes. Yes. No."

Ari grunted. "We're back to one word answers?"

"Yes."

"Seriously?"

He exhaled wearily, his head dropping in a groan. "Ari-"

The phone rang beside her, cutting him off. Throwing him a grumpy look, Ari reached for it, hoping it was Charlie. As the voice on the other end explained who they were and why they were calling, Ari felt the room tilt a little as she forgot to breathe.

"I'll be right there," she replied hoarsely and dropped the phone without hanging up.

Jai's concerned face suddenly hovered above hers. "Ari, you OK? What's happened?"

Ari blinked, feeling nauseous. The sounds of sirens on the television made her head pound and the flicker of blue across the living room walls from the picture disorientated her. As if he had read her mind, Jai reached across for the remote and shut the television off.

"Ari?"

"It's my dad," she told him, standing up on shaky legs. She fumbled for her cell, looking around for her shoes and keys. "He collapsed at the office. He's in the hospital."

Jai cursed, snatching her keys up from the windowsill. "I'll drive."

In the car, Ari called Charlie and was thankful that this time he picked up. He promised to meet her at the hospital and she felt better just hearing his voice. As Jai drove them through town, Ari tried not to hyperventilate. They just said he'd collapsed. Was it a heart attack? A stroke? A really bad flu virus? As her mind wandered into the morbid, she started berating herself for the way she'd acted over the last few days. She'd blamed her dad for her real father's crimes and that was completely unfair. What if something really terrible had happened to Derek and the last thing she remembered him saying to her was how disappointed he was in her? That could not be their last conversation.

She was jolted out of her dark thoughts by the rough and hot touch of Jai's hand as he reached over and thread his fingers through hers, squeezing her hand comfortingly. "Stop," he said quietly, glancing at her quickly. "Stop beating yourself up."

Looking down at his large hand in hers, Ari squeezed it back. It was so surreal. "Can you read my mind or something?"

"No. I just know what you're thinking."

"How?"

He smiled sadly, an expression she wasn't used to seeing on him. It tugged at something in her chest and she gripped his hand even harder. She felt warm, safe even, as his fingers flexed, tightening his hold on her too. "Spending 24/7 with someone tends to give you some insight into their thought process. He's going to be alright, Ari. He'll be alright and you and he can sort out all of your problems."

God she hoped so.

Any hope Jai had given her evaporated when the doctor led them to her dad's room in the ICU.

Derek had fallen into a coma and the doctors so far couldn't determine what had caused it. They were doing a number of tests but for now he was stable.

That was it?

Ari had felt like screaming, the pale blue room tilting to the right like a canted camera angle as Jai led her into her dad's room. Derek was a tall man, but lying there in that cold, white bed, he had seemed smaller somehow. His skin was a horrible ashen grey color, and the dark circles under his eyes were purplish and unreal. The skin on his arms seemed papery and translucent, even his hair looked thinner and lank. A sob caught in the back of Ari's throat as the doctor left them alone. She grabbed for her dad's hand, hoping that would magically awaken him. It didn't. His touch felt cold and empty. Ari had never believed in auras but standing there looking down on him it was as if she could feel him dying. There was no vibrancy, no life pulsing around him and she gasped, feeling as if the wind had been knocked out of her. She gulped for air, tucking her head into her chest, ignoring Jai's comforting hand on her back, his hoarse voice telling her to breathe.

"Where is he?" she whispered. "He's not in there, Jai. What's going on?"

"Ari… this is… this is Jinn enchantment."

"What?" she gaped up at him.

He nodded grimly. "Jinn have done this to him."

The door of the hospital room squeaked open and Ari looked over her shoulder sharply. Charlie strode in, his hair askew, his face pale. "What kind of Jinn?" he asked fiercely, looking from her to her dad on the bed.

Her heart thudded in her chest at the sight of him, so glad to see him, so grateful to him for coming when she knew he hated hospitals. He hated the walls and the smell and the squeak of linoleum under foot. All because of Mike. Without thinking, Ari flew at him, throwing her arms around his waist and crushing herself against him. His strong arms came around her, holding her fast, his lips in her hair. Wanting to immerse herself in him, Ari inhaled a lungful of him and then promptly pulled back frowning. He smelled like a bar.

Ari tried not to grimace as she stared up into Charlie's bloodshot eyes. "Thanks for coming. Where were you?"

Charlie's eyes cast about, as if he couldn't meet her gaze. "I was hanging with Rickman."

Bitter shock jarred her and she stumbled back a little from him. He was still messing around and getting wasted with Mel? She shook her head, dazed, not able to deal with her disappointment. It was too much all at once.

God, how naïve she'd been to think that Charlie could change overnight.

Her pride was bitten as her face crumpled. "Thanks for coming," she whispered, fighting hard not to cry as she pulled away from him, leaning on her dad's bed, her hand wrapping around his white blanketed foot. "This isn't happening."

"Ari," there was a world of regret in Charlie's voice and she watched from the corner of her eye as he reached out for her. Something stopped him, however. Perhaps the brittle tension in her body. "Ari, I'm sorry about your dad. What can I do?"

Apparently nothing. She shook her head at him and shot a look at Jai. "What kind of Jinn would do this?" Strangely, at this moment, he seemed like the only one she could rely on.

"I don't know. There are many Jinn capable of causing physical illness in humans, physical illness that no modern medicine can cure."

Trying not to fall into a panic attack, Ari whirled on him, finding it difficult to look at her dad's face and wishing like hell that Charlie hadn't disappointed her once again, that all she had to worry about was getting her dad well again. But no. Now she was back to worrying about Charlie too, like she had been for the last two years.

She shook him off, trying to project the anger she felt. "What do you mean there's no cure?"

Jai's eyes glittered as he looked over her shoulder, his face tight with determination. "We could try Tellicherry Bark. It's usually the only thing that brings a human back from Jinn poison."

"OK." Ari nodded, breathing too fast. "Good. OK. Where do we get it?"

"It's hard to come by but my tribe *should* have some."

"Then go get it."

His eyes returned to her face, washing over her features. There was sternness in them where only moments ago there had been sympathy. "I can't leave your side."

Another burst of rage shot through her. Rage at her own dependency on the three men in this hospital room who all seemed bent on letting her down. "This is my father we're talking about," she growled, glaring up at him.

His expression didn't change. "I've been hired by The Red King, Ari, to protect you with specific instructions not to leave your side. Ever. Do you think I usually spend 24/7 joined to the hip of a client? No. But that's what your uncle wants and so I do it. I can't leave your side, Ari. It's breaching my contract with The Red King."

As his words sank in, Ari's jaw locked. She was trying desperately not to cry angry, hateful tears. Her eyes swung to Charlie wishing he could help her just this once. This was the moment she had somehow talked herself into believing wouldn't happen. This was the moment she was pulled into the Jinn world. It was overwhelming. It was all too overwhelming. And it would have been nice if Charlie had shown up, not wasted, but together, so she had one less thing to worry about. And Jai. Ari glanced sharply back at him, surprised to see his eyes soft on her, watching her carefully, almost unsurely. Jai always projected this image of a guy who knew what he was doing. Like he could take care of any situation. Like... she could be safe with him. Why did he have to destroy the person she'd built him up to be in her head when she needed him now the most?

"Please," she begged, throwing pride to the wolves. "Please, help me. Jai, he's my dad."

He was silent a long time. His vivid eyes locked on hers. Tension manifested between them, rippling in the air around them, locking them in a cocoon together. Finally, he stepped back from her, shaking himself, clearing his throat, blinking away whatever there was between them. Ari's cheeks felt hot, her heart was pounding. "OK." He nodded, his features grim. "I'll go get it."

The crushing weight on her chest eased and Ari had to wrap her arms around herself to stop her from diving into Jai's arms in gratitude. "Thank you," she breathed in relief.

Without another word the air around him flickered and he went up in a blaze that brought a surprised curse from Charlie's lips. The silence when he had departed was thick and uncomfortable. Ari didn't know what to say to Charlie.

How was it possible to miss someone when they were standing right next to you?

When he took a few steps towards her and wrapped his arms around her, pulling her back into him, Ari let him. She couldn't speak.

At this moment Charlie was trying.

But what about an hour ago?

What about all the times I don't know about?

He was trying now. But was that really the best she could ask for?

Little more than two minutes later, the air in the room crackled, the lights flickered, and shadows seemed to slither across the walls. Flames erupted in the space on the other side of Derek's bed and both Ari and Charlie stumbled back at the unexpected appearance of The Red King. He stood in a black t-shirt and jeans, his massive frame seeming to occupy the entire room. His red hair shone under the fluorescents and his blue eyes cut through them like shards of opal.

"What the..." Charlie breathed, stepping in front of her.

Ari made a huffing noise as she pushed him gently aside. "Charlie this is..." How should she introduce him? She made a face, feeling awkward.

The Red King, however, merely smiled at her. "Nice to see you again." Then he turned those eyes on Charlie and they narrowed to ice chips. "This must be Charlie Creagh. I am Ari's uncle, The Red King. You may call me your highness." He shifted his eyes back to

Ari. "Jai doesn't trust this guy." He gestured to Charlie. "I'll remain wary of him."

It came as no surprise to Ari that Jai didn't trust Charlie. He was under the impression that everyone had an agenda about everything. That The Red King respected Jai's opinion and intuition did surprise her. She frowned, seeing Charlie's jaw flex with anger. If she didn't say something quick Charlie might and she didn't know if she could stop her uncle from doing anything to harm him. If he did he could kiss any kind of relationship with her goodbye.

"Look-"

The door to the hospital room squeaked open again and this time a nurse came in quietly. Her eyes widened at the sight of The Red King, her mouth falling open and shut like a fish gulping bubbles. When it became apparent she was paused on astonishment, Ari hit the play button and strode over to the nurse, drawing her attention. "Is something wrong?" she asked worriedly, her gaze jerking back to Derek on the bed.

The nurse swallowed hard, her head turning towards Ari and her eyes following slowly as if they couldn't pry themselves from The Red King. It was like pulling bubblegum off a desk. "Um..." she made a weird, hysterical little noise in the back of her throat, glancing down at the papers in her hands, her face flushed lobster red. "I have hospital forms you need to fill out, insurance etc."

"My niece has already filled those out," The Red King said before Ari could take them. His voice was warm, as were his eyes, as he walked towards the nurse with a charming smile on his face.

"Uh." The nurse shook her head in confusion. "No. Forms haven't been filled out for Mr. Johnson yet."

"Yes they have," he assured her, tapping the papers in her hand. "Check them again."

Nodding shakily, the nurse flipped through the papers, her eyes widening and her cheeks turning an even darker shade of red. "So she has. So sorry for intruding. I'll leave you alone with your father, Ms. Johnson." She spoke to Ari but still continued to stare open mouthed at The Red King. Ari couldn't blame her. "Visiting Hours are over in about an hour."

When the nurse made no move to leave, Ari began to feel bad for her. Her uncle kept smiling at the poor woman and it was hypnotizing her. Finally he sighed, gesturing to the door impatiently. She blushed hard again before stumbling back and fumbling for the door. Ari breathed a sigh of relief when she left, uncomfortable with witnessing the effect of the Jinn on a human.

"So." She took a step back, standing next to Charlie, silently telling her uncle that he may not trust Charlie but of the two of them the human won her vote. "Why are you here?"

The Red King strode back over to Derek, his eyes washing over her dad's slack face. "Jai contacted me to tell me he had had no choice but to leave you unattended. I came to watch over you while he retrieves the Tellicherry Bark from his tribe."

"You're The Red King?" Charlie suddenly asked, taking a step towards him, his eyes round with awe. He had that same rapt look on his face he'd had when the Aissawa Brothers were doing the exorcism.

Instead of answering right away Ari watched nervously as The Red King took slow steps towards Charlie. He began to circle him, his eyes narrowed and calculating. The energy he projected seemed to wash over Charlie, who shivered visibly. Finally, just when Ari was sure she would stop breathing altogether, her uncle drew to a halt in front of Charlie, a strange smile on his face that reminded her way too much of The White King. "You scream of pain," he whispered, suddenly seeming just as fascinated by her friend. "No wonder Jai is wary of you. There is so much power in your pain, Charlie Creagh."

"Really?" Charlie asked hoarsely, desperately.

The Red King nodded and they shared a silent long look that sent an indecipherable shiver through Ari. She didn't know what passed between her best friend and the Jinn but whatever it was she didn't like it and she didn't like how spellbound Charlie seemed to be by everything Jinn.

She took a step forward, wanting to throw herself between them. "Do you think this was The White King?" she asked her uncle, gesturing to her dad's heartbreaking stillness.

In a whiplash of movement, The Red King was suddenly on the other side of the bed, staring down into Derek's face. Ari had squeaked in fright at his supernatural speed and he glanced back up at her with a smirk.

"So cool…" Charlie breathed.

Ari made a face at him and he tried to cover up his awe, his features evening out as he attempted somber.

Taking a calming breath, Ari looked back up into The Red King's face. "Well?"

"We won't know until Jai arrives with the Tellicherry Bark," he muttered noncommittally.

~16~

A Destiny That Tastes Like the End

Sweat rolled down Jai's forehead and he squeezed his eyes shut, pinching the bridge of his nose as the pain exploded out of his sinuses and down the back of his skull. Giving in to Ari's pleas meant summoning The Red King, which meant telepathing over the realms, which meant agony for those too young and not powerful enough to handle it. His legs trembled as he stood in his father's office, the two of them waiting for the healer with the stock of Tellicherry Bark to arrive.

What was taking so long?!

All he wanted to do was lean against his father's desk and have someone pour a bucket of cold water over him but he refused to appear weak in front of the old man.

Luca stood also, with the desk between them. Jai had noticed long ago that his father never sat in a room when he was facing someone he considered a competitor in a pissing contest. For once he wished they could just be father and son. That he could fall into his dad's Chesterfield armchair while Luca brought him a bottle of water.

Willing some strength into his quickly failing body, Jai ignored the fresh outbreak of sweat.

"Oh for the love of... sit down before you fall down," Luca snapped, coming out from behind the table. "Contacting The Red King in Mount Qaf and not even for an emergency!"

Ignoring his antagonistic tone, Jai finally gave in and slumped into the armchair he'd been coveting. Now he had to *will* himself not to fall asleep. "It's her father, Luca. It is an emergency."

"It's not her real father," Luca grumbled. "Poor bastard should know the truth."

Oh of course, Luca *would* find empathy with Derek. No surprise there. Jai rolled his eyes. "How long is your healer going to take?"

"Don't take that tone with me, boy. The healer will get here when she gets here. Why are you so antsy about it? It's not *your* father."

Yeah, if it was my father I might not be so antsy.

Instead of being a smartass comment, Jai shifted in the chair, trying to preserve some element of cool professionalism in his demeanor. "Ari begged me to help. I'm trying to help. As quickly as possible."

"Ari?"

Oh shit.

Luca Bitar was all pleasance and niceties with his clients to their face but he had a strict policy of professional distance, including how his guardians referred to them. When discussing a client behind their back one was always to use the term 'my client' or 'Miss so-and-so'. Never were first names used.

Jai had effed up on the first question. It was the telepathy. His concentration was nearly dead. "I mean Ms. Johnson," he corrected himself.

Luca wasn't the type to let it go though, especially not with Jai. He grunted. "Typical. What... you think because this one is important to the Jinn Kings that you can play up to her, get in good with her and go places?"

"Don't be ridiculous. *Sir*."

Luca shook his head. "I knew something was up when you came tearing in here to tell me that Jinn had gotten into her party. You were upset. Upset that she'd been taken."

Jai grunted. "Of course I was upset. I was supposed to be guarding her."

"No." Luca smirked disdainfully at him. "It wasn't upset and concern for your failure to guard your client, it was genuine anxiety and worry. Should have known my half-breed would be the one to cross the line when it came to a pretty girl."

Rage rushed through Jai's veins at the look in his father's eyes. This was what Luca Bitar had been waiting for. A moment for Jai to mess up so badly he could finally say 'he's nothing like me'. Mixed in with the rage was the panic that Jai was handing him that moment right here, right now. He never, ever wanted Luca to have that satisfaction. Struggling to his feet, Jai squared up to Luca, enjoying the disdain seep out with disappointment.

"I displayed concern for a client I was supposed to be guarding over. That's it. Ari Johnson is nothing more than an assignment."

His voice grew colder than ice, so cold it was a wonder his breath didn't puff out after each word. "But let's not forget, *Dad*, this is the biggest assignment Bitar Security has ever landed. I'm guarding The Red King's niece. And we both know she's so much more than that. If I have to endure migraines and vomiting to contact her uncle, or use the *Peripatos* to pick up some herb that will pull her father out of a coma then I will. Because it's part of the assignment. The Red King isn't pissed off I contacted him. I'm not pissed off and I'm the one feeling like I've been dragged fifty blocks by a mail truck. So why are you so pissed off?"

Luca's eyes narrowed. "You're forgetting who you're speaking to, boy."

Jai didn't have time to reply. The air shimmered near the door and out of the flames stepped their healer, Kammi. She rushed over with a pouch in her hand and handed it to Jai. "Sorry, it took me so long, Jai," Kammi apologized. "This stuff was hidden right at the back of my stores. I'll need to order more. I made up the entire remedy for you so all you need to do is apply it. Remember massage it into the head and chest."

"Thanks, Kammi." He grinned wearily taking it from her.

She nodded at Jai and then at Luca before Luca gave her the nod to leave.

Before the last of her flames had even dissipated Jai turned back to his father. Fear still gnawed at him that his father would discover an inadequacy with his dealings in this assignment. And he knew the fear was born from the fact that there was some truth in what his father had said.

He wasn't treating Ari like every other client.

Ari *wasn't* like every other client.

She was unlike anyone he'd ever met.

But she was caught up in something huge. And she was in love with a basketcase. And she was only eighteen years old.

And she was a client.

He shouldn't have told her all that stuff about his relationship with his father. He shouldn't have let her in like that. Why did he do that? It was stupid. It was crossing the line. It was making her think he was some kind of friend. He wasn't a friend.

Determined to somehow put their relationship back into reverse, Jai's blood ran cold and he poured the chill into his next words, "Your attempts to find a fault with my work in this assignment are transparent and beneath you. If we're going to fight, Luca, try and base it on something real."

Leaving his father red-faced, Jai used the last vestiges of his strength to channel the *Peripatos*. He had a human to save.

For forty five minutes Ari sat by Derek's bed, her shoulders hunched to her ears, her dad's cold hand clasped in both of hers as she waited on Jai's return. She ignored the frequent looks Charlie and The Red King passed one another. She ignored the monitors beeping beside her dad's bed and even somehow tried to ignore The

Red King humming the theme song to the television show *Pretty Little Liars* . *Sh*e tried to ignore that but… it was just too weird. Ari had a shot him a stunned look, her eyebrows nearly hitting her hairline. The Red King, who sat across from her on a plastic chair with his right ankle caught casually on his opposite knee and his flame red hair draped across his shoulder, had grinned at her expression and winked. "Gotta love that Aria chick, no?"

Bemoaning the weirdness of her life Ari had groaned, pressing her face to her dad's hand. Not even Charlie's comforting touch on her back helped. He was too close, too close smelling like yesterday's laundry basket and cheap beer.

The first hint at Jai's arrival was the flicker of the lights. The space at the bottom of the hospital bed buzzed and glimmered before the flames appeared, swimming towards the ground like a jacket unzipping, unveiling Jai. Ari jumped to her feet, heart thudding in her chest at the thought of waking Derek up. The thump of her heart only strengthened when Jai had to catch onto the bed to keep himself on his feet. His face was pale, and there were dark purplish circles under his eyes where only an hour ago there had been none.

Worry sliced through her. More worry than she expected to feel for him. Ari was by his side in seconds, her arm sliding around his shoulders as he coughed, a harsh wracking cough that only tightened the coil of panic in her chest. "Jai," she murmured softly, bending down so they were eye to eye.

He slanted a look at her, shrugging away from her touch. "I'm fine," he told her coldly.

Hurt by his inexplicable chilliness Ari pulled back only to catch Charlie's suspicious gaze. His eyes flickered between her and Jai and, as if coming to some unpleasant conclusion, his expression darkened.

"Don't worry," The Red King suddenly said before Ari could work out what Charlie's damage was. "Jai will recover soon. He used telepathy to contact me while he was in the mortal realm and I was in Mount Qaf. Only the most powerful of Jinn can do that without it causing physical weakness."

Despite Jai's coolness with her, Ari couldn't help but place a hand on his shoulder as he straightened. He looked so drained, so young. "Are you sure you're OK?"

This time, as his green eyes flashed angrily at her, there was no mistaking his annoyance. "I'm fine," he snapped, backing out of her touch before reaching into his pocket. He pulled out a pouch and opened it. Inside it was a greyish paste. Sighing heavily, not quite meeting her eyes, Jai's tone returned to neutral. "My tribe healer made the mixture up for you. You have to massage it into Derek's head and chest."

Still hurt, angry, Ari put her messed up feelings for all the conscious men in the room aside so she could concentrate on saving the one in the bed. Taking the pouch from Jai, Ari made sure she didn't make contact with his skin. He noticed and Ari questioned the way his jaw flexed as she pulled away. Still he wouldn't meet her eyes. Annoyed, Ari turned to Charlie. "Can you pull back the covers for me?"

"Sure." Charlie's eyes brightened, seeming glad to be of use.

After she'd massaged the paste into her dad's skin, she watched as it miraculously dissolved, seeping into his flesh, journeying in to pull him back from the Jinn enchantment.

"How long do we have to wait before it takes effect?" Ari asked The Red King, worrying about the nurses coming back in. Visiting Hours were going to be over soon.

A sick feeling rose into her throat from her gut as The Red King and Jai shared a grim look. Finally, just before she was about to explode with impatience, her uncle turned to her gravely. "It should already have worked. He should be awake."

Panic began wriggling in her veins and Ari gripped the mattress of the bed, curling her nails into it in an effort to hold onto reality. "What... what does that mean?"

"It means The White King has begun his campaign to get what he wants."

Confused, she shook her head. "No. I don't understand. How is hurting my dad going to accomplish anything?"

When silence fell over the room again and Jai and The Red King continued looking at each other, both their eyes narrowed in concentration, realization dawned on Ari and she slapped the metal bars on Derek's bed, the ting of it echoing around the room with as much significance as a water gun. Still, it drew their attention. "You're talking to each other with your minds. Stop it. Speak to me! What the hell is going on? Is this blackmail? Will The White King help my dad if I agree to go live with him or something?!"

When The Red King began to nod Ari was surprised by the outraged growl that ripped from Jai. It was so animalistic, so frightening.

They all looked at him but his fierce eyes were glued to The Red King. "Tell her the truth."

Heart pounding so hard and loud, Ari was sure they all must hear it as she turned to her uncle, trembling. "Tell me what?"

After shooting Jai a venomous look, The Red King sighed wearily, slumping back against the wall and gazing at her through shuttered lids. Drawing out the drama seemed to be a thing with the Jinn and Ari was this close to screaming at him when he finally asked, "Have you heard of King Solomon and the Seal of Solomon, Ari?"

Glowering at him, wondering what evasive crap he was pulling, Ari nodded tightly. "Solomon was bestowed the Seal, a ring that enslaved the Jinn. It was made of brass and Iron and with each side - can't remember what was what - he could stamp commands to the good Jinn and the evil Jinn. He was dethroned for it and Azazil's right hand man, Asmodeus, took over his reign and was allowed to keep the Seal. He tried to hand it over to Azazil who tried to destroy it but it can't be destroyed. He commanded Asmodeus to protect it and according to legend Asmodeus wears the ring around his neck."

The Red King looked astonished by her knowledge. His jaw locked and he stood up away from the wall, his height somehow magnified. She wondered if he was doing something magic to make him even more intimidating than usual. "How did you know that?"

She shrugged. "Jai gave me a book about the Jinn."

Her uncle turned on Jai with an incredulous look. To Ari it seemed as if he was warring between wanting to kill him and being impressed by him. "You gave her a book?"

Jai crossed his arms over his chest defiantly, looking ready to take whatever The Red King threw at him despite his weakened state. "She deserved to know the truth."

"You're not contracted to tell her the truth. You are contracted because your tribe owes me."

"Wait, wait." Ari tried to defuse a confusing but clearly dangerous situation. "What's going on?"

Jai barely looked at her. "I conjured that book so that when this day came you would have a better understanding. So maybe it... wouldn't feel so confusing. So overwhelming."

"What the hell is going on?" Charlie snapped, coming up behind her, his hands clamping protectively down on her shoulders.

Jai glared at him but refused to respond. Instead he turned back to The Red King who watched Ari with those calculating eyes.

"What did my brother tell you? What reason did he give for your birth, Ari?"

Leaning back into Charlie, Ari gulped, sensing something huge on the horizon. "He said he was looking for meaning."

The Red King guffawed at that although his blue eyes remained serious. "My brother was looking for power."

"I don't understand."

"Your mother, Sala, he told you she was a powerful Ifrit, yes?"

Ari nodded, mute with growing fear and anticipation. She slid a hand up to clutch Charlie's fingers, needing an anchor to the real world as she waited for the revelation she knew would try to blow her off her feet.

"Sala is the most seductive Jinn we've ever come across. Even more seductive than the Lilif like Jai's mother. My brother believed he could use her to steal the Seal of Solomon from around Asmodeus' neck."

"By seducing Asmodeus," Jai explained before she could ask.

Ari nodded, looking back and forth between them, wishing they would stop drawing this out. "So did she?"

The Red King pinned her in place with his electric gaze. "To our utter surprise, yes. She returned to The White King with the Seal. He promptly made her swallow it and that night he mated with her, using enchantment to conceive a child within her womb, a child whose life force - the greatest power on this earth - broke the seal down into its basic properties, stealing its magic and winding it into the child's DNA."

This time, when the silence descended around the room, Ari knew they could all hear her heart banging in her chest. It raced even harder at the feel of Charlie's own heart pounding against her back. He was probably confused but he could feel the air of expectation, the crackle of legend sparking in the air.

Ari sucked in a deep breath, a hysterical laugh desperate to erupt out of her. She controlled herself though and met The Red King eye for eye. "Are you telling me... are you telling me *I'm* the Seal of Solomon?"

~17~

My Name is Not Mine but I Wish it was Yours

*T*here was nothing that could prepare a person for discovering they were a pawn in a war between mythical beings.

Unless you know... you were Frodo. But Ari wasn't Frodo. She was just Ari.

I'm just Ari!

"Wait... what?" Charlie asked, his hand sliding around her shoulders as he stepped around to peer down at her with alarm and confusion in his dark eyes. Not even the warm familiarity of his face was a comfort at that moment.

Ari felt frozen with fear as the full reality of what The Red King and Jai were telling her hit her. When it became apparent she couldn't form words, she heard Jai sigh impatiently. "Look, I'll give you the book I gave Ari to get you up to speed but right now-"

"At least tell me what this means and why Ari looks like she saw the demon out of *Jeepers Creepers* come to life?"

Gripping Charlie's bicep, Ari squeezed it tightly, her fingernails pinching into his skin. "Not funny," she whispered, unfreezing but falling into a panic attack. She gulped for breath, her lungs shutting down on her, her brain fuzzing up and tilting the world at a hell of an angle. Fighting nausea was difficult when you were busy trying to keep your balance so you didn't pass out on top of your dad who happened to be in a coma. She swayed, tightening her grip on Charlie, who swore.

I'm dying. Oh God I'm dying. Air. **Air.**

"She's having a panic attack," Jai cursed and the next thing Ari knew she was sitting on a chair breathing in and out of a brown paper bag. "Slowly, Ari, slowly," she heard Jai coach her. Sure enough after a few minutes she was breathing again, the tension in her muscles easing.

"Perhaps giving her the book was a bad idea," The Red King mused, a whisper of anger in his tone. "If she hadn't known what the Seal was she might not have taken the news so badly."

"Yeah because she wouldn't understand what the hell it meant... *Your Highness.* Her reaction? Fairly understandable under the circumstances if you ask me."

As she sat there trying to come to grips with the truth, to really, truly understand what it meant for her and the people she cared about, it occurred to Ari what a chance Jai took standing up to a Jinn King like that. Her watery eyes rose from the floor to see the death look The Red King was shooting at her guardian. Yup, definitely taking a chance with his life.

"Look, I hate to already add to the confusion," Charlie said from his position on the arm of the chair, "But what does this mean?"

"Ari." The Red King moved around her father's bed almost like he was floating on the foggy cloud bank of Mount Qaf. "What do you think it means?"

Her chest tightened again but Ari drew strength from Charlie, reaching for his hand and squeezing it tight. She should take comfort in his presence while she still could. "It means..." she looked up at her best friend, at the boy she loved, at the one person who despite his continued attempts to disappoint her, had been her only anchor for the longest time. "The Seal is the only thing in existence that can command the Jinn to do anything. Any Jinn, any time, anything, no matter how powerful they are. What my real father did, The White King, he used magic to break the properties of the Seal down into my DNA. Meaning..." she glanced back up now at Jai and her uncle. "...meaning that if I decide to use my Jinn abilities, it's more than likely that I'll also be able to command the Jinn. All Jinn. And The White King wants to use me to dethrone the Jinn Sultan Azazil. And he's..." her voice broke off as her eyes began to glisten, falling on Derek lying hollow on the bed. "... he's going to hurt the people that I love to make sure I do what he wants since he can't make me do it any other way."

They were all silent a moment, Ari's heart thumping out of time with her father's heart monitor.

"Well... shit," Charlie breathed, squeezing her hand and looking down at her in awe and sympathy and fear. "Ari..."

"Worse," The Red King spoke up, "What he has done to Derek can only be reversed by you."

Ari blinked rapidly, her pulse leaping in fear as she watched Jai and the King share a grim look. "What... what do you mean?"

"The only way to cure Derek is to have the Jinn who did this, reverse it. There are many Jinn capable of doing this but my bet is my brother used a Shaitan, the original servants of Azazil. Evil personified. The only way to have a Shaitan reverse it is for *you* to command him to do it. The White King knew *you* would have to do this. This is his way of making sure you become true Jinn and embrace your power as the Seal."

The empty, soulless darkness of The White King's eyes flashed through her mind and Ari shuddered with rage.

"I could ask Azazil for help. He should be able to tell us which Shaitan did it and where to find the offensive Jinn. I'd ask him... as a favor to me."

Looking up into The Red King's suddenly soulful eyes, Ari wondered how he could possibly be related to her real father. He seemed to genuinely *feel* for her situation. To want to help. God she hoped he was sincere. Right now she needed all the allies she could get. "Thank you... but I just..." she turned her eyes from him to Jai to Charlie, pulling her hand from her friend's grip. "I just really need to a moment alone with my dad."

It took them a minute to realize she was serious and both The Red King and Charlie opened their mouths as if to argue. Jai beat them to it. "Out fellas." He nodded at the door, waving a hand for them to move. Ari's heart thud thud thumped a little as she met his gaze, telling him with her eyes that she was grateful. He seemed to get the message, giving her a brittle little nod, his demeanor still odd and cold. Ari didn't really have time to worry about that at the moment.

"You're lucky you're already in pain," The Red King said to Jai as he swept out of the door before him. "Or I'd seriously considering lighting a flame under your ass."

"Apologies, Your Highness." Jai grinned wearily as he shut the door behind him.

Left in the quiet of the hospital room with just her dad, Ari pulled one of the plastic chairs over to his bedside, reaching through the bars to grab his cold hand.

His touch felt alien. And distant. Not just because his body lay there on that bed like a shell of the true man, but because the way she felt about him was somehow different now too.

Not that she didn't love him. She did. That would never change. When she was younger she used to worship the ground Derek walked on. Back then of course he had more time for her. They would spend entire weekends together, sometimes just hanging out in the backyard, or taking off to Cincinnati. When Jude Scott tripped her on the playground deliberately, she'd swung at him and hurt her hand. Instead of getting mad, Derek had taken her aside one Saturday afternoon and taught her how to punch, showing her where to place her thumb so she wouldn't get hurt again. He'd driven her to Little League with Charlie and had gone to all their games. He'd read her bedtime stories when he could, including her beloved collection of the *Harry Potter* books, and listened and talked to her as if she were his friend and not just his kid. Then, when she started growing breasts and wearing skirts he'd grown a little distant, clearly not sure how to deal with a teenage girl in his house. He'd shown her in his own way that he loved her. That he cared. That she was his daughter. But the truth was he hadn't been a good dad to her these last few years. It was only now when she was so close to losing him that she was really able to accept that. If this had never happened, Ari would have waited for him to come home from Boston, would have bit back her complaints as he talked her into going to Penn and she would have argued away his reasons, making excuses for him as she had done for years. Now, if she saved him, she may never get the chance to stand her ground, to ask him to be the dad he should have been, to prove to him she was still the little girl that he loved but…

….the truth was she wasn't. For months now Ari had been panicking, looking out into the black, trying to uncover who she really was.

Well now she knew.

"I'm not your daughter," she told him hoarsely, her wet eyes sliding across Derek's deathly pale face, her thumb brushing back and forth comfortingly over his papery cold skin. "I'm…" she laughed stupidly, letting the tears spill down her cheeks for the first time in a long time. "I'm not anyone's daughter. He made me to use me. You raised me and yet our blood is like water. You know what though? I always thought we had the same smile. Kind of goofy, a little crooked," she huffed tearfully, letting the silence fall over the room again.

Finally she sighed. "I guess what I'm trying to say is that I'm not anyone's daughter, dad... but I am still your kid." She burst into hard tears now, pressing his hand to her salty cheek. "I am still your kid and I'm going to protect you even if that means becoming *his* kid. I am so sorry. I'm so, so sorry." She broke down now, sobbing hard, deep painful cries into his pillow. Feeling more alone than ever.

After a while a knock sounded at the door and the nurse from before popped her head around the doorframe. Her eyes grew round with sadness as Ari lifted her red-rimmed eyes from Derek to her. "Sweetheart, I'm sorry, but visiting hours are over for today."

Nodding numbly, terrified of what awaited her outside the hospital room door, Ari slowly drew to her feet. She gazed down at the man in the bed she would die to protect, wondering if and when she saved him, if she would ever be able to call him 'dad' again.

"I love you, Dad."

For a moment she could hear his deep, rich voice in her ears. *I love you too, kid.*

Sucking back more tears, Ari turned sharply away from him and followed the nurse out of the room. She wasn't surprised as Charlie, Jai and The Red King snapped away from their places leaning against the nurse's station. They strode towards her determinedly, Charlie's face tightening at the sight of her. Ari sighed, dragging a hand through her hair. She knew she must look a mess. When her eyes flicked over Jai she was stupidly hurt by the lack of expression on his face. The Red King just stared at her expectantly. It was to him she nodded. "Let's do this."

~18~

Could I Be Read if I Were See-Through?

*H*e could pretend to not be worried about her. Didn't mean he wasn't.

Jai had to stop himself from rubbing a hand across his short hair in frustration. He eyed Charlie, who bristled outside of Ari's bedroom door, practically bouncing on the balls of his feet in his impatience to see her. Jai didn't need the human kid to see Ari had any effect on him. Like they didn't have enough problems already.

But hell, last night, when she'd come out of her father's hospital room, pale and frightened, those gorgeous eyes of hers red-rimmed from crying, it had taken everything he had not push the other two out of his way and pull her into a hug. Jai cursed inwardly, hitting a fist quietly into the wall behind him. At that moment he'd hated himself and Luca more than he ever had before. The hurt in her eyes when he'd snapped at her before it, then when he'd looked through her during it when she was so clearly upset, when she so clearly needed to be comforted…

He'd done crappy things before but up until that moment he'd never actually felt bad about them.

That's why he was her guardian. Not her friend. Not her-

"That's it, Ari, open up!" Charlie yelled into the door. Jai glared over at him.

"Back off," he growled, pushing off from the wall to face the kid. Charlie was built for a human, only an inch or two shorter than Jai, but Jai was Jinn and Jai was trained in four different martial arts. He could take the idiot on if it came to a fight.

Charlie's eyes narrowed on him and Jai felt a frisson of excitement at the challenge in them. He'd been looking for any excuse to punch this guy for days now. "I'm worried about her, and standing out here trying to hear if she's breathing isn't doing jack!"

Rolling his neck, feeling the satisfying crack, Jai had to draw on all the patience and professionalism he could. Punching Charlie would just upset Ari even more than she already was and that was last thing he wanted. After she'd told them she was going to allow them to show her the way to her magic last night, they had all returned to the house. Without a word, Ari had locked herself in her bedroom, and The Red King had assured Jai that for tonight he was allowed to leave her alone in her room. Charlie and Jai had slept downstairs. The Red King had left after promising Jai he'd contact him as soon as Azazil gave him the information on the Shaitan. For now he left Ari in Jai's 'capable' hands. He was the one who was to show her the way to her abilities - a prospect he did not look forward to as he was still suffering a splitting headache from the contact he'd made through the realms.

It was ten in the morning. Jai and Charlie had already washed and eaten breakfast, and had been waiting and waiting for Ari to open her door. Still nothing.

Not that Jai could blame her. He would have hoped after giving Charlie a copy of the book he'd conjured for Ari to read that he *too* would now understand the gravity of Ari's situation. He'd cursed enough about it last night as he read the book, keeping Jai from a good night's sleep every time he came across something that affected Ari directly. If Jai had had to listen to him mutter, "Ari's father is such a dick' one more time he had seriously considered finding an enchanted bottle and trapping the douchebag in it for good.

Understanding Ari's state of shock, the crazy, unbelievable reality of whom and what she was didn't seem to be affecting Charlie like it should. Jai didn't like the look in his eye, his impatience, his excitement.

"Give her time," Jai hissed. "She said she'd do this and she will, but back off and give her time to deal with this stuff."

Charlie shook his head, shooting another concerned look at the door. "Giving her time will just make her think about it too much. She might decide not to go ahead and then what'll Derek do?"

Jai narrowed his eyes, his suspicions crawling in his veins and nudging his intuition awake on their journey. "Derek? Is that really what you're worried about, Charlie?"

"What the hell does that mean?"

"It means I don't think you give a damn about Derek. I don't know what you're game is here but I will find out."

The kid took a step towards Jai, his jaw clenched, his eyes blazing at the accusation. "Who the hell do you think you are? I'm here for Ari. *Ari!*" He shook his head, his eyes washing over Jai disdainfully. "I'm not fooled by you, dude." He leaned in to Jai, whispering his next words, "But just so you know... she's been *mine* for a long time."

You little piece of fu-

Ratbag little-

Jai took a deep breath, trying to control the desire to deck the jackass. Instead he leaned in just as threateningly as Charlie had and cocked his head mockingly. "Yours?"

When Charlie pulled back, his expression changing, softening, as if he realized he was acting like a dick, Jai unfortunately could see the glimmer of the good kid in his eyes that Ari was so hung up on. He shook his head, his messy hair flying around his face, his dark eyes full of self-directed derision. "I meant she's my friend. She's been my friend for a long time. Long before *you* came into her life."

I can't get caught up in this crap.

Before Jai could say something, anything to assure Charlie (and himself) that his only part in Ari's story was that of the guardian, Ari's bedroom door swung open. She looked more together, her hair freshly washed, her eyes bright with determination. Jai dropped his gaze, not needing to look at her for too long.

"I've been in there trying to psyche myself up for this," she explained, coming out and shutting the door behind her. "That would have been easier if I hadn't had to listen to you two bicker outside my door for the last half hour like two old woman fighting over the last can of corn." She brushed past him, her bare arm sliding against his and sending the hair on his forearm up in tingles. She smelled of the rich, exotic *Dior* perfume she wore all the time, a scent Jai would never be able to smell again without thinking about her. As he and Charlie followed her down the stairs he noted the change in her gait. Ari was one of those rare girls who seemed to float from place to place when she walked, graceful and feminine. Today her steps were heavier, as if the emotional burden of discovering who she was, was an actual physical weight. He felt a sharpness in his chest at the thought and ignored the splice of some unknown but ugly feeling rip through him as Charlie caught up to her at the bottom of the stairs, pulling her into a hug before she could say anything more.

Her small hands slid around his back and for a moment she held tight to him. Jai felt the ugliness grow darker and deeper, like a stone caught at the back of his throat. He eyed the floor determinedly, waiting for the rustle of clothing to tell him they'd stopped embracing.

"I'm fine, really," Ari told them quietly and Jai raised his head to see her eyeing him warily. "I'm ready to learn."

Glad for his stoic professionalism, Jai jerked his head towards the living room. "Let's go in there, sit down, relax into this."

She heaved a sigh and turned to Charlie. "You should go."

Ha-ha, loser.

Oh real mature, Jai. Real mature.

Charlie's jaw dropped, his comical expression giving Jai more satisfaction than it should. "What? No way!"

"Charlie." Ari's face crumpled as she reached for him, her palm pressing on his chest above his heart. She was so comfortable and affectionate with him it made Jai want to gnash his teeth on something. "I can't have anything happen to you. And being around me... not good. Starting now I have to walk away from all of this. From Ohio. From dad and Rachel and Staci... and you."

Panic lit Charlie's eyes and for a moment Jai almost felt bad for the guy even if he did think Ari's sacrifice of her friends and family was the logical thing to do.

"No!" Charlie shrugged away from her. "You can't-" he threw a dark look at Jai, cutting off whatever he was about to say. To appease him somewhat, Jai took a stroll into the kitchen where he could still hear them arguing in the hall, but at least it gave Charlie the pretense of privacy. "You can't do this, Ari. You've spent the last two years being there for me even when I didn't deserve it, even when I didn't want you to. I get it, OK, I do. After Mike, I knew how messed up I was and I wanted you far away from me, from *that*. I wanted the best, purest thing in my life to remain that and I couldn't guarantee that would happen if you stuck around. But I couldn't get rid of you. You wouldn't let me. You have been there for me, Ari. And I didn't realize how much I need that until the night you disappeared. I took you for granted and I'm sorry. But please... please don't give up now. Please don't push me out of this."

"I'm trying to protect you."

"By leaving me?" he asked hoarsely. "You're all I have."

"Charlie-"

"I'm all you've got. It's always been us. I'm not scared of anything. And I take full responsibility for whatever happens to me, for whatever goes down. Just please... Ari... you're my best friend."

Jai groaned inwardly when he heard her whisper 'OK'.

He'd thought he was rid of the tool.

"OK then." Jai clapped his hands, striding back into the hall. "If the after school special has come to an end...can we get on with this?"

Although her heart was still racing too fast at the thought of Charlie being caught up in the enormity of her situation - her very *dangerous* situation - the selfish part of her was glad he wanted to stick around. He followed her into the living room as she took a seat opposite Jai. He stared back at her emotionless, waiting for her signal to begin. It was so nice of her guardian to turn into a cold asshat just when she needed him to be her friend. Ignoring the hurt that spiked through her every time she thought of the way he looked at her now, Ari drew in a shuddering breath.

Jai's face softened infinitesimally, the sun beaming in through the window turned his eyes a startling golden green. "You ready?"

She nodded and then glanced over at Charlie one more time. "Last chance to get the hell out of here."

He grinned at her, that yummy, adorable smile of his that never failed to make her feel good. "I'm not going anywhere. I called my mom last night and explained about Derek, said I'd be staying with you for a while."

Ari quirked an eyebrow. "So you're still getting wasted at Rickman's but communication with your mom has improved. That's good, right?"

"Are you seriously going to lecture me about that right now?"

"No, she's not," Jai snapped. "Come on people, let's focus."

He was really starting to piss her off. Ari shot him a hateful look. "What crawled up your butt? Did you find out you were the Seal of Solomon and the most sought after weapon in the history of the Jinn?" she mocked. "Oh no, wait, that was me."

Rolling his eyes at her Jai made her feel about six years old. "You're breaking rule number one."

Another stab of hurt.

Nice.

"What, we're back to rules again?" she huffed at him, ignoring Charlie watching them cautiously. "And technically I wasn't insulting you, I was mocking you."

"Technically will you shut up so we can do this?"

"Hey don't talk to her like that," Charlie snapped.

Ari shrugged. "Jai doesn't mean anything by it, Charlie. He was raised like a wolf among people."

The deeply hurt look Jai used to pin her to the couch stuck through her like a big sharp pointy needle. She gaped wordlessly, remembering him confessing his upbringing with a family who didn't want him. Jai hadn't gone into the details but she could guess it hadn't been good. Or affectionate. Probably like a wolf among people. *Crap.* He thought she was throwing his vulnerability back in his face. Despite his earlier, baffling coldness, she wanted to reach out and touch him, to reassure him. To apologize. "Jai..."

He smoothed his features again and when he spoke his voice lacked any emotion. "Forget it. Let's just get started."

Still feeling awful, Ari bit down the nerves and exhaled. "What should I do?"

"Speak to me," he said matter-of-factly.

"Huh?"

"Using your mind."

"OK what?" Charlie interjected.

"You." Jai pointed a finger at him without breaking his concentration from Ari's face. "Can't be doing that. You read that book last night, right?"

"Yeah... I just... I guess I keep forgetting Ari is Jinn. It's too weird."

"Gee, thanks Charlie."

"You know what I mean."

Ignoring him, Ari leaned forward, her elbows braced on her knees as she stared deep into Jai's eyes, trying not to flush at the immediate tension she felt coiling within herself trapped under his exotic gaze.

"So… I what?" she whispered hoarsely. "Just direct thoughts at you?"

"Exactly."

"It can't be *that* easy."

He smirked arrogantly. "Try it."

OK, what do I say to him? Um… you look nice in a towel? She flushed. *Jesus Christ don't say that!*

Clasping her hands together and bracing her chin on them Ari bore her eyes into his, imagining the words floating out of her brain across the living room and in through Jai's forehead. ***What's up with the grumpy?***

His mouth quirked up at the corner ever so slightly. ***Didn't get much sleep last night.***

"Holy-" Ari slid back in her chair in fright as his voice echoed around inside her head as clear as if he'd spoken right into her ear.

"What? What did it work?" Charlie asked excitedly, but Ari couldn't even look at him. She was amazed. In awe. A bubble of laughter floated up out of her and tinkled into the air and there was no mistaking the little spark of something in Jai's eyes at the sound.

Curious, and eager to continue, Ari leaned back into him. ***Seriously. What did I do?***

The spark promptly sputtered out of his green depths. ***Nothing. I'm just doing my job, Ari.***

You're being a tool.

What did I say about the name-calling?

Jai.

Ari.

"OK, guys this freaking me out," Charlie said, finally drawing Ari's gaze. His eyebrows were practically at his hairline. "Can you do it? Are you a telepath now?"

A slow smile slid across her face and she nodded. Yeah she was a telepath. And it felt weird and strange and unbelievable.

But it also felt right.

Like something that had been right in front of her all this time.

Ari laughed again. "Yeah, I'm totally a telepath."

She slanted a look at Jai. *What next?*

You're Jinn, Princess. You can do pretty much anything you want.

~19~

This Lifeboat Isn't Big Enough for Three

The act of telepathy to Jai was an exercise. He believed it would be the most straightforward way to unlock Ari's abilities and she couldn't disagree with him. It came naturally to her, and although she was more than thankful that Jinn could not read minds, she had to admit there was something mega cool about being able to communicate with Jai through the power of telepathy. To keep her exercising her Jinn muscles he was making her speak to him mostly that way. It was pissing Charlie off, she could tell. It would piss her off too if she were the only one out of the loop, but the excitement of using such a weird and unique gift kind of over-rode her concern for Charlie. Tapping into her abilities wasn't at all what she imagined. She'd thought Jai would set her up in the living room and start testing her and making her conjure stuff, but according to her guardian that was a pointless exercise. Since she was one of the Jinn, like himself, with a wide scope of power and ability to conjure, Jai insisted that she use her magic for everyday things. He said there was no *one* muscle that needed to be worked, no inner power that had to be tapped into or explored. It was all about believing. It was as simple as that. Ari had to believe that if she wanted a glass of water that she could conjure it. Or a bag of chips. Or be able to grab the remote for the TV without moving. She even managed to turn a cushion to ash when Charlie threw it at her for cracking a joke about his feeble mind not being able to handle anyone else inside it. She just thought about what Jai did and raised a hand, believing it was ash. Suddenly it was.

As she conjured, the act becoming more natural as the day progressed, Ari began to feel the heat build in her skin. At one point she felt as if she were emitting the heat of a thousand suns, her mouth was constantly parched, her skin was too hot to the touch and she felt weak. Jai had assured her it was normal, and sure enough by the time late afternoon rolled around she could no longer feel how enflamed her skin was. She had Charlie run ice cubes down her skin and she couldn't feel the cold, and she waved a hand over an open flame and couldn't feel the heat. Well… it wasn't that she couldn't *feel* the temperature changes it was just it had no effect on her comfort anymore. It was weird.

The whole experience was overwhelming and Ari had to stop herself from over-conjuring stuff when she realized she could have practically anything she wanted. It was kind of a high. *But a dangerous one*, Jai had warned. It was too easy to get drunk on power. Ari had thought she could use his concern to her advantage. What she really wanted to do was learn how to use what Jai called the *Peripatos*. The *Peripatos* was Jinn form of travelling. You could literally travel from New York to Sydney just by concentrating on where you wanted to go. However, Jai had said it was pretty exhausting the first time around and he wanted her to build her abilities before she did any of the big stuff. Turned out there was no using *anything* to take advantage of Jai.

Getting to use the *Peripatos* was just one of many things Ari felt like she was waiting on. Waiting to learn the 'cool' Jinn stuff, waiting on word back from The Red King about the Shaitan who had put Derek in a coma, waiting on Derek coming *out* of the coma, waiting for the day in the not so distant future when she'd have to cut ties with her friends and family.

Now that she knew what she really was.

There were moments throughout the whole day when she had to shake herself because she found her thoughts climbing over her like creeping ivy, scratching and biting into her skin and entangling her in their morbid clutch. Because… wasn't it true now that not only was she not human but she was kind of a 'thing' rather than Jinn? The Seal was an object with no emotion or thought or feeling. It had one purpose. To command the Jinn. What did that really make her then?

It got to the point where she was deliberately drawing on all the bad stuff that broke her heart just to remind herself that she was more than an object. That she was a being with thought and emotion. It was completely masochistic and not at all who she was.

Realizing how dangerous her position was among the Jinn, Ari was certain that walking away from her life once Derek was well again was for the best. She couldn't stick around and put the people she cared about most in jeopardy. The plan was to walk away from Ohio and her friends and Derek. No matter how heartbreaking.

But Charlie…

It was so selfish but Ari was glad the stubborn idiot didn't want to leave her. Asking him to leave, to walk out of her life and never come back was the hardest thing she'd ever done. She was impressed with her poise when she tried to do it (maybe she had inherited a little Jinn decorum after all) but her heart had been slamming like a wrecking ball against her ribs the whole time as she waited for his response. It had been weird with Jai eavesdropping, weird for many different reasons that she didn't want to think about, but in that moment she and Charlie had shared something new, a spark, something Charlie hadn't allowed before. He'd actually looked like he had been leaning into kiss her before Jai came out of the kitchen, interrupting them.

Ari hadn't known what she would have done if Charlie had kissed her.

She'd wanted his kisses for like a zillion years but right now was sooo not the time. Plus… she really needed to know where he stood. He was still hanging out with that idiot Rickman after all.

Come on, Ari, her inner voice scolded as she followed Charlie and Jai into the hospital, *is that really the problem? You had no issue with hooking up with Charlie a few weeks ago, Rickman or no Rickman. Are you sure this hasn't got something to do with a pair of green soulful eyes you can't get out of your head?* Growling at her inner monologue, Ari's eyes darted away from Jai's back and she picked up her stride, overtaking the boys in the hospital corridor and smiling serenely at the nurse outside her dad's room. Physical distance would put him out of her mind.

The nurse said there was no change with her dad.

Of course there wasn't.

Even though Ari knew Derek wouldn't come out of the coma until she had commanded the offending Shaitan to reverse the enchantment, she was determined to visit her dad every night. She didn't want him getting lonely. Irrational perhaps, but this wasn't exactly the most rational experience Ari had ever gone through.

Charlie and Jai followed her tentative steps inside and her heart plummeted into her stomach at the sight of her father. She had forgotten how small and vacant he looked lying there. She clasped his hand in hers, no longer feeling the chill of it like yesterday. It was temperate. Like everything. Distantly, Ari wondered if she would start to miss the heat and the cold.

"I'm going to get a coffee," Charlie said quietly, edging towards the door. He was still uncomfortable being in the hospital. Ari had told him he didn't need to join her and Jai for visiting hours but her best friend had looked at Jai dubiously and he'd shaken his head, determined he'd be there for her. Ari was beginning to think Charlie was jealous of Jai. Which was silly.

Really.

Ari flicked a look at her guardian who sat down on a chair in the corner, pulling out his book, and casually opening to his placeholder. "Black, one sugar."

Charlie sighed and threw him a dirty look before he turned to Ari, his features softening into something so loving the transformation was comical. Ari bit back a smile. "Ari?"

She shook her head. "I'm good, thanks."

"OK. Be back in five."

When he was gone, Ari glanced back over at Jai who was determinedly reading his book, pretending she didn't exist. Not for the first time in the last twenty four hours Ari wondered what she had done to make him so cold towards her. And worse... she hated that it bothered her so much; she hated that last night, as she tried to drift to sleep, one of the things playing over and over in her mind was the wintry look in his eye when he returned from his Ginnaye tribe with the Tellicherry Bark for Derek. She tried to tell herself the reason his attitude bothered her so much was because, after her dad woke up, Jai would be one of only three people she'd have left in her life.

Wincing pain, like a sharp claw cutting a deep scratch across her chest, flared for a minute as she stared at this seemingly cold stranger in front of her, and she knew that it was more than that.

You like him.

Crap.

You more than like him.

But you love Charlie!

I do love Charlie.

But Jai is...

Jai was what? She frowned, edging closer to Derek and squeezing his hand as if his very presence, despite how hollow, could bring her some support, some clarification, some comfort. As she let her gaze travel over Jai, she felt that warm, excited flush take over her again. Maybe it was just physical attraction. Really strong physical attraction. The kind of *really* strong physical attraction she'd never experienced before.

But it was more than that. Even when he was being Mr. Cold and Distant, she loved talking to him. She loved sharing her new abilities with him and teasing him and learning what she could about him. And Ari wanted to know more! She wanted to find opportunities all the time to make his eyes spark like they did sometimes when he couldn't help it, or make his upper lip quirk at the corner as he fought off a smile *she* had prompted.

Ari realized she was grinning at the thought and blushed, dropping her gaze.

She was acting love sick.

This is so not good.

In fact this is so bad.

Ari blinked, her own musings falling away at the sound of a familiar voice outside the hospital door.

"...Derek Johnson. We're friends of the family."

Rachel! She was here?! Oh crap.

Ari trembled, her wide eyes flying to Jai who was already on his feet. She hadn't called Rachel or Staci about Derek. She had been trying to prepare herself for meeting them as their next meeting was to be their last. Ari's stomach flipped at the thought of turning her friends away. Turning them against her.

Could she really do this now?

I'm not ready.

"I'm going into the *Cloak*," Jai whispered, nodding at her militantly.

She gulped, nodding back, her eyes widening even more as the air around him rippled and warped, until she could no longer see him. Ari could still feel him though, and she shook out her hands, disbelieving that this was about to happen and Jai was going to witness it.

It was something Ari had discussed with Jai and Charlie only hours before: leaving her life behind. They both thought it was the right thing to do (Jai thought it was smart, Charlie didn't care what she did as long as she didn't try to leave *him* behind) and Ari drew strength from their support.

Turning her friends against her, though? Not the easiest thing Ari would ever have to do.

She waited, bracing herself against Derek's bed, as the nurse's voice grew louder as she approached the door. The nurse, Lucy, thrust it open and stepped in to peer with confusion around the room when she saw Ari was now alone.

"Oh, your father has visitors, Ms. Johnson."

"I heard, please let them in."

Lucy nodded and disappeared back out of the door, the shuffling of clothes and feet making Ari's heart pound in her ears. Rachel's small figure strode into the room, her blonde hair scraped back from her face with a blue bandana. Staci trailed in at the back of her, her dark eyes sad as she took in Ari standing by her dad's bedside.

"Oh, Ari," she whispered before throwing her thin frame into Ari's arms. Ari hugged her back, bending down a little as she always had to when hugging Staci and Rachel. Staci pulled back and Ari was immediately enveloped in the scent of rose water from Rachel's perfume. Ari tightened her hold on Rachel, knowing this was the last gesture of affection that would ever exist between them. Choking back the ball of burning anger in her throat, that her life had come to this, Ari stepped back, pushing Rachel gently away from her so she didn't breakdown.

"What happened?" Rachel asked, her brows creased in concern. "Why didn't you call? I found out from my aunt."

Oh shoot. Of course. Ari had forgotten Rachel's aunt was a nurse in the hospital. News travelled fast in Sandford Ridge.

"Yeah, and my dad found out from Mr. Wilshire that works with your dad," Staci added. "They say he just collapsed at work?"

Ari nodded, finding it difficult to meet their eyes. She hated lying. "Yeah. They don't know what's wrong. Or if he'll wake up."

"Oh God, Ari, I'm so sorry," Rachel breathed, tears shimmering in her clear baby blue gaze. "You should have called. You shouldn't have to go through this alone."

OK, Ari, time to put your game face on.

She smoothed her features, attempting the expressionless mask Jai was so good at donning. "I'm not. Charlie's here, he's getting coffee."

"You told Charlie but not us?" Rachel couldn't hide the hurt. Even Staci looked upset and confused.

"He *is* my best friend."

"Oh."

"Well…" Staci shrugged, trying to breeze past the awkward moment. "We're totally here now. What can we do?"

"Nothing," Ari perfected her monotone. "There's nothing anyone can do."

"Well." Rachel smiled, a watery smile that broke Ari's heart. "We could take your mind off of it. There's nothing you can do, sweetie, but the let the doctors figure this one out, so me and Staci are here at your disposal." Her eyes lit up. "What if we took you across state to Penn? We could check it out together. Your dad would want you to do that, no?"

A part of Ari was genuinely mad at the suggestion. Did they really think she was going to head out of Sandford Ridge while her dad lay dying in a hospital bed? Was college all Rachel ever thought about?! Even though the rational side of her knew Rache was just trying to find ways to comfort her and take her mind off of a bad situation, Ari drew on that angry part and shot her best friend a disgusted, disdainful look. "Is that all you think about? College? My dad is dying, Rache!"

"Ari, no, I didn't mea-"

"And I'm not going to college. I never wanted to go to Penn in the first place."

Rachel shook her head, perplexed. The look she shared with Staci was one Ari knew well. She thought a screw had come loose in Ari's head. "Wait. No. Of course you want Penn. Ari you can't let this hurt your future. Your dad wouldn't want that."

Do it, Ari. Just do it.

She curled her lip mockingly. "You don't know what he'd want. How could you when you don't even know your supposed best friend?" She scoffed and narrowed her eyes on them, watching her two friends pale with shock at her aggression. "I've been freaking out for weeks about college, but I couldn't even talk to my best friend about it because she would have turned her back on me the second I said I didn't want to go."

Rachel snapped her head back as if she'd been slapped. "Ari, that is so not true. I would have been there if you'd just talk to me. You blame it on me but you don't talk to us! You didn't even tell us your dad was in the hospital! What is wrong with you?" Her lips trembled and Ari had to hold herself back. Rachel was so close to crying. Ari couldn't stand to see anyone cry.

She shrugged, remaining strong. "I just know who my real friends are, is all."

"What? Charlie Creagh?!" Rachel cried, tears now spilling down over her lids. "Yeah, Ari, he's such a good friend. He's not even been there for you for the last two years! He's a loser! And if you keep going this way you're going to end up just like him." Her last words were caught on a sob as she whirled around and fled out of the hospital room.

Staci stood frozen for a moment, staring at Ari as if she'd never seen her before. Finally, she cleared her throat, "I don't know what that was about but I know this isn't you. So does Rache. She'll realize when she stops crying that this... this isn't you." She gave Ari a soft, heartbreaking smile. "I want you to know that when you're ready to deal with all of this, we'll still be here, Ari. We'll be waiting."

Her promise almost broke Ari's resolve. She wanted to fall into Staci's arms and hug her friend and ask her to take away the last few weeks. She wanted to go back and have everything be the way that it had been. But her life was never going back. There was no friends, no parties, no college talks in her future. There was good and evil, magic and danger. And Rachel and Staci were too vulnerable to be involved in that.

Throwing her shoulders back, Ari gulped down the nausea brought on by her grief. Her eyes deadened as they looked right through her friend, and she replied in a clear, unemotional voice, "Don't bother."

What little color had been left in Staci's cheeks fled and her own eyes glistened with hurt tears before she nodded, a little puff of disbelief escaping her lips as she turned on her heel and followed in the wake of her friend's departure.

As soon as the door closed behind Staci, Ari sagged, a sob catching in the back of her throat as she bent over her father's bed, groaning in heartbroken fury.

A hand slid across her back, a spicy familiar cologne tickling her senses. "You OK?" Jai asked her quietly.

Frustrated at everything, Ari shrugged away from his comforting hand and felt him step away from her. She shot him a look over her shoulder and found him gazing at her blankly, although his features were taut. She hoped he was hurt. Hoped he was mad. She wanted someone to be as mad and as hurt as she was. "What do you think?" she bit out, kicking the hospital bed with her foot. "How would you feel if you had to cut Trey out of your life?"

He shrugged uncomfortably, shoving his hands into his jeans pocket and looking like a little boy who had just been scolded.

Ari scoffed meanly, "God, between you and Charlie it's a wonder I haven't gone into frickin' dentistry."

"What does that even mean?"

She snorted. "It's like pulling teeth to get anything out of you two."

Jai shrugged, still looking bewildered. "We're guys."

Ari shook her head, hating everyone and everything at that moment. "You're asshats."

~20~

I Don't Want This Heart, It's Split in Two

Sunlight poured in through the kitchen window like an interrogation spotlight on the unbreakable. Ari turned her head this way and that, catching the beams of hot light on her face and feeling nothing but the temperate tingle of its touch.

She missed the heat.

She missed the cold.

She missed... her dad. Her friends. It was weird but she'd spent half of her time complaining they weren't really there for her. As it turned out they were there enough to have created an ugly dent in her bumper now that they were gone. Charlie and Jai sat behind her at the kitchen table. Charlie had gone out to the store and gotten some eggs. Jai had cooked omelets. They existed together in a strained state of peace for Ari's sake. Ari felt just as tense around them as they did around one another.

Feeling the way she did. About them both.

It wasn't enough to be worrying constantly that The Red King hadn't contacted them in three days, or that Rachel and Staci were gone from her life (and so easily – it was a little insulting), or that she was exhausted from using her Jinn magic twenty four hours a day. Who knew that conjuring random crap out of thin air instead of having to get off your ass and get it could get boring? But it did. Ari could see why Jai lived like a human, fetching glasses of soda and cooking omelets. Not that she talked to him about it. Since the hospital she had been distant with Jai *and* Charlie. There was just too much to think about. Too much to feel and right now she was just...

...angry.

Angry at her dad, at The White King, at The Red King, at Azazil, at Rachel and Staci for walking away after a five minute dispute (yeah, yeah rationality wasn't really factoring into her rage), mad at Charlie for being a teenage delinquent for the last two years, and mad at Jai for making her feel a certain way about him and then treating her like some one night stand he couldn't wait to get rid of. Finally... she was just angry at herself. Surely she should be coping with all of this waaaay better than she was? She should be strong enough to protect the people she loved rather than have to push them away; she should be smart enough to find some way around The White King's plans for her rather than playing directly into his hands; and she shouldn't be so flaky as to fall for a guy when she was supposed to be in love with someone else.

She groaned inwardly, pressing her nose against the window pane. *Sucks.*

Ari was close to giving up on feeling the heat through the glass when Jai's voice cut through the room, commanding and steely, "I think it's time we test your other powers."

Nervous little cretins awoke in her stomach, dancing and partying around in there, not caring that she was this close to throwing up.

Ari knew what Jai meant when he said 'other powers'.

Stealing herself, she turned around slowly, her eyes falling on the table. Charlie sat looking at her, a forkful of egg inches from his mouth as he waited on her answer. Jai was finished eating, his plate pushed from him, his arms crossed over his chest so his muscles flexed almost threateningly. "Why now?" she asked quietly, afraid.

"Because The Red King is taking a while. I don't know what that means but I do know that time is running out. I think we should use what time we do have sensibly. To me it makes sense that we test the powers of the Seal." His eyes narrowed at the petulant look she threw him. "Hey, I'm not happy about it either. The only way to test those abilities is to test it on the Jinn. The only Jinn we have in our midst is yours truly. I'm putting a lot of trust in you that you won't command me to do something asinine."

Ari grunted. "Asinine?"

"Ari…" he warned, standing up.

Charlie had been watching the byplay between them, his head swiveling back and forth. Now he grinned wickedly up at Jai. "Do I get to choose what she commands you to do? Come on, let me, it'll be fun."

Jai laughed humorlessly. "I said I don't want her commanding me to do something asinine, kid."

Charlie's grin disappeared as quickly as it had surfaced. "I told you not to call me, kid, Jinn boy. I'm what… two years younger than you, douchebag?"

"Try five. And that's only in physical years."

"What, you trying to say I'm not mature?"

"Oh those socks you're wearing definitely are. Have you heard of detergent? Showers? Hygiene?"

"I shower, you militant, glorified fucking babysitter."

"Watch it, kid."

"Kid? I am this close to taking a swing at you, you overblown piece of-"

"Oh for the love of God!" Ari cried, throwing her hands up, her head pounding. So much for their strained peace treaty. "Shut up. Shut up. Shut up!"

Despite their matching glowers, both of them slammed their lips closed and glared at one another. Ari heaved a sigh of relief as she pulled a chilled can of soda out of the refrigerator. At least the soda still felt nice sliding down her throat. Not the same as an ice cold Coke on a blazing summer day but still nice. She took a refreshing swig and turned towards her male companions once again. Blasts of frost shot out from Jai's eyes only to be met by the simmering black heat of Charlie's angry gaze. Rolling her eyes and biting back the guilt that she was somehow responsible for the animosity between the only two people she could count on right now, Ari spilled into the chair between them and Jai slowly sunk back down into his.

"So what will I command you?" she asked quietly, ignoring the way her fingers trembled as she played with the tab on her soda can.

When she got no answer, she glanced up to see Jai's face going red, the veins in his head throbbing.

"Dude, what's wrong?" Charlie asked quietly, looking at Ari in alarm. "Is he choking?"

Ari's heart flipped in her chest at the thought and she reached across the table to grab his arm. "Jai?"

His eyes widened and he waved a large hand at his throat and mouth and then pointed at her.

What the hell?!

"Jesus Christ, he can't talk?" Charlie asked incredulously. "Is this a joke?

Ari, your power! Jai's voice blasted into her head in a shout, probably born from his frustration. It knocked her back in her chair with a painful wince. ***You commanded me to shut up!***

Holy macaroons, so she had! "And it worked?!"

"What?" Charlie blinked in confusion.

"Telepathy," she muttered, staring at Jai wide-eyed. Curiously she reached a hand out, her fingers brushing his warm throat without thinking. His eyebrows hit his hairline at her touch and as quickly as she had reached out to him his own hand trapped hers in a tight grip, pushing her away. Hurt, Ari pulled out of his grip, ignoring the flip in her stomach and the tingles down her spine at the feel of his work-roughened hands sliding against her skin.

Guess it works. His voice sounded quieter, more subdued.

She nodded, at once creeped out and unsure of herself. *I can really command Jinn to do anything?*

Looks that way.

Her mouth twisted at the possible consequences of this verification. *I am so screwed.*

Looks that way.

She shot him a dirty look. *You want to be able to speak again or not, Jinn Boy.*

Hey!

She smiled teasingly. *What? I think Charlie came up with a super nickname.*

When he smirked at her, Ari felt relief pour through her, glad to see his features soften a little. *I think Charlie better watch his mouth.*

Why? No matter what he says it's not like I can command him to shut up.

Shame.

You really should try to get along better.

Hmmph. That's as likely as humans rediscovering the lost city of Palmyra.

I have no idea what that means.

Jinn thing.

Ahh what else. The bitterness must have been apparent in her eyes and tone because his whole demeanor changed.

Ari...

Noting his concerned look, Ari smiled softly at him. *I can never tell with you, Jai... do you actually care or not?*

He froze, his green gaze pinning her to the spot. *I'm your guardian. I care.*

Because you're my guardian?

Why else? And why do you care if I care? He cocked his head, his eyes narrowing. *You're in love with the kid... right?*

I... I-

"OK, this is getting old," Charlie snapped, jerking Ari out of the little bubble she'd gotten caught up in with Jai. Her heart was pounding against her ribs, blood rushing in her ears, and she was pretty sure in her face.

What the hell did that mean?!

Did... Jai...

Oh my god, what did that mean?! She eyed him, frustrated as all hell when his gaze dropped. *Can you uncommand the whole shutting up thing?* he asked blankly.

Huffing in annoyance at the interruption, not only at Charlie, but at herself for being annoyed with Charlie, Ari nodded. "Jai, I command you to be able to talk again. Or whatever."

He made a face at the 'or whatever' part and cleared his throat. "I... great, I can talk again."

"Well." Charlie shrugged. "Paradise could only last so long, right."

Getting up from the table, shaking a little at her unraveling, Ari cuffed Charlie across the head. "Be nice."

"Tell him to be nice!"

"I can't," she snorted, looking back over her shoulder at them. "If I did that he'd actually *have* to be nice... it would be like re-writing his entire personality."

Jai grunted. "Funny."

Charlie chuckled. "I thought so."

Rolling her eyes, Ari strolled out of the kitchen, not surprised at the scrape of kitchen chairs across tiling as the two of them rose to follow her out. Jai was still contracted to be glued to her hip and Charlie had taken up residence in her home and life as a guardian in frickin' training. Not for the first time, Ari wished she could have just one moment of alone time so she could gather her thoughts and work out what the hell was going on with her and how she really felt. About everything.

It was the stalemate. The waiting.

Where's a Jinn King when you need one?

If there was one thing being an immortal Jinn King had taught him it was patience. For days The Red King awaited news from his father after requesting an audience with him. His father, the all-seeing, all-knowing, powerful Sultan of the Jinn, Azazil, was most assuredly aware of The Red King's reason to request an audience. Azazil enjoyed drama, conflict, tragedy, destruction - he liked to manipulate a situation into place, then draw it out and glory in the carnage that resulted from frustration and impatience and misunderstanding. It came as no surprise then to The Red King that he heard no word from Azazil for seventy two hours. And now he was summoned while he sat in a darkened movie theatre in Stockholm watching a reshowing of a Swedish horror movie that made *Interview with a Vampire* look like *Nosferatu*. Disgruntled at the call during an especially chilling scene, The Red King stepped into the *Cloak* before descending into the *Peripatos*. Unlike his brothers, The Red King was still quite enamored with the mortal realm. He liked the movies and technological gadgets they were forever creating. Their science and inventiveness was a form of magic even they themselves did not appreciate.

He thought them rather clever.

He even (although he would never admit so to his brothers or father) *liked* some of them.

Granted access to Azazil's compound in the furthest reaches of Mount Qaf, The Red King appeared in the Receiving Room with grace and aplomb, automatically conjuring robes and hand-sewn leather trousers more befitting to this realm and his father's tastes. His hair he let loose and he strode towards his father's throne at the farthest end of the room with his red robes and hair billowing out behind him like a flickering flame. He was an impressive, intimidating sight, and his vanity preened a little as he relished the awed looks that crossed the faces of the hundreds of servant Jinn who stood in formation, one after the other, on each side of the room. They were garbed in white pants and loose white shirts, no accessories adorning their bodies. They were all Shaitains, immensely powerful, but completely under Azazil's command. Despite their own power and their subjection to the Sultan Azazil the sight of one of the Seven Kings of Jinn could still thrill them. The Red King remained expressionless as he passed them, the Receiving Room stretching an impressive few hundred yards, the glass ceilings and floor only interrupted by cuts of precious stones that winked back in all of the reflections, creating a chaos that only the Jinn could see through without becoming befuddled. The ceilings arched high above him and the dais that housed Azazil's throne stretched way before him. The Receiving Room was as vast as an airplane hangar, designed to confuse the unworthy and intimidate the ignorant.

Using enchantment to silence the sounds of his bare feet slapping on the glass floor, The Red King swept along, eager to discuss Ari's predicament with his father.

Finally, he drew to a halt several paces before the throne. The throne itself was constructed entirely of black flawless marble, the hard, harsh lines undisturbed. There were no arabesques or curlicues or chiseled reliefs. Its high back rose a good ten feet in the air, the overawing light of the Receiving Room seeping into its deep black like a sponge soaking up water. Azazil eyed him, his black eyes narrowed. He gave his son a tiny nod and The Red King took the steps up to the dais with ease and confidence. His father held his hand out and he took it carefully, bowing over gracefully to place a respectful kiss on his father's knuckles. Nodding approvingly now, Azazil waited for his son to retrace his steps back down from the dais before waving a hand across the air in front of him. The Red King felt the heat of the enchantment at his back, crawling on his robe like little secret spiders.

"We have privacy now, my son," his deep voice, so like The White King's, rumbled around them like the thunder of an avalanche on a snow-covered mountain. "You need my help? It is time?"

He nodded. "My brother has had a Shaitan place an unbreakable enchantment upon Ari's human father Derek Johnson."

Light glittered in Azazil's black eyes and he smiled. Although the smile was sinister, Azazil's power was such that his smile made you warm and eager to stretch your own lips into a matching expression. "Clever. It seems my son has played into my plans every step of the way."

The Red King gave a sharp nod. "Yes, Father. It appears he has."

"His arrogance will be the death of him. It pleases me. His arrogance. As does your loyalty to me."

"Yes, Father."

Azazil abruptly burst into raucous laughter, the harsh and unearthly sound making even The Red King wince. "Is it not humorous, son, The White King believes my greatest lieutenant would be fooled by an Ifrit?"

"It amuses me greatly."

"I will have to take your word on that since you show no mirth."

"I laugh inwardly, Father. My brother believes Sala stole the Seal of Solomon from around Asmodeus' neck when in truth you commanded Asmodeus to let her take it."

Not without his own conceit, Azazil enjoyed having his trickery repeated over and over again so he could glory in his own cleverness and manipulative genius. His humor, however, dissipated as his eyes took on a contemplative look. His moods were as mercurial as the sea. "The White King must never be Sultan, son. He is not cool-headed enough to claim mastery over the Fire Spirits. But sometimes I do admire his intelligence. Transforming the Seal into human form was one of his better notions. Why did I let his plan play out?"

Patience, The Red King reminded himself, *patience is my greatest ally when dealing with the Sultan.* For perhaps the tenth time, The Red King found himself reiterating Azazil's words of wisdom when he discovered The White King's plans to create Ari. "Many have sought the Ring of Solomon over the centuries. If one of those seekers were to be successful in finding the Seal they could have commanded us all and ripped Chaos from its Master's hands. But if the Seal is a child, if the Seal is Ari, she can be manipulated, she can be swayed, and her loyalty to you can be won."

He smiled, pleased with his son's passionate oration. "Such fine words I weave."

"Yes, Father."

"So." He straightened, his huge seven feet tall frame moving sinuously on the throne. "The next phase is in place. Ari has been forced into using the powers gifted to her at birth?"

"Yes, Father. And I promised I would ask you to help her find the Shaitan who has hurt her mortal father."

Azazil nodded slowly. "She has begun to trust you?"

"I believe so."

"Good."

"If Master would see fit to do this for her, I believe Ari would also come to trust *you*."

Like a serpent slithering across Azazil's face, another smile slid into place. "Excellent."

~21~

The Realm of Truth and Lies

Charlie had a way of taking Ari's mind off things. Jai might not like that but he admitted the truth in it as he watched the two of them laugh through a foreign movie without the subtitles, translating for the actors on screen and coming up with ridiculous lines that made even Jai snort with amusement. Sitting together on the couch, close, their arms brushing, Ari's chin tilted up as she laughed into Charlie's face, Jai could suddenly see the years of friendship between them. They were comfortable, in sync. Jai was still suspicious of Charlie and his interest in the Jinn, but it hadn't taken him long in close quarters with the teenagers to see that the kid genuinely cared about Ari. Probably loved her even.

And right now she needed that familiarity, and that comfort that Jai was unable to provide her. All he could do was sit back and watch as she grew sadder and angrier over all the changes in her life. It had made him panic, that darkness in the depths of her forever-changing eyes. The last thing they needed was for Ari to spiral into the black, especially when she was just getting a handle on her powers. So it was a relief to see her acting like Ari again. Even if it *was* this little douchebag bringing her back to the light.

Keeping his eyes trained on his book, Jai sighed, wondering when and if The Red King was ever going to show up. Despite his tendency to distrust everything and everyone there was something about that particular Jinn King. If Jai didn't trust him he at least *liked* the ancient immortal. Had he been wrong about him? Was he going to leave Ari's dad to die? Sliding a furtive glance Ari's way, he felt a pang of anxiety creep in. What would happen to Ari if Derek died?

Are we irritating you? Ari's laughing voice suddenly echoed around his mind and Jai bit back a smile, focusing his gaze down on his book.

Not at all. In fact, I'm amazed at your ability to rewrite a script on the spot.

Her laughter glittered in his brain like champagne bubbles, making his heart throb. Jai slid his hand over his chest on the place that ached, wanting to contain the feeling somehow.

We used to do this when we were kids. She was getting good at using telepathy. As she spoke to him with her mind, she was still engaging in conversation with Charlie. It was difficult to do. Not many could.

Ah years of practice then.

Yeah. It's nice. Feels like old times.

You know your boy hasn't had a drink or a smoke in days? Why was he telling her that? He wasn't supposed to be encouraging her with Charlie. *Well you can't encourage her with you so...*

I know. At least one good thing has come out of all of this right?

Hearing the melancholy creep into her voice again, Jai hurried to reassure, *Ari, everything will be fine. I promise.*

For a moment he didn't think she'd answer but then…

If you say so, then I believe you.

Something in her voice caught him, making his heart pound, and he twisted his neck around to look at her across the room. She gazed back at him, her expression unreadable but serious. Jai gave her a soft nod.

If she believed in him there was no way he was letting her down.

Ari was mentally berating herself for not being able to spend five minutes without having some kind of interaction with Jai – using her telepathy to talk to him behind Charlie's back?! What was that?! She had little time to yell at herself, however, her attention caught by the dark, writhing shadows that suddenly came to life across the living room walls. The atmosphere in the room grew charged and the spot in front of the television screen shimmered.

Jai muttered, "Incoming," springing up on to his feet and placing himself between Ari and the shimmer.

Orange, reds and yellows burst before them and this time Ari barely felt the heat of the flames as they licked at them before their smokeless dissipation, revealing The Red King. Relief poured through her and she shot to her feet, stumbling to Jai's side and

286 | SAMANTHA YOUNG

feeling Charlie behind her, his strong hand on her lower back, giving her silent support.

"Hey guys." The Red King grinned cheerfully at them. "How's it going?"

As if sensing her sudden burst of fury, Jai gripped her arm tight, his fingers biting into her skin as he stopped her from launching forward at the Jinn King. She knew it was a smart move on his part but right now she just wanted to tear the red-head to shreds for making her suffer this long.

Jai cleared his throat. "We've been waiting. We're anxious to help Derek."

The Red King nodded sympathetically. "Of course you are. Sorry about the delay but Azazil doesn't exactly jump when you say 'jump', you know." His blue eyes found Ari and they winked at her brightly under the dim light. "You been working on your magic?"

Clenching her teeth tight together in an effort to control herself, Ari nodded tightly.

Once again Jai spoke for her, "Ari's got a handle on telepathy and she's been conjuring, using her magic for everyday things."

"Good, good. What about enchantments or using the *Peripatos* or the *Cloak*?"

"No." Jai shook his head. "I felt that would be too much too soon. She did a few basic enchantments... turning a cushion to ash and locking Charlie in the bathroom but-"

"I knew that was you," Charlie grunted behind her and Ari had to bite back a nervous laugh.

"And the Seal?" The Red King took a few steps towards them, his eyes narrowed, his whole body pulsing with energy and power. "Have you used your powers as the Seal yet, Ari?"

Finding her voice, Ari replied hoarsely, "I commanded Jai to shut up. It worked."

Her uncle burst into laughter, slapping a strong hand against Jai's biceps. "Oh dude, that's funny."

And just like that Ari relaxed, sensing her two companions ease beside her. Smiling now at the king, Ari explained, "I didn't mean it. These two were arguing and I told them to shut up and Jai literally couldn't talk until I reversed the command."

Blue eyes sparking like electricity now, her uncle drank her in with amazement. "So it is indeed true. That's crazy! Well... we better put Derek back together again then huh?"

Her knees almost buckled with relief at that pronouncement and she had to stop herself from throwing her body into The Red King's arms in gratitude. "Did Azazil tell you who did it?"

And just like that the air around them changed, compressed, as The Red King's face grew dark. He took a few steps back and shook his head. "He wants to meet you first."

"What?" all three of them asked and she could feel both Jai and Charlie bristling beside her. Her own pulse had increased in tempo and this sick, wary feeling was toying with her gut.

"Azazil wishes to speak with Ari directly." Noting their worried eyes and the way Jai surreptitiously began easing his body in front of Ari's, The Red King's own eyes narrowed. "Ari isn't going to get hurt for the love of Shaitans. Azazil's just curious. And he wants Ari to know that he's doing what he can to protect her, even if it is just to piss off my brother. So… you meet Azazil and he'll give you the scoop on the Jinn that hurt Derek."

"No wa-"

"You gotta be ki-"

"I'll do it!" Ari raised her voice over Jai and Charlie's protests. Jai glared at her and Charlie whipped her around to let her know he was glaring too. Shrugging out of his hands, Ari stepped away from her companions. "Don't look at me like that. I'm doing this. If meeting Azazil will save Derek them I'm doing it."

Charlie threw his hands up in frustration. "What part of this doesn't say 'it's a trap!' to you?!"

"Hey!" The Red King's voice thundered around the room. Ari blanched at the danger in the sound and glanced cautiously over at him. For the first time since she'd met him he looked truly annoyed and truly… *scary*. "Are you questioning my word of honor?" His now black eyes bore into Charlie.

"Say no," Ari whispered.

Charlie crossed his arms over his chest and Ari's heart fell, recognizing the defensive stance. Before he could say anything, Jai thrust an arm out pushing Charlie back. "No, he's not. He's just a kid worried about his friend. But if you say Ari is safe going to Mount Qaf to speak with Azazil then we believe you."

There was a tense moment as they all waited to see if Charlie would disagree with Jai. However, he must have remembered that he was owner of a modicum of intelligence for, to Ari's everlasting relief, he remained silent.

"Good." The Red King skewered them all with another severe look. In that moment Ari knew he was silently telling them that although he might be a nice, easy-going guy, he was also a guy who could kill them in a snap of his fingers. Drawing the moment out his demeanor slowly transformed from scary to cheerful again, which was in itself sinister. Ari shivered when his blue eyes alighted on her again. "When I ask you to repeat these words I need you to truly mean them. No being enters Mount Qaf under duress."

"Got it," Ari agreed.

"OK. Repeat after me: I, Ari Johnson, wish to request an audience with Azazil, Master and Sultan of the Jinn."

Feeling stupid, like some lost cast member of *The Wizard of the OZ*, Ari blushed but repeated the words, infusing meaning and belief behind them, "I, Ari Johnson, wish to request an audience with Azazil, Master and Sultan of the Jinn."

Almost as soon as the words were out of her mouth pins and needles started in the tips of Ari's fingers. *Oh crap, not this again.* Ignoring the uncomfortable pain that began as a tingle and turned into a nip, Ari lifted her eyes from her slowly disappearing limbs to Charlie and Jai's faces. "I'll be OK. I'll be back soo-"

An exhausting blackness dripped into her eyes like thick paint and the accompanying sickly fumes and Ari gave into the overwhelming sensation, letting her body relax and float away into the ether.

Her cheek was smooshed up against something hard and smooth. Not just her cheek but her whole body. Her chest ached, flattened against the hard surface and Ari groaned, shifting her torso at an angle to relieve the pressure. Just that slight movement felt exhausting. And familiar.

Reality swamped over Ari as the dam broke, the memory of The Red King in her living room unfurling fear in her heart. She was terrified to open her eyes.

"I haven't got all day, Seal."

That voice.

Horror pried her eyes open and she jerked up from her prone position on the floor at the warped reflection of herself in the glass tiles. The White King?! Pushing herself up with more strength than she thought she'd have, Ari glanced around, her eyes almost crossing over at the warring, clashing reflections that collided with one another in the monstrosity of the glass room she found herself in. Focusing, Ari fought her way through the confusion, her eyes zooming in on the huge figure before her. Not The White King.

Thank the ever loving gods.

"Will you not stand before your Master, Seal?"

This was... Ari's gaze started at his huge bare feet, travelling up the long legs clad in black hand-sewn leather, to the bare chest inked with tattoos of ancient script, to the billowing blue silk robes and the startling face upon a thick neck. Like The Red King Azazil's head was unshaven, his long silver-white hair loose and flowing around his shoulders. His skin was a dark contrast to the pure brilliance of his hair, as were the deep black abysses that qualified as eyes. Those eyes were narrowed on her between a strong nose and a hard mouth.

He was huge.

Standing next to a black marble throne that must have stood at least ten feet tall, Azazil was an awe-inspiring and intimidating figure. The Jinn was at least seven feet tall, the largest she had yet to meet.

She guessed it made sense that the daddy of them all was the biggest of them all.

Coming to her senses, Ari struggled to her feet, her sneakers squeaking on the glass floor, making her wince. When she glanced up at Azazil for a reaction he merely frowned and the next thing Ari felt was glass against her bare feet. She blinked, stupefied, down at her tan toes and chipped nail polish.

He'd taken her sneakers.

Shoving down her indignation at that, Ari drew her head back up. How was she supposed to address this guy?

As if reading her mind, Azazil stuck out a hand and she noted that every finger was bejeweled. Guy likes his accessories huh? "You may kiss my hand, Seal."

Seal? That was a creepy-ass nickname.

Gulping down her trembling nerves, Ari took a few tentative steps forward, placing her feet carefully, one in front of the other, as she headed up the dais. She didn't know why but she kept expecting something to jump out at her and attack her. Despite her resolve to be cool, when Ari reached out a hand to clasp his, her fingers shook like she was on her first ever date. Her hand looked tiny gripping onto his, the heat of him no longer affecting her like it once would have before she'd tapped into her own powers. The butterflies in her stomach raged a war as she pressed her lips to his knuckles, darting back so quickly she nearly fell down the stairs. Glancing up at him, petrified at his reaction, Ari was surprised to see humor glittering in the black depths of his gaze. Unlike his son, The White King, Azazil's features were warm with emotion. Oh, Ari had no doubt he was terrifying when enraged, and cruel and spiteful when he wanted to be (she'd read the book Jai had given her cover to cover after all), but she also could see that he had the ability to feel. The White King, for some inexplicable reason, didn't have that. He was the darkest, soulless being she had ever met.

Trembling at the bottom of the dais, Ari waited for Azazil to speak.

"You are quite lovely." Azazil smiled and Ari felt the warmth of that smile seep through her, her muscles loosening and relaxing. "But then if I remember correctly so is Sala."

Like always the mention of her mother felt like the crack of a slap across Ari's face. The warmth dissipated and she grew tense again.

Sensing it, Azazil waved his hand dismissively. "But that is not why you have come. You wish to save your human father?"

"Yes... Your Highness."

He nodded. "A noble quest. One that..." as he trailed off, his eyes flicking over her shoulders, Ari felt the atmosphere within the humungous room shift and change, like the cap on a bottle of soda twisting, trapping all the gas inside. Ari felt choked by the sensation. Inexplicable fear exploded through her and she whirled around, her eyes fighting through the sparkling reflections to the end of the room. She strained her eyes, noting the Jinn servants in white all staring towards the massive thirty feet double doors at the end of the hall. "Have you mastered the art of the *Cloak*, Seal?"

Whipping back around, the fear transparent on her face, Ari shook her head. What the hell was coming?!

"Well." Azazil smiled. "You better learn it fast. I invited my son, The White King, today. I wanted you to hear from his mouth what a scheming, manipulative bug he is."

Ari's teeth chattered as she jerked around again, watching the doors slowly swing open. "I already knew that." Feeling betrayed she shot Azazil a watery glare.

He tutted. "I just wanted you to be sure. Don't panic," he now coached her soothingly. "Just believe you are hidden, that no one can see you. Just believe."

Drawing in shuddering gulps, Ari tried to calm, turning her thoughts inwards. *I am invisible. No one can see me. I am invisible. No one can see me. I am invisible. No one can see me.* She shut out the sounds of the doors creaking wide and kept chanting.

"It worked," she heard Azazil murmur and she shot a look at him in surprise. "Don't break your concentration. Just move up to behind the throne. My son will never know you were here."

Shocked but too petrified to question him, Ari followed Azazil's directions, moving forward and up towards the throne. A gasp escaped her when she looked down and right through her body. Where was her body?! *Holy macaroons!*

"None of that," Azazil muttered under his breath, shooting her a venomous look. "Don't make a sound."

Cowed, Ari moved fluidly behind the throne, placing her invisible hands against the chilled marble for support and peering around its back. Her eyes widened at the sight of her real father's face peering back at her from all directions around the hall. He seemed to glide along the glass floor towards Azazil, his purple robes trimmed in gold, his shaven head shiny under all the brilliant light created by the glass. As he grew closer, Ari noted the diamonds winking in his ears and the rings bejeweling his fingers. He'd dressed up to meet his dad, she mused.

Without a word, The White King strode up the dais. He grasped his father's hand in his and placed a kiss upon his knuckles. Militantly, he returned to his stance at the bottom of the dais. For the first time, as Ari glanced between father and son, she wondered why on earth her 'father' was The White King when Azazil was the one with the white hair? She got why The Red King was The Red King - he had that blindingly passionate mane of his. Her real father, however, was bald.

She guessed the Seven Kings of Jinn hadn't been titled after their looks, then.

For what seemed forever, Ari held in her breath, watching Azazil and The White King stare at one another. Peering around, she caught the tension in Azazil's jaw that said he was amused. He seemed perpetually, scarily amused. The White King, however, looked just as he had before. Emotionless. Blank. Soulless.

And suddenly it occurred to Ari why he might be titled The White King. There was a purity about him.

A purity of evil.

"Are we just going to stare at one another?" The White King cocked his head, for one moment seeming almost introspective.

The amusement fled Azazil's eyes and the air seemed to pulse around him, like waves rolling out tumultuously and crashing against rock. The rock in question was The White King and to Ari's awe he actually stumbled back against the attack. She shot Azazil a giddy, impressed look before reminding herself she was supposed to be concentrating on remaining in the *Cloak*.

"How dare you address me so disrespectfully."

The White King looked up at Azazil from under his lashes, his features still cruelly blank. "Apologies. Master."

Accepting the apology with a brittle nod, Azazil settled down into the throne, causing Ari to flinch back. The tart, citrusy scent of pomegranate washed over Ari as her nose missed being buried in his silver white hair. She felt pressure against her skin, like a strong wind was trying to blow her in the opposite direction. Heart thudding, Ari held her feet against Azazil's unconscious power and tried to concentrate on the conversation taking place. What had she missed?

"...Master has requested an audience with me to ask if I had Pazuzu curse the human, Derek Johnson?" The White King asked, pursing his lips.

"Yes," Azazil replied calmly. "That's exactly what I am asking?"

Her father shrugged elegantly. "Even if that were true, Master, there is nothing anyone but the Seal can do about it."

"What a heartless child I reared that would cause his daughter so much strife."

Surprised at the admonishment, Ari waited with bated breath for her father's reply. As before, The White King betrayed no emotion. Instead he eyed Azazil carefully. "It shocks you that your son has learned from your behavior, Master?"

A chuckle rumbled from the back of Azazil's throat. "I never harm those who my children call family."

"Then that is where you and I differ in strategy, Master. Perhaps my ability to set aside emotion will act in my favor in this-"

"Usurpation," Azazil supplied angrily. "You are an arrogant, festering boil."

"Must we have this same disagreement every time we meet, Master?"

Ari had to suck in a gasp as she was forced to skitter back from the throne at the angry vibration of power that throbbed from Azazil's body at The White King's disrespect. He leaned forward in his throne and hissed at his son, "I want you to know that I will do everything in my power to aid the Seal against you."

As if expecting such The White King nodded. "You may try, Master. But the girl is my daughter and I have no doubt that once she is left with no one, she will come running to her father, to her family."

"You seem confident of this."

The bitter smile that curled The White King's eyes almost blasted Ari off her feet she was so surprised by the slip of emotion. "Every child needs their father, Master."

The growing heat of rage began to thicken between father and son and Azazil abruptly stood from the throne. "You will never have the Seal. I promise you that. You are dismissed."

With his blank mask perfectly back in place, The White King offered a 'deferential' nod and turned, his purple silk robes snapping in the air like a wild animal, the reflection and explosion of amethyst rippling back at Ari from every direction. She waited, quietly in pain at the physical reminder of her parentage, as he strode along the immense hall towards the exit.

She knew now why Azazil had invited her to witness this interaction with her father. He wanted to reiterate the impression she'd already gained from The White King. He was cruel, merciless, unloving, and she should never be drawn or manipulated to his side by anything he said or did because he spoke and acted with one goal in mind: to use her to usurp his father.

The room seemed to breathe a sigh of relief as the giant doors glided closed with impressive silence. Letting her concentration fade, Ari stepped out of the *Cloak* and quickly moved down off the dais to face Azazil. As soon as he took in her expression he nodded with satisfaction. Holding her emotions inside, Ari gave him a careful look. She may know now to never trust her father but that didn't mean she trusted this alien creature before her either.

"Pazuzu, Your Highness?" she asked quietly.

He raised an eyebrow at the question and smiled. "Your determination and bravery is entertaining, Seal. Pazuzu is not like other Shaitans. He is an ancient Mesopotamian Jinn we call a Wind Demon; he's older than many of his kind. The Wind Demon is loyal to The White King despite his ex-servitude to me. Thousands of years ago The White King created an entire city, spent decades spinning destinies and watching it grow and flower into something beautiful and productive." He pinned her to the spot with a dark look. "My son built it up specifically to let Pazuzu terrorize it once it was in its glory. That patience, dedication, and artful evil is seductive to our kind. It is his way of gaining very loyal followers."

There were no words to describe the despair Ari felt as Azazil depicted the horror that was the man she was born of. It seemed unreal. It was sickening. Hollow. Painful. Heart wrenching. She wished she were anywhere but where she was just so she could run and hide from the truth.

"Pazuzu is a desert spirit. He never strays far from the sand. He cannot." He gave her a small nod and an amused smile. "You will find him in Roswell, New Mexico."

Ari had no chance to reply, to thank him, to tell him how grateful she was for his help despite the fact that he had crushed her even more and terrified the living daylights out of her. Almost immediately upon his words, Ari felt the darkness crawl over her eyes. She drew in a deep breath, preparing herself for the wind tunnel.

~22~

My Wings Are Yours, Are Your Wings His?

𝒫omegranates. She couldn't get the smell of pomegranates out of her head. Despite her best efforts to step out of the cloying, nefarious shade her visit to Mount Qaf and Azazil's home had dragged her into, Ari couldn't. The gloom, the truth of how her life would be once Derek was healed, was determined to cast out the sun.

Trying to focus, Ari's head swiveled back and forth between Jai and Charlie and The Red King who oversaw their discussion. After returning to the house by smacking into the floor like last time, Charlie and Jai had been blustery and over-concerned and vying for authority over her. Exhausted yet determined, Ari had shoved them away from her and recounted her visit with Azazil, including The White King's appearance. To her surprise The Red King looked perturbed when she mentioned Azazil had invited his brother. As if he hadn't known about it. Somehow, it made Ari feel better, that perhaps out of all the Jinn Kings there was one she could count on.

"I agree with Jai, Charlie," The Red King was saying, pulling her attention back in like a thread through the eye of a needle. "Pazuzu is not an easy creature to deal with. In fact he's effing hard to take down. If I go on this little mission he'll sense my energy right away and take off. If you go you might get killed. Only Ari and Jai should go."

Agreed.

"No way," Charlie growled, slanting a sleepy dangerous look her way. "Ari, I'm not letting you do this without me. Why can't *I* help when *you're* the one who needs a 24 hour guard?"

"Oh yeah." The Red King slapped Jai on the back. "Your contract has changed since Ari here came into her gifts. You're still her guard but you don't have to be hanging around all the time. If she needs you, she can contact you using this." He tapped a finger to his forehead.

At that news, Ari caught Jai's gaze, hating the strange ache and panic that was suddenly spreading across her chest and lungs. Like always Jai's eyes revealed nothing and he dropped them quickly, nodding. "OK, no problem."

No problem?

It was sooooo a problem.

Feeling guilt rip through her Ari shot a look at Charlie only to find him smirking. Of course he was happy with that turn of events. Annoyed, Ari punched him on the upper arm. "I don't know what you're smiling about, you aren't coming to Roswell."

Glowering, Charlie slapped her hand away. "What if it was me? You'd be tailing my ass whether I liked it or not."

"Probably true," Jai replied before she could. "But since I'll be flying us there I think you're out of luck."

Flying us there? Ari's jaw dropped. "As in… flying *flying*?

"You forgot we can fly?"

"Was that in the book?"

"Yeah."

"No." Charlie shook his head adamantly. "It wasn't in the book."

"Huh." Jai frowned. "Sorry about that."

"We can fly?!"

The Red King winced at her screech and took a step back. "Hysterical woman. That's my cue to leave."

Before she could say a word or question when she'd see him again, The Red King went up into the fiery *Peripatos* leaving Ari staring at the empty spot he left behind with disbelief. Finally, she unlocked her jaw and picked it up from the ground. "Do *I* have to fly?" she asked, feeling more than a little queasy at the mere thought.

Jai shook his head. "No, like the *Peripatos*, that's something that will take time for you to learn how to do, time we don't have. And since it's impossible to take someone into the *Peripatos* with me, it looks like I'm flying us there. It takes a lot of focus because you have to go into the *Cloak* at the same time. You'll have to hold on to me."

Ignoring Charlie's disgruntled mumblings beside her, Ari stuck out a hand to Jai, feeding off her nervous butterflies and adrenaline to get her through. "OK. Let's do this."

"What, now? You've just been to Mount Qaf. You've been gone a whole day. Don't you want to sleep first?"

"No. As far as I'm concerned I was gone like an hour. I want this done. Now."

Heaving a sigh, Jai nodded. "OK." The air around him pulsed and suddenly he was wearing a black leather jacket over his white t-shirt.

"Show-off," Charlie muttered sullenly.

Rolling her eyes at him, Ari shoved him playfully only to be surprised as he grabbed her arm and hauled her into a fierce hug. Feeling his muscles tremble beneath her and his heart pound against her ear, Ari held on tightly, breathing him in. He smelled like the tropical detergent she used. At the feel of his lips against her forehead, Ari sighed, melting into him.

"You come back in one piece, you hear," he demanded hoarsely.

Afraid if she held on any longer she wouldn't let go, Ari pulled back and smiled up at him as confidently as she could. It was only when she let her gaze flicker over his shoulder she flushed, caught in Jai's turbulent green eyes. Another pang of guilt cut through her for some inexplicable reason and Ari stumbled back, this torn in two feeling really not working for her at all. "I will," she murmured her promise.

"You'll need a jacket," Jai said, coming around the coffee table to stand before her.

His familiar heat and strength did funny things to her when he stood this close and she had to concentrate extra hard to conjure a jacket. She chose a brown leather biker jacket like the one she saw in *Cosmo* last week, the one she'd been lamenting over at the fact that it would cost her three months allowance to buy it. Now it fit, sleek and snug, like it had been made especially for her.

Being Jinn had its perks.

"Outside." Jai strode out into the hall. He pulled the door open with a flourish. "Let's do this."

~23~

The Coppery Scent of Death

*F*lying wasn't Ari's thing. It wasn't ever going to be Ari's thing. Ari thought she'd just have to hold Jai's hand and they'd zip up into the air together. Instead Jai had slid an arm around her waist, drawing her tight against his side and murmuring for her to hold on tight. She'd done so, trembling shyly as she was pressed against his hard body, one of his strong hands gripping her shoulder, the other sitting comfortably on her hip. Ignoring the way her body lit up like a Christmas tree around him, Ari nodded one last goodbye to a seriously pissed off Charlie before she felt the vibration of Jinn enchantment as Jai pushed into the *Cloak*. Ari had followed suit, barely having hidden herself when Jai shot them into the sky at a blurring speed that made her scream. Her stomach had bottomed out and the vacuum of air that had rushed into her mouth momentarily suffocated her. Panicking Ari had clung tighter to Jai, squeezing her eyes closed and praying for the sensation to end.

And here they were.

The flight was painful with the wind hitting her skin like little rocks skipping over water, not to mention her muscles burned from the tension of holding on so tightly to Jai. It seemed to last forever and all Ari could do was tuck her head into Jai's neck and wait it out.

Superman and Lois Lane made this look like so much fun. It is sooo not fun.

Jai's chuckle bounced around in her mind, making her bury deeper into him. *I'm getting that. I have claw marks in my skin now.*

Oops sorry.

Don't be, I'm fine.

With the superhuman speed they flew at, it came as no surprise when Ari felt her body take a dip hours before a plane would arrive across country. Prying her eyes open, she peeked out from under her lashes to see they had slowed and that the ground was moving closer and closer towards them.

Her eyes widened as the earth below her burst with color - greens and reds and blues and purples and glinting diamond light - all of it moving, like multi-colored bugs scrambling around. If Ari wasn't mistaken they were heading for a ton of people. Sure enough, Jai eased back on the accelerator even more and as they approached ground she nipped her nails into his shoulder in her anxiousness.

What the hell is that?

It looks like... a parade.

A parade? A parade of what?

Uh... people?

Bracing herself for impact, Ari was glad for the graceful landing Jai made, her feet hitting concrete with little reverberation through her body. She staggered out of his arms only to be shoved back into them.

"Hey, what was that?" A girl in costume shrieked, glancing around for her invisible 'attacker'. Ari and Jai broke apart, their gazes taking in the madness around them.

Come out of the Cloak, now.

Following his instructions, Ari stepped out of it only to be slammed into Jai again by a giant green alien. Dodging the next stream of people, Ari cursed under her breath at the sparkles and glitter and multi-colored faces and masks. Everywhere... there were aliens.

Eyes alighting on a banner spanning the entire width of Main Street, Roswell, Ari cursed loudly this time.

Welcome to Roswell's Annual UFO Festival 2011!

"You have got to be kidding me," Jai growled, moving out of the way of a huge guy dressed in silver spandex. The beat of drums crashed around them and the song Spaceman by *Babylon Zoo* blared from someone's beatbox. The air smelled of burgers and cotton candy. Laughter and singing mingled in with the raucous celebration and Ari had to catch her breath, fighting the disorientation caused by the parade. A laughing alien face appeared inches before her and she bit back a yell, stumbling into Jai to get away from the face that smelled of hot rubber and sweat. Jai caught her and she looked down in surprise when his hand tangled in hers, holding it in his unrelenting grip.

She gulped. "What now?"

Now we find Pazuzu. You'll feel him, Ari. You'll sense Jinn among us. He's old and powerful so whatever you do... don't let go of my hand.

OK.

Jai shoved into the crowds, ignoring the yells as they walked in the opposite direction. They sidestepped some floats and a couple of cars and plunged back into the crowds again. Keeping her senses alert Ari couldn't help but begin to feel drained. There were just so many people there. How were they ever going to find Pazuzu?

Jai glanced back at her squeezing her hand. *Crazy huh?*

Too crazy.

He's gotta be here somewhere, Ari. Just hold on.

I am. I am.

Flexing her hand in his, Ari realized how safe she felt with him. Safer than she even felt with Charlie. It was nice. Very nice.

As they passed people melting under the New Mexico sun in their heavy makeup and costumes, Ari was actually glad her body ran at such a stable temperature. Looking for Pazuzu in these crowds and dehydrating at the same time did not sound like fun. Not that this was-

What the...

Jai's hand tightened again. *You feel that?*

Yes, she replied. Her head swiveling around this way and that, checking over the crowds. *What is that?*

Jai drew to an abrupt halt, pulling Ari to a standstill. He groaned. *This isn't happening.*

What? She eyed him apprehensively before following his gaze through the parade.

There. He nodded his head and Ari squinted trying to see what had caught his attention. Focusing, she searched the energy she had felt only moments before and her spidey senses zoomed in on a young woman in a skin-tight, bright green catsuit beckoning two young men down a dark alley. The boys grinned at each other before following her in. *Another Jinn.*

No way.

Yes way. And not just any Jinn. He looked down at her now, his eyes hard. *A Ghulah. A flesh-eating Jinn. They prey specifically on travellers.*

Ari's stomach flipped at the thought of the carnage the Jinn was about to unleash. She hadn't even known there were flesh-eating Jinn. Wow... she really was born into something freaking horrible. *Travellers? What...?*Her eyes widened as she looked back at the UFO festival sign. Of course. People travelled from all over the world to enjoy the Roswell UFO Festival.

Ari, I have to stop her. I can't just stand by and let that happen when I can do something about it.

I know. But I'm coming with you.

No.

Yes.

Ari, I don't have time to argue this.

Neither did she. Tugging out of his grip, Ari began pushing through the crowds towards the alleyway. Feeling the heat of Jai's growl at her back Ari looked over shoulder defiantly. ***What do we do?***

You do nothing. Just stay out of the way.

Not even given time to roll her eyes, Ari gaped as Jai shot by her in a blur, disappearing into the dark of the alley. Panic suffused her at the thought of the Ghulah hurting him and Ari gripped asphalt, dashing into the alley after him, the smell of garbage and beer flooding her nose and tickling awake whatever it was that made a person want to be sick. Stopping at the mouth of darkness, Ari's gasping breaths sounded overly loud and she clamped a hand over her mouth, willing her eyes to adjust to the light.

A yell rent the air and Ari dove forward, the sounds of glass smashing and loud rustling setting her heart to pounding.

"Jesus Christ!" a guy cried out in fear, his voice reaching Ari only seconds before he appeared out of the dimness, blood seeping from the fleshy bite in his neck. Pale and weak, completely discombobulated by fear, he fell past Ari and out into the streets.

Screw this!

Petrified, Ari strode into the alley, the shapes of dumpsters and garbage bags spilling out into the dirt infested space forming before her as her eyes adjusted. Stepping tentatively over what could have been anything from water to urine, Ari wrinkled her nose, trying to hear past the rushing of blood in her ears for sounds of Jai.

Her eyes widened at the sight of a bloody hand lying limp on the ground and as soon as she saw the blood, the strong thick, nauseating scent of copper overwhelmed her and she gagged. Disbelief and screaming unreality wept through her as she followed the hand to the rest of the body. It was one of the boys. Hurrying forward, Ari was just about to fall to her knees to inspect him when a gust of wind blew past her, carrying Jai in it. He slammed into the wall beside her, dirty garbage bags breaking his fall as he slid down it with a wincing scrape of leather against brick.

"Jai?!" she squawked, making a move towards him only to be stopped by a large hand wrapping around her throat. Clawing at the hand, Ari was turned by it and lifted off the ground, her feet dangling helplessly as she struggled to draw breath. The Jinn's female façade smiled up at her sweetly, her mouth covered in gore from where she'd been eating the boys. To Ari's horror her jaw elongated unnaturally, revealing huge sharp teeth. Ari closed her eyes shutting out the image of blood and flesh dripping from the Ghulah's mouth.

"Another Hunter from the Guild I presume. I don't know why you bother when you know you're not allowed to kill us."

She squeezed tighter and black spots started popping up all over Ari's vision. Biting her nails into the Ghulah's hand, Ari raked them deep and the Jinn winced just before Ari lost consciousness.

Jai pounded a fist against the enchantment the Ghulah had placed around him while she choked the life out of Ari. Before she'd gripped Ari, Jai had been able to think. The Ghulah was more powerful than she should be, almost as if she were borrowing power. When the barrier went up around him his eyes had zeroed in on the talisman she wore around her neck. A Sorcerer's talisman. She was drawing power from it. His only thought had been of removing the talisman from her neck and destroying it, that is...until he was unraveled by her attack on Ari. The emotions that rushed through him as he banged and punched the invisible wall keeping him from rescuing her was nothing like how they described. There was no *one* thought in a moment like this. There was terror and fury and panic and vengeance. It was unrelenting and painful as it clawed and clouded his brain, reducing him to a saliva-ridden animal desperate to eviscerate the Jinn who dared to hurt what was his.

When Ari's eyes rolled back in her head, Jai stilled, staring in disbelief as the Ghulah released her, her hand unwrapping from around her throat. Ari's body hit the concrete with a thud as she collapsed, sprawled out on the dirty ground, unconscious, her long limbs seeming dead, her hair spread out in a pillow around her head, her throat red raw from strangulation. The rise and fall of her chest, however, eased him, rationale seeping back into his thinking.

The Ghulah took a few steps towards him, a smug smile on her painted face. Jai found the fury, drawing a foot across the ground like a bull readying to charge.

"I'll deal with the girl once I've gotten rid of you for good. What say I lower the barrier and we play this nice and fair half-breed?"

No way was he telling her he wasn't a half-breed Hunter. He needed the advantage the element of surprise would provide. The barrier dropped immediately and Jai fell back on good old fashioned human training.

He threw a punch. Her nose breaking under his fist.

Howling the Ghulah clasped her face, clearly having expected something in the way of a magical attack from her opponent. Her retaliation, the buzzing that erupted in Jai's ears, almost made him laugh. It was a wasp enchantment - a hallucination that wasps were crawling in his ears and into his brain - to make him think he was being eaten alive by them. With a wave of his hand he killed the enchantment, something a half-breed would never be able to do.

The Ghulah's eyes narrowed at his defense, the blood dripping out of her mashed nostrils. "What are you?"

Without another word he shot a leg out, his foot connecting with her solar plexus. She stumbled back in outrage and Jai lunged at her, his fist pummeling into her face again and again. At the hum of power emanating from her neck, Jai swore and snatched at the talisman, ripping it from her neck and melting the stone in his bare hand. The act cost him, the Ghulah pushing her own magic out to cast him back into the air. He slammed into the wall again, the breath whooshing momentarily out of his body as he slumped to the ground.

"You're not The Guild," The Ghulah snarled. "You're full-blooded Jinn!"

Huffing, Jai drew to his feet, shrugging at his leather jacket. He would be reeking by the time he got out of here. "Yeah. So that kind of leaves us at a stalemate. Neither of us can kill the other without being taken before the Jinn Courts. So what do you say you get the hell out of Roswell?"

She curled her lip. "I was here first."

Narrowing his eyes, Jai crossed his arms over his chest. "Look, I may not be able to put you in the ground like I want to but I sure as hell can do something to make sure you never walk again. So what's it going to be?"

"You don't frighten me."

"Yeah well I don't have all day and my patience is wearing thin since you tried to choke my friend to death."

"She didn't though," Ari croaked, and Jai shuddered in relief as she clambered to her feet. Her face was pale, her neck red and swollen, and she swayed unbalanced on her feet. She touched her neck, wincing, before drawing those eyes of hers up and at the Ghulah.

"You OK?" he asked quietly, wishing he could just grab her and hide her somewhere where nothing bad could happen to her ever again. How the hell was he going to get them out of this?

"I'm fine," she reassured him, taking a few tentative steps towards him, her hair falling into her face. She tucked a few strands behind her ear with trembling fingers, revealing intense eyes narrowed solely on the Ghulah in front of them. When she pressed her side up against him it took everything within him to resist putting an arm around her. She coughed, tears of pain pricking her eyes before she threw her shoulders back, looking every inch the battered Princess. "More than I can say for this bitch."

The Ghulah grinned, cocking her hip confidently. "Like you could do anything to me, sweetheart."

"Actually…" Ari smiled back at her, a dark smile he'd never seen before. It made him shiver, as did the pulse in her aura that told him she was about to use her magic. "I command you to leave Roswell and to never eat the flesh of any living creature again."

The smug smile on the Ghulah's face slipped as the force of Ari's command seeped into her. "How…?" she blinked, her body automatically walking her out of the alleyway. She stepped over the boy's body next to the dumpster, and as she strode towards the mouth of the alleyway, her neck was still craned back over her shoulder as she gaped at Ari in utter disbelief.

That is some seriously wickedly creepy power she has going on. Jai eyed Ari, not sure what to say.

Catching his look Ari shrugged wearily. "I know. It's creepy."

He couldn't help but smile. "A little."

"It worked though, right?"

"That it did."

Frowning Ari whipped back around, her eyes falling on the body of the guy. "We should help-"

"He's gone, Ari." Not wanting her to see the mess the boy was in Jai caught her arm, pulling her back.

"But-"

"He's dead."

Hating the way her lip trembled with confusion and distress, Jai wished there was something he could say or do but there was really no way to comfort someone during their first experience with death, especially a violent one.

"We need to get out of here," he told her quietly, trying to draw her gaze away from the young man. "We need to step into the *Cloak* and get back out there and find Pazuzu. You OK to do that?"

~24~

What's the Use of the Wind if It Won't Take You Away on It?

Accepting that there was nothing to be done for that one boy was harder than Ari ever could have imagined. Numbly she followed Jai into the *Cloak* disappearing out onto Main Street just in time. Two deputies were approaching the alley with cautious and sober expressions. Feeling sick at the thought of what they'd find, Ari turned away, gripping tight to Jai's hand. The garish costumes and masks - some seriously scary – as well as the pounding music and riotous flurry of the crowds felt difficult to manage after what had just happened. She was quiet, not even using telepathy to talk to Jai. After ten minutes of causing freak outs bumping into people while invisible, Jai squeezed her head. *Come out of the Cloak.*

You sure? People might have seen us go into the alley.

We'll have a greater chance of feeling Pazuzu if we come out.

She didn't need much persuading after that. She so wanted this over. She wanted to find him. She wanted to cure her dad.

And then what?

Thankfully Ari wasn't allowed to fall into a teenage/Jinn version of a mid-life crisis because a ripple of power suddenly flooded over her, the unpleasant taste of dirt filling her mouth. *What is that?*

Pazuzu.

Heart pounding Ari clasped her other hand around Jai's wrist, feeling the vibrations grow deeper, stronger, nearer. She twisted her neck around, checking the people strolling past.

"Watch it," a voice growled as a body slammed into her. Jai pulled at her as her eyes washed over the tall figure before her. A grey alien mask with its pointy chin and huge black almond-shaped eyes stared down at her blankly and Ari screamed inwardly at the pulsating power that was coming off of the guy in waves.

IT'S HIM!

I know!

"Damn," the voice cursed and Ari blinked in disbelief as he disappeared into the *Cloak*.

Hauled into Jai's arms Ari didn't even have time to squeeze her eyes shut as he took off. *Ari, CLOAK, CLOAK!*

HOLY MACAROONS! She bit her lips, focusing on stepping into the *Cloak*, although she was pretty sure it was too late now.

Holy what? Jai teased as they blazed through the air.

Not the time!

This time when they landed it was with a bump. The impact ripped her from Jai's arms and she collapsed on her ass in the sandy dirt. Gaping up at Jai who had somehow managed to keep his feet, Ari's heart throbbed, seeing him stare off into the distance like a gunslinger getting ready to duel. She followed his glower and scrambled back to her feet to face the Jinn who stood, legs braced apart, before them. Around them was nothing but open New Mexico desert. The scent of sage hit her nose in the muggy atmosphere, lifted by the musky scent of animal. There was no road near them, hardly any plantation, just red clay-colored rock mountains looming in the background like bored spectators. There wasn't even a breeze to send a shiver of foreboding down her spine.

When her eyes focused on the Jinn before them, the Jinn that moved towards them on taloned feet, Ari's jaw dropped. He was almost as bad as the Nisnas. Freaked out, Ari backed into Jai, wishing she was more graceful. His feet must be black and blue by now. At the parade she had been pretty sure the Jinn looked like... well... a guy. Dressed bizarrely in a shirt and jeans, the Jinn smirked, his face part human, part lion. The flesh of his mouth curled like an upside down love heart, reminding Ari of the Lion from *The Wizard of Oz* except this guy had huge fangs peeking from between his lips. He had human shaped eyes and nose, except where the bridge should be - like the Nisnas' it was completely flat. His skin was almost black in color, his amber eyes glowing eerily against the rich dark chocolate of his flesh. He pointed a long, twig-like finger at Ari and it was then she noticed that even more strange, his left hand was twisted downwards, while his right hand seemed to be perpetually twisted upwards, the bones pushing against his flesh, making Ari feel queasy.

"You shouldn't have come for me, girl. Have you no idea who I am?" his voice to her surprise was... *normal.* For some reason she'd expected it to be screechy, like nails across a vinyl.

Pulse throbbing visibly, Ari threw her shoulders back, pulling on all the bravery she could muster even though her legs were shaking so badly it was a wonder she could still stand. "You're Pazuzu."

He smiled. "I am Pazuzu!"

At the pronouncement a gale force wind rushed in around her and Jai, the desert storm blinding her, stinging her eyes and beating into her mouth. She clamped her lips closed and threw a hand up to shield her eyes, wondering how the hell they were going to get out of this.

Ari! Jai shouted.

I'm here. I'm right here! What do we do?!

Try and reach for me. I'll get us out!

I don't know where you are!

Beat out your arms around you, I'll do the same!

OK! Ari began flapping her arms around her like a blindfolded idiot determined to hit the piñata at a child's birthday party.

I don't think so, little girl. Pazuzu's voice echoed into her mind. *How dare you HUNT me! I'll show you what it feels to be an animal caught in a trap.*

A slice of pain cut through Ari's cheek and she cried out, sand and wind whipping up against the open wound. Another one, another one, another! Slice, slash, gash after gash, laceration after laceration ripped into Ari's skin until she was screaming, collapsing to the ground in agony as her whole body went up in torturous stings and flames.

ARI! Jai was yelling frantically in her head at the same time Pazuzu filled it with his laughter.

She was in too much pain to call back to Jai, shuddering on the ground as the desert storm ate at her wounds. Agony writhed through her, so much so, she was barely even cognizant when the storm dissipated.

Jai was leaning over her, his face pale, his hands hovering above her, afraid to touch.

"Ari," he choked, his eyes so full of worry and horror her heart might have exploded in panic if it weren't already slamming against her ribs in outcry against the pain. She wanted to reassure Jai but she could only bite her lip, tears streaming over her lids. It felt as if the whole of her insides had been laid bare.

Darkness crept over Jai's face and she watched in blurry disconnection as he stood to his feet and faced Pazuzu. No! Her brain attempted to fight through the pain. He couldn't face the Wind Demon. Not alone!

Pazuzu's laughter echoed around the desert, a manic, forced sound that seemed to enflame her wounds. Ari tried to shout out to Jai only to cough up a thick gunk of blood, her throat raw and unusable. Jai jerked around at the noise, his eyes widening, his jaw tightening with rage. Ari tried to plead with her eyes for him to leave. Instead he turned to Pazuzu, whipping his hand out like he was throwing an invisible curve ball. Pazuzu screamed as his eyes bled pure white, his awkward and grotesque arms flailing out in front of him as if he couldn't see.

Jai had blinded him?

Yes, she choked on her momentary triumph, more blood bubbling up between her lips and cutting Jai's victory short. *I'm dying. Oh god I'm dying.*

"This won't hold, you child!" Pazuzu snarled before he began muttering something under his breath. At the same time, alien words met Ari's ears as they escaped out from between Jai's lips. She had no idea what he was saying, but as he rose his arms like a conductor at the orchestra the ground beneath her began to shake, scraping against her wounds. Biting back silent screams, Ari watched as Pazuzu rocked on unstable talons. He cursed and began muttering faster.

Just as the white began to melt from his eyes, the ground finally gave way beneath his feet and water gushed up out of it like a geyser. As it descended, cascading down over his head, Pazuzu screamed as if someone was sawing off his twisted limbs. Ari's eyes widened at the bloody pustules that popped up on his skin where the water touched, smoke pouring from his pores like cold water on hot asphalt. His screams nipped Ari's ears and she curled deeper into herself. When he fell to his knees, she almost breathed a sigh of relief, despite her wounds.

Desert Spirit. Jai turned to her to explain. ***Water is poison to them.***

If she could have, Ari would have nodded at him. She didn't care why Pazuzu was going down. All she cared was that Jai was safe.

Afraid to move, Ari waited for Pazuzu to pass out, but instead he howled into the New Mexico desert with hatred fuelling his power. A gnarled hand struck out towards Jai and Ari watched in horror as Jai clasped his throat, his face turning purple as he, too, dropped to his knees. Petrified, Ari slid a hand towards him, the sickening agony of her torn skin matching her sickening fear as Jai began coughing up desert dirt, thick with his saliva and insides. The gooey dirt began seeping from his eyes and nose, even his fingernails. Pazuzu was suffocating him, filling his insides with desert.

No. No! NO!

In all the pain and confusion Ari knew there was something she was supposed to be doing. What? What was it?

Suddenly Pazuzu was kneeling before her, his vile, wounded face grinning at her evilly. "So this is the Seal. What a disappointment you are, child. So easy to kill."

The Seal! Ari screamed inwardly. She choked, trying to force the command out but she only ended up spitting up more bloody globules. Fury and helplessness gripped her as she saw Jai collapse onto his back, his eyes closing and hands falling limply to his sides.

JAI! Her mind screamed.

Pazuzu laughed again.

Eyes widening as she realized what she'd done, Ari slid her narrowed gaze back to Pazuzu and whatever he saw in her face made him freeze. *Got you, you piece of crap.*

Pazuzu, I command you to release and heal Jai.

Mouth hanging in horror, Pazuzu immediately turned like a robot at the telepathic command and crooked a hand out at Jai. Her guardian's eyes flew open and he coughed, spitting up the rest of the dirt as he sucked in shuddering breaths, his eyes wide with panic.

Pazuzu, I command you to heal me.

Furious now, the Jinn spun back on her, his legs collapsing beneath him as his mind gave into her. The palm of one of his twisted hands pressed against her forehead, the slide of his skin reminding her of the feel of the lizard's skin she'd touched at the zoo in Cincinnati years ago when she'd visited with her dad. Relief washed through Ari as the wounds began to close and heal, the pain dulling to a throb, to a sting, to nothing. Before he could disappear, Ari clamped a hand over his and pinned him to the spot with her unrelenting gaze.

Pazuzu, I command you to undo the illness you placed upon Derek Johnson. Heal him. And afterwards, never come near me or mine again.

Despite the rage burning in his eyes, Pazuzu nodded deferentially and she let him step back. The New Mexico air burst into fire as the

Wind Demon disappeared into the *Peripatos*, where she had no doubt he would head to the hospital to revive her father.

Relief crashed over her, deadening her limbs, and Ari had to drag herself across the desert dirt to Jai who was crawling his way towards her. His face was pale, his eyes slightly haunted as he reached her, a large hand cupping her cheek. Ari nuzzled into it, shocked by the depth of her fear of losing him. "You OK?" she croaked, her throat still raw from being shredded from the inside.

For a moment Jai didn't say anything and when he leaned into her, her breath caught, her heart crashing against her ribs. He was going to kiss her! *He's going to kiss me!*

The excitement fizzled out into something deeper as Jai pressed his forehead to hers, his green eyes seeking something – she didn't know what – in hers. Frozen, afraid to move, to talk, to break the moment between them, Ari merely waited. For what... she didn't know.

At last Jai pulled away, nodding jerkily. "I'm fine. You?"

"I used the telepathy to command him."

"Good thinking." He coughed again, a spittle of dirt landing on his hand. He grimaced, groaning as he eased onto his feet, reaching a hand down to help her up. "We need to head back."

Ari frowned, swaying into him as his arms banded around her. "Have you got the energy?"

He nodded, the color still frighteningly absent from his cheeks. "We have to make sure Derek is OK."

She wanted to kiss him. She wanted to reach up and tug his lips back down to hers so she could enjoy the deliciousness of his mouth this time feeling the way she did about him.

But she wouldn't.

Not yet.

~25~

One Plus One Equals Two Walking Away

*I*t was a miracle they made it back to Sandford Ridge in one piece. The flight had been slow because Jai was still suffering from the effects of having desert try to kill him from the inside out. When they touched down on solid ground they both wobbled, clinging to each other for balance. Smiling abashedly, Jai made sure she was steady on her feet before taking a few steps back from her. Ari would have taken the time to frown but as she glanced over at the hospital the need to see if Derek was awake was far more compelling than whatever was going on with her and Jai at that moment. Stepping out of the *Cloak* Ari nodded tightly at Jai and moved to head into the hospital. His hand on her arm stopped her and she turned back impatiently. He tugged her back into the shadows of a skinny Buckeye planted next to a large sign with the hospital name on it. Following him behind the sign Ari sighed. ***What?***

"Your clothes." He gestured to her torn and dirty appearance. "Conjure something clean so people don't ask questions."

Focusing took a lot of energy she didn't have but as Jai's appearance rippled, transforming from 'biker in accident' to 'clean guy' Ari conjured a fresh t-shirt and jeans too. With a quick glance to make sure no one had seen them, she strode out from behind the tree and sign, dashing across the ER line to the hospital entrance. She barely looked at anyone as she hurried along the corridors and into the elevator that would take her to ICU. Jai kept pace with her, quietly supportive, as her adrenaline shot her body into the stratosphere. Her heart beat out of time with her steps, her limbs not quite able to keep up with the speed it was racing at, and as she neared the nurses' station it almost exploded when her father's nurse, Lucy, came out of his room, her eyes widening as they caught sight of Ari.

Her pretty face blossomed into a bright smile and Ari choked on a sob. Jai's hand pressed against her lower back as the nurse came towards them, and the delicious warmth of his touch shot through her.

"Ari, he's awake," Lucy announced happily. "He woke up an hour ago and the doctors are doing tests just now. You'll be able to see him soon, I promise."

"Is he going to be alright?" she asked dumbly, knowing for a fact that he would be. But wasn't that something a normal relative would ask?

Lucy bounced her head cheerfully. "It's looking good. His vitals are great and there is no sign of brain atrophy. The doctors just want to make sure they haven't missed anything and to ask your father some questions. He's a bit of a medical mystery."

Ari gave her a weak smile as Lucy gestured for her and Jai to take a seat in the small ICU waiting area. "I need to call Charlie," she said, turning to him with tired eyes. "Do you have a cell?"

"Ari," he whispered, leaning into her, "You can conjure one."

Grimacing at her own mental deficiency, Ari nodded. "Right." Making sure no one was watching, Ari tucked a hand behind her chair and let her magic focus on creating a cell phone with Charlie's number in it. Feeling the solid object take shape in her hand, Ari took a moment to ponder the weirdness of her life.

Yeah, Ari, making a cell phone appear out of thin air is so much weirder than being eviscerated by a Wind Demon older than Jesus Christ.

She shuddered, not wanting to think about the fact that she now knew what parts of her insides looked like. A bubble of bile rose up in the back of her throat and she gulped for air, jerking the cell up to her ear.

You OK? Jai's concerned voice floated soothingly into her mind.

Not really. Trying to concentrate on the good stuff. She smiled sadly. *I'd rather think about my dad being awake than what went on in that desert.*

He squeezed her shoulder in silent understanding before dropping his hand back into his lap, flexing it like she'd burned him. Frowning, Ari pressed speed dial one on the cell, not surprised when Charlie picked up on the first ring.

"It's me."

"Oh thank God," he breathed. "What happened? Are you OK?"

"I can't really talk right now. I'm in the waiting room at ICU. The doctors say dad's awake though."

"I'll be right there."

"OK. See you soon."

She hung up, letting her head loll back against the wall. "Charlie's on his way."

Like the never-ending stretch of Azazil's Receiving Room it had felt like forever since Derek had stood in their living room. He looked great. He had color in his cheeks, meat on his bones - he looked as if nothing had ever happened to him. He could even walk. No dizziness, no muscle weakness. The doctors couldn't work it out and since their tests were inconclusive and Derek was feeling absolutely fine, there was nothing they could do when he ignored their advice and told them he was discharging himself. Ari had stood by, giddily, watching him as he signed a form saying he was leaving against medical advice.

She had her dad back.

Although, hours before it felt as if that was never going to happen.

Sure enough Charlie had raced down to the hospital, crushing her up into a giant bear hug right there in the ICU in front of everyone. Ari had blushed at the way he stroked her hair off her face, his eyes narrowed and dark, as they drank her in. It had been that look again. That look he never used to give her. Before he could do anything to complicate her already complicated feelings, Ari had pulled him aside down an empty corridor to tell him what had happened. For a minute she expected Jai to follow her, before remembering he was no longer contracted to be glued to her hip.

After that it was literally just an agonizing wait to see her father.

When she had been allowed into the room, she'd rushed in alone and thrown her arms around him. Ari had tensed at the tentative pat he gave her on the back, expecting him to squeeze her close. Surprised and a little hurt, she'd had to remind herself that he had just come out of something extremely weird and scary. She'd pulled back and quietly watched as he went about organizing things as he always did.

Now midnight... and they were home. Jai had transformed back to the Great Dane instead of going into the *Cloak* since Derek was used to seeing him as a dog anyway. Ari stood facing her dad unsurely, Charlie on one side and Jai in dog form on the other.

"Can I get you anything?" she asked quietly.

"Yeah, sir, anything you need...?" Charlie added.

Derek snorted, a noise of disbelief that set alarm bells ringing in Ari's head. He was acting weird. Even for someone just out of a coma. He hadn't said a word in the car and every time she'd reached for him he'd flinched away from her touch. For the last few days Ari had gone over and over again in her mind that when her dad woke up she would have to leave him. But despite her fallout with Rachel and Staci, leaving Derek had seemed unreal, some distant unthinkable act that might never happen. Now, watching him refuse to meet her eyes, avoiding her touch, it was like she was already gone. And the thought made her want to shrivel up and die.

"Dad?"

Finally he lifted his head, his eyes boring into her, his expression completely unreadable. "I know, Ari."

Her whole body froze with shock and she felt Charlie move closer to her. "What?"

He threw up his hands, shaking his head like he couldn't believe whatever was going on.

What is going on?

Ari, I think he knows, knows.

She glanced down at Jai in horror. ***What?***

"In the coma," Derek's voice brought her head back up, "I heard everything. What you were all talking about. I heard it all." He took a few steps back, lowering himself to the arm of the couch. He narrowed his eyes on her, his mouth hanging open as if he were finding it difficult to reach the right words. "When I woke up I just... I just sat there... thinking it couldn't be true. But that *thing...*"

Heart palpitating, Ari whispered, "What thing?"

"The thing." He flicked a hand at his face in disgust. "Face like some kind of hybrid lion."

"Oh my God."

"Yeah oh my God." He nodded at her. And then he shook his head, his eyes growing glassy with tears, his face red as the tendons in his jaw flexed. "I knew there was something off about Sala. I knew it. But it was like I couldn't control myself around her."

"Dad..."

"I'm not that though, am I, Ari?" A tear escaped, dripping down his cheek. He wiped it away roughly. "My little girl..."

Fighting back her own tears, Ari trembled. "I'm still your little girl."

He frowned, seeming in pain. "I know, I know. And what you did for me... I am so grateful... I just..." heaving a sigh, looking as if he'd lost the most precious thing in his life, her dad stood to his feet. "For being in a coma for days I'm kind of beat. I'm going to head to bed."

"But, Dad-"

"Let him." Charlie grabbed her arm, stopping her from following Derek out of the room. They watched him ascend the stairs like a man twice his age. "He's learned a lot of weird crap in the last few days and coming from personal experience, the guy needs time to adjust. Just let him sleep on it. You can talk in the morning."

Ari bit her lip, feeling numb. "He hates me."

"Listen to me. That is not a guy who hates you. That's a guy who's messed up. And you can't blame him. But he still loves you, Ari. Eighteen years of being your dad doesn't just go away overnight."

"As much as I hate to admit it, Charlie's right," Jai added as the flames disappeared around him.

To Charlie's credit he bit back a retort, glaring at Jai as he pulled Ari into another strong, warm hug. "I've got to get home. My mom has been calling non-stop today and I haven't been answering because I was too worried about you. But I'll be back in the morning."

"Of course." Ari pulled away. "Go, she'll be worried."

"Yeah." Charlie grinned in surprise. "What's that about right?"

"I'm glad… that things are getting better for you."

He gave her a sad smile before pressing a soft kiss to her forehead. "Yeah, we'll see."

When he was gone, the house seemed to ring and vibrate in the quiet. A forlorn feeling knotted in her chest before she turned around to find Jai staring at her. She took one step away from the front door as Jai strolled towards her, his face flashing in and out of the darkness as the moonlight streamed in through the windows.

The need Ari felt just looking at him was overwhelming, her chest tightening so much so she could barely breathe.

"Well… I should go," he said softly so Derek wouldn't hear. "Just use your mind if you need me OK, and I'll be back to check in tomorrow. You still have a lot of decisions to make. This isn't over, Ari."

She barely heard anything after the words 'I should go'. Desperate to keep him with her a little longer, Ari smiled up into his face, finally letting her feelings shine out of her eyes. "I want to thank you for coming with me, for protecting me."

Jai's eyes widened just a fraction before he could stop himself. Clearing his throat he took a wary step back. "Just doing my job."

Frustrated and feeling reckless after everything that had gone down, Ari reached out, gripping his arm and taking advantage of his surprise by hauling him close. The spicy, musky scent of his cologne made her stomach flip. In that moment, as she gazed up into his face, Ari just wanted to let go and drown in his eyes. "Don't," she whispered, almost pleadingly, throwing away pride and guilt in the face of what she was sure they shared. Charlie's eyes tried to probe their way into her mind but she pushed them out, focusing on the man in front of her, the man who made her feel things no one had ever made her feel before. Truthfully... not even Charlie. "Don't act like you're not my friend, Jai. After everything... you *are* my friend." Unconsciously, her eyes dipped to his mouth and she flushed remembering the way it felt against her own. Licking her lips Ari began to tremble as her body fought with her brain.

Jai cursed and she snapped her gaze back up to his eyes just as he took hold of her upper arms, pushing her back into the door behind her. Leaning close, his eyes blazed into hers. "Stop it," he whispered harshly, his breath teasing her lips, his chest rising and falling rapidly. Heat exploded through Ari. "Stop looking at me like that."

"Like what?" she whispered back, leaning in just a little closer so her top lip brushed his bottom lip.

He jerked back, another curse slipping out of his mouth as his grip became almost painful around her arms. "You *know* what," he replied hoarsely. "I'm your guardian, Ari. Ginnaye. You and I... we can't..." Shuddering he let go, abruptly stepping back from her, and for the first time since becoming Jinn Ari felt the cold wrap its arms around her. "We can't and we won't." Jai lowered his gaze now, taking a deep breath, taking a moment, before he was able to meet her eyes. "I don't... look... you are... beautiful. You're really beautiful and you're...great. But you're only eighteen and you love Charlie and I... I... well, there's someone else... in my life."

It was like he had slapped her. One hard crack across her face. Heat bit into her cheeks and shock slammed through her body. Painful shock. Sickening shock. In all of her confusion over Charlie and Jai, not once had she considered that Jai might be in love with someone else.

How stupid did that make her?

She made a sort of disbelieving, huffing sound, wrapping her arms around herself protectively. Taking a moment, she nodded, trying to find the right words. "I'm sorry... I'm sorry if I made you uncomfortable... I-"

"Ari, it's fine," he interrupted all business-like again. She wanted to punch him.

"Yeah," she laughed humorlessly, staring somewhere over his shoulder. "Should I ask my uncle for a replacement or something?"

"What? No." He seemed shocked by the suggestion and Ari finally found the courage to meet his gaze. There was slight hint of anger in the flex of his jaw that made Ari almost smile. Jai was nothing if not professional. He wouldn't want a girl's teen crush on him messing up his ability to do his job.

Although it was so much more than just some stupid crush.

Stop thinking about it! If she didn't, she'd end up crying right there in front of him.

"I'm still your guardian. OK. We'll just forget about this and move on."

Ari nodded numbly. "OK."

"OK. I'm going to head out. I put my number in your cell but remember you can use telepathy. Don't try anything stupid while I'm gone. I'll be back tomorrow after I take care of some things and we can discuss your future, maybe train you in using the *Peripatos* and flying."

Not able to say anything, Ari just nodded her agreement, desperate for him to leave when only five minutes ago she'd have done anything to make him stay.

"See you, Ari."

She blinked back at him dumbly, hating him for sounding so unsure. Two seconds later he went up in flames into the *Peripatos*. Ari burst into tears as soon as he was gone. Sliding down the door to land on the floor with a bump, Ari pressed her face into her knees and cried the million tears she'd locked inside since this had all begun. She cried for the dangerous and unknown future she had ahead of her, for a dad who may not love her anymore, for a boy who was starting to want her the way she had always wanted him just when she begun to move on and fall in love with someone new. And for that, Ari was surprised to realize, she cried the hardest - the place where her heart beat in her chest ached like mad as she relived the moment with Jai. Jai who loved someone else. Bitterly she wondered who could have caught Jai's interest. Someone older and more sophisticated than some stupid Jinn girl who was more weapon than heart.

But that couldn't possibly be true.

Otherwise why did hers hurt so much?

~26~

This Vengeance of Mine

*D*espite the Marid's assurance he had placed an enchantment around the room that acted as a sound barrier and would deter his mom from wanting to come into his bedroom, Charlie still couldn't help glancing anxiously at his closed door. As if coming out of some two year dream, his mom had started paying attention to him again. It was weird. It had coincided with him finding out the truth about Mikey's death. Like his relief, his release of the guilt that had been killing him had physically and mentally changed him... so much so it had affected his mom even – she was actually acting like she cared again. She'd also mentioned something about Ari. Ari had said something. He smirked at the thought. Beautiful Ari. Couldn't keep her nose out of his business. Now his mom called him. A lot. Made it hard for him to hang out at Rickman's - not that he wanted to do that so much, now that all of this weirdness had gone down with Ari.

Now that he had a chance at revenge.

When The Red King came back yesterday after Jai and Ari had left for Roswell, Charlie had been shocked to discover he 'wanted to talk'. He told him he saw how much he was suffering, feeling useless while Ari and Jai worked their voodoo magic to take down the dick that had hurt Derek. He said he knew Charlie wanted to do the same thing to the person who had killed Mike. He said he could give Charlie what he needed. All he had to do was promise not to tell Ari that The Red King was the one who handed him the key to it all and to be there when The Red King called in the debt.

Charlie wasn't stupid. He knew it would be like making a deal with the devil.

But he was offering him a chance to destroy the bitch that killed Mikey. That's all he wanted. He knew that this would bring him peace. He'd spent too many nights fighting his own rage, hating himself for killing his brother. No one could know what real self-hatred did to a person unless they'd been through something similar. And to discover that he wasn't to blame, that he *had* been paying attention to the road, that magic – Jinn – was responsible for taking Mikey, for destroying his family's life, left him with a new kind of rage. He needed vengeance. He needed it like he needed oxygen.

The Marid The Red King had sent stared down at him from his great height, dressed in a dark, charcoal suit that really ruined the whole 'genie' image for Charlie. "Do you know what you would like to wish for?" The Marid growled and Charlie felt the hum of his dark, angry energy. This guy was not cool.

Remembering the epiphany that had come to him in his dream, Charlie had jolted out of bed that morning to grab the book Jai had given him about the Jinn. Some of the wording made him frown as he looked over what he wanted but... but surely this was the only way? Plus - he grinned inwardly, feeling warm and sure at the thought of Ari - if he did this he'd be strong enough to protect her, maybe not strong enough as a certain guardian he'd like to punch, but strong enough to be what she needed. Finally, to be what she needed.

"Yes," he replied, clearing his throat when it came out all husky and nervous. "I wish to be a Sorcerer."

The Marid raised a thick dark eyebrow before he nodded slowly. "I grant you this wish, Charlie Creagh."

~27~

Kiss of Darkness

Ari hovered outside her dad's bedroom, glancing at the hall clock again. It was noon and he still hadn't made an appearance. For the fiftieth time she raised a fist to the door, ready to knock, ready to face him. And then the nerves caught hold of her gut again like vicious little gremlins playing with her insides, and Ari fell back, taking deep breaths, trying to pull herself together.

Just as she was sure she was ready to knock for real this time, the doorbell rang downstairs. Hoping it was no one else but Charlie, Ari almost threw herself into his arms when she swung the door open to find him there. But the memory of the night before, of crying herself to sleep over someone else, stopped her short. Charlie grinned at her, striding into the house, an electric energy seeming to buzz around him. He placed a proprietary hand on her waist, his lip curling in that sexy, arrogant way of his. "Can we talk?"

Curious, Ari nodded. "Sure."

She headed upstairs, hearing them creak behind her as he followed her. Suddenly she was conscious of the fact that her ass was in his face and she hurried up the steps, bemoaning how easily she blushed. It was just... Charlie had been acting so differently around her lately. She wasn't sure what it meant and right now she wasn't sure she could deal.

Wow. She never thought she'd ever doubt wanting to be with Charlie.

Feeling inexplicably guilty again, Ari let him into her room and shut the door quietly behind them.

"Have you spoken to your dad yet?"

She shook her head, staring at him as he stood before her, his eyes warm, his hair all mussed up as usual. He stood with his hands stuck lazily in his pockets. He looked casual, relaxed.

Happy?

"He'll come around."

"Yeah." Ari wasn't so sure. "So... what did you want to talk about?"

He sobered, taking a step towards her. "First, I want to apologize."

"Apologize?" *For what?* What did he do?

"Yeah. For all the times in the last two years I turned my back on you. I was messed up and I didn't want to drag you down. I didn't think I was good enough for you." He took another few steps until he was standing inches from her, the lemon detergent his mother used on his clothes tickled her senses, reminding her of those two lonely years. "I'm sorry, Ari," he whispered, leaning in and making her heart pound. "For hiding from someone so special and taking you for granted. And on that note... the second thing I wanted to talk about..." When his lips came down on hers and his strong arms pulled her close, Ari froze. Probably assuming it was surprise, Charlie grasped the back of her neck, his fingers threading through her hair. The soft pressure of his lips began to unwind her and Ari found herself holding on to him, kissing him back. Thoughts of Jai pushed in on her, screaming at her that she was acting unfairly. *But Jai doesn't want me,* she argued. *And Charlie does. And I love Charlie. I do.* Sighing into his mouth, Ari let her lips fall open and Charlie took the invitation, his tongue teasing hers in a wet, deep kiss that flushed her cheeks rosy red.

So she didn't feel the overwhelming, unbearable, nerve shattering heat she felt with Jai.

But this was good.

This could be so good.

This was Charlie.

Kissing him back harder, Ari almost smiled when he groaned, the vibration shooting through her body. He gripped her closer, her shirt straining against her chest as he scrunched the back of it in his fists, aiming to press as much of his body against hers.

"Ari," he moaned, pulling back to look at her, his eyes bright with desire. He just took a moment - almost as if he couldn't be away from her lips any longer -but that moment was all Ari needed to be reminded that his eyes were brown.

Not green.

And as awareness of what she was agreeing to came down on her like a ton of concrete, so did her awareness of everything else. She felt the hum of energy above Charlie's skin, the hum that she'd attributed to lust.

But it wasn't lust.

It was familiar.

It was...

NO!

She pulled back from Charlie, her mouth falling open in disbelief, her hands shaking as they slid across his chest feeling the power pulsate from him. "What did you do?" She croaked, horror filling her mind.

His wide eyes grew less panicked as he realized she had sensed it on him. He grinned, tugging at her arms and folding her hands in his. "I made a wish, Ari."

"What?" *NO! NO! NO! This isn't happening!*

"I'm a Sorcerer now. I had to Ari." He pulled on her hands as she tried to tug out of his hold. "I have to get that bitch that killed Mikey and this was the only way to do it."

"No!" she cried, disbelieving he had done this to himself. "Didn't you read that stuff about them, Charlie?! This isn't a way to get revenge for Mike. This is a way to destroy yourself!"

The screaming in her head only grew louder as her heart pounded in panic. There had to be away to fix this. There had to be? How did this happen? How did he make this happen?

About to voice the question, Ari jerked back from him as flames erupted at the bottom of her bed, and Jai dove out of the *Peripatos* with a look of pure fury on his face. He lunged at Charlie and Ari moved fast, putting herself between the two of them.

"What the hell did he do to you?!" he yelled, completely disregarding the fact that her dad was down the hall.

Terrified of the look on Jai's face, Ari held him back with a forceful hand pressed against his chest. She felt his own heart pounding beneath her palm and was surprised by his reaction. It occurred to her when she was recoiling in horror at Charlie's admission she may have telepathed that horror to the one person who made her feel safe. Stupid. Stupid. Shaking her head at herself, Ari slapped her other hand against Charlie's chest. "He made a wish."

Jai looked momentarily stunned, his rage deflating at the revelation. "A wish?"

"To be a Sorcerer," she added pointedly.

Rearing back at that, Jai eyed Charlie over her shoulder, his vivid gaze focusing on him, searching. When he found what Ari had, he shook his head in disgust. "You are such a dick."

EPILOGUE

Moving the Players into Position

"So the rumors were true, brother?" The Gilder King asked from his place beside The Lucky King. Like The Red King and his brother of The Glass, those two were on truly friendly terms, and truly comfortable with one another, because they were the only two brothers neutral in The War of the Flames.

The Red King lounged before them on his leather chaise longue, the huge fire behind him having no effect on the room's occupants other than to add a shadowy, secretive ambience he thought fitting for the occasion. Rarely did the Jinn Kings meet with one another these days, and never all at once. But before him was a nice gathering of his brothers.

Everyone but The White King. The White King who was mad. Delusional enough to believe he could possibly be Sultan. No one had Azazil's power. No one. And only one had the ability to manipulate Azazil. A girl… an innocent…

They all stood around his living room with its dark red painted walls and gilt-laden furniture. His taste differed from most Jinn. He liked texture and color and luxury. The cold decorative tastes of the general masses seemed in complete opposition to their fiery natures and he refused to bow to convention.

"Yeah. The White King stole the Seal and now it's a girl. His daughter."

The Gleaming King cursed viciously. "Why would he not tell me of this?"

The Red King grinned. Yeah, that had to sting. The Gleaming King and The Shadow King were allied with The White King. They shared bitter looks, making no effort to hide the fact that they were surprised the king they backed in the war hadn't seen fit to confide something so important to them. He hoped it effed up that sick little "Triple Alliance". "I guess he was playing this one close to the chest, boys. But it's true. With the Seal of Solomon alive and kicking and literally up for grabs, the war has become a whole new ballgame."

"Why are *you* telling us?" The Lucky King narrowed his eyes suspiciously.

"Because Azazil wished it."

They all shared a knowing look, their lips curled in understanding. Trying not to think of Ari, or let his cocky smile falter, The Red King murmured dispassionately, "You know Father likes a good drama. You better choose your sides again, brothers. Our Father is not about to lose this one."

Without even a 'by your leave', as if their minds thought as one, The Gleaming King and The Shadow King fled into the *Peripatos*. Ignoring the press of worry that gnawed at his chest, The Red King grinned over at The Gilder and Lucky King. "Well… in or out?"

"Still out," they said in unison, although they couldn't help but looked intrigued. They were of course their father's sons. But with one last wary look, The Red King was unsurprised when they too stepped off into the *Peripatos* to return to their palaces to live out their lives away from the conflict.

Remaining before him was the brother who looked most like him and acted most like Azazil. The Glass King. His deep, cerulean blue hair slid across his shoulders as he strode towards him. Unlike Azazil and the others, The Glass King favored stark leather vests that matched his trousers instead of colorful robes. He wore no earrings, no rings, had no tattoos. His eyes that could be mistaken for being dyed to match his hair shone fiercely out of his exotic face. He dropped to a knee, clasping his hands together, the leather cuffs around his wrists straining with his intensity. He bowed his head, his blue hair shimmering in the light from the fire as it fell over his face. Feeling less alone, The Red King placed a weary hand on his brother's shoulder, silently asking him to lift his head. He did and they shared a long look of resignation.

The Glass King nodded in understanding, perceiving things within The Red King that none of the others ever had. His grim façade softened and he placed his own hand on The Red King's shoulder. "How may I serve you, brother?"

THE END

New York Times and USA Today bestselling author, Samantha Young, is a 26 year old writer from Stirlingshire, Scotland. After graduating from the university of Edinburgh, Samantha returned to Stirlingshire where she happily spends her days writing about people she's keen for others to meet, and worlds she's dying for them to visit. Having written over ten young adult urban fantasy novels, Samantha took the big plunge into adult contemporary romance with her novel 'On Dublin Street'. 'On Dublin Street' is a #1 National Bestseller and has been re-published by NAL(Penguin US).

For more info on Samantha's adult fiction visit http://www.ondublinstreet.com

For info on her young adult fiction visit www.samanthayoungbooks.com

Printed in Great Britain
by Amazon.co.uk, Ltd.,
Marston Gate.